CUMBRIA LIBRARIES

3 8003 04509 5148

D1354104

*Be*

*Beirut*

Cumbria County Library
Carlisle Group H.Q.
The Lanes
CARLISLE
CA3 8NX

WITHDRAWN

# *Beirut, Beirut*

SONALLAH IBRAHIM

*Translated by Chip Rossetti*

دار بلومزبري-مؤسسة قطر للنشر
BLOOMSBURY
QATAR FOUNDATION
PUBLISHING

مؤسسة قطر
Qatar Foundation

First published in English in 2014 by
Bloomsbury Qatar Foundation Publishing
Qatar Foundation
PO Box 5825
Doha
Qatar
www.bqfp.com.qa

First published in Arabic in 1988

Copyright © Sonallah Ibrahim, 1988
Translation © Chip Rossetti, 2014

The moral right of the author has been asserted.

ISBN 9789992194522

*Beirut, Beirut* is a work of fiction. Names, characters, places and incidents are either
the product of the author's imagination or are used fictitiously. Any resemblance
to actual persons, living or dead, events or locales is entirely coincidental.

All rights reserved. No part of this publication may be reproduced or
transmitted or utilized in any form or by any means, electronic, mechanical,
photocopying or otherwise, without prior permission of the publisher.

Printed and bound in Great Britain by CPI Group (UK) Ltd, Croydon CR0 4YY

# I

They searched me twice: the first time at the customs gate, and the second time before the exit leading to the tarmac. Between the two, my leather carry-on bag and I passed a closed-circuit television and an airport scanner. One of them was waiting for me at the door of the plane, probing with his hands under my arms, between my legs, and inside both my carry-on and duty-free bag. Finally, I was allowed to board the plane.

I stopped beside the first empty seat I came across. I stowed the plastic bag in the overhead compartment and sat down, after putting the carry-on on the floor between my feet.

There was an empty seat between me and the airplane window through which the feeble afternoon sun shone. Beyond it appeared the enormous billboard for Cairo International Airport. I sat back and stretched my legs out beneath the seat in front of me. Soon enough I had to move them to one side to clear a path for a passenger in a flowing white robe who sat down beside me. Out of the corner of my eye, I noticed the Saudi *ghutra* headdress hanging down over his shoulders.

I heard him sigh loudly as he spoke to me: "They treat you like you're a terrorist or a *fedayeen*."

I was busy fastening my seatbelt around my waist, and didn't bother answering him.

In a few minutes, the plane filled up. Flowing robes and bulky clothes from the countryside were spread all over the interior, topped by dark-brown faces that spoke of fear and worry. I noticed some of them wearing chic European clothes, their eyes hidden behind dark sunglasses, with reinforced Samsonite bags resting on their knees. There were a few women; some of them revealed delicate arms carrying handbags that looked like shoeboxes or jewelry boxes. There wasn't a single *fellaha* among them.

The plane finally made its ascent, and my neighbor finished the prayers he had been muttering under his breath. A little later, the "No Smoking" sign turned off, and we heard the sound of the pilot's voice as he introduced himself, telling us our cruising speed and altitude, and how long it would be before we reached Beirut.

I undid the seatbelt, and took out of my pocket my pack of Egyptian cigarettes. I lit one. I realized from the first puff that smoke was seeping out of it from several holes, so I stubbed it out on the tray table. I decided to put off smoking for a while, to reduce the risk of getting cancer.

My neighbor addressed me as though he were continuing a conversation between us.

"Didn't the war end two years ago? So why all those procedures?"

I didn't understand at first which war or which procedures he meant. Then I realized he was referring to the Lebanese Civil War, and the repeated inspections we were subjected to.

I turned to him. "They're just precautions – there's no sinister motives behind them."

The brown face of an older man, around sixty, gazed back

at me. At the center of it were two cunning eyes, surrounded by a light-gray beard with a tapered end.

His eyes roamed over my clothes and hair, and lingered over my finger, which had no wedding ring, and the glimmers of white hair on my head. An intense focus appeared in his eyes as he observed the leather bag placed between my feet.

I felt an urgent need for a drink, so I turned in the other direction, leaning into the aisle to ask one of the flight attendants. I mentally calculated how many dollar bills I had on me, and decided to order a beer. Then I remembered that it cost more than fifty cents, but less than a whole dollar. Usually, the flight attendant wouldn't give back change for a dollar, because the plane was Arab, and we were all Arabs. But for this dollar, I could get a glass of whiskey or gin that would put a little life in my veins.

One of the passengers in the opposite row turned toward me, clutching his armrest with fingers covered with an overlay of yellow. He was addressing the passenger behind me in an Egyptian accent, asking him if he had bought his tape recorder at the duty-free shop.

"These fellows are all heading off to work in Iraq," the Saudi said, gesturing at him. "They're forced to travel by way of Beirut. Baghdad Airport is closed, and Amman Airport can't handle the overflow any longer."

My need for a drink grew stronger. The flight attendant walked by and I asked her for a glass of whiskey. I ignored the look of disapproval from the Saudi.

A moment later, he asked, "Is Beirut your final destination or are you headed somewhere else?"

"No," I said, "Beirut."

"East or West Beirut?"

I was about to answer automatically that I was going to East Beirut. But then I remembered that Beirut was the only place in the world today where political alignments are just the opposite of their geographical locations.

"West Beirut," I replied. "And you?"

"I have business in a lot of places."

The flight attendant brought me an extremely small bottle containing enough for one glass, and a glass with some ice cubes. I opened the bottle and poured the whiskey into the glass, then shook it around several times and raised it to my lips.

Warmth coursed through my insides. I lit myself a cigarette and took some slow puffs.

"Business or pleasure?" he asked.

"Business," I replied.

"First time?"

"No."

I emptied the glass, and instantly felt the desire for another one.

"Do you have a job lined up, or are you going to look for one?" he went on.

"You might say I'm going to look."

"What kind of work do you do, exactly?" he asked with interest.

"Writing."

"You're a journalist?"

"Not exactly."

"So you're not going to look for a job at one of the newspapers there?"

I shook my head.

"Then are you looking for a political organization you can write for?"

"Not at all. I'm looking for a publisher for a book I've written."

He lapsed into thought, so it was my turn to ask him: "And you . . . what kind of work do you do?"

"As you Egyptians would say, I'm a *contractor*."

"A contractor for what?"

"Everything."

He gestured with his hand, pointing to the Egyptian passengers on the plane, adding, "I have hundreds of these people in Saudi Arabia."

I began to imagine that second glass of whiskey.

"Do you know a movie director named Sobhy Tawfiq?" he asked me.

I thought about it, and then answered that I didn't.

"I was with him at the Hilton this morning," he told me.

I made no response. He was silent for a moment, and then continued with his questions: "Why didn't you publish your book in Egypt?"

"No one wants to publish it," I replied.

"Is it your first book?"

"No."

"It must be a political book."

"Just the opposite," I said. "It's a pornographic book."

He blinked quickly, then went quiet. After a little while, he hesitantly asked, "Do those books . . . make money?"

"Oh, a lot."

I felt that I deserved another glass, so I decided to sacrifice a second dollar. I signalled the flight attendant as she walked by, passing out newspapers.

I took two Lebanese newspapers from her, handing one of them to my neighbor. I noticed she had several American newspapers, so I helped myself. I glanced at the lower half of the Lebanese paper, and found it was divided into three main articles: the first was about the press conference that Reagan held after his election as president of the United States. The second was about a recent Israeli bombardment of South Lebanon. As for the third, it contained a statement by the foreign minister of Iraq, in which he defended the war that his country had launched against Iran, saying that Iraq's military and economic forces would be liberated from the Iranian "distraction", so that it could counteract the Israeli menace.

I spread out the newspaper and looking up at me in the middle of the page was a large headline that read: "Decisive resolutions for a ceasefire in West Beirut". I looked for the date, and found it was November 7, 1980 – today's. I went back to the news item and read: "In the last few hours, firm decisions have been taken to clamp down on the clashes that have taken place in the last two days in West Beirut, following a series of calls between leaders of Lebanese parties and groups, Palestinian organizations and Syrian authorities."

Below that I read the full details of the events it referred to. They had begun when the car belonging to the president of the greengrocers' syndicate in West Beirut (whose name was Munir Fatiha) was at an intersection and tried to pass in front of another car driven by a member of the *Syrian Social Nationalist Party (SSNP)*. The two drivers exchanged curses, then both pulled out guns and aimed them at each other. The driver of the second car fired first and shot the syndicate president, killing him, then fled.

As soon as the victim's son – who was one of the leaders of the Nasserist organization known as the *Mourabitoun* ("the *Sentinels*") – learned what had happened, he assembled a military team and attacked the house of Bashir Ubayd, one of the leaders of the SSNP. There the attackers found another party leader, the poet Kamal Khayrbek and his young niece Nahiya Bijani, and killed all three of them. Clashes broke out between members of the two parties immediately afterwards.

I searched all over the paper for new details, but only found a reference to a lead article in the Lebanese paper *al-Safeer*, which said that armed militias in West Beirut – who were followers or allies of the Lebanese National Movement, the Palestinian resistance or the Syrian government, or who were (to use the newspaper's expression) "operating on their own account" – were responsible for the security vacuum and the chaos, as well as the crimes and lawlessness that take place under those conditions, from murder and armed assault to extortion, illegal appropriation of apartments and buildings, and the piling up of uncollected trash.

I put the newspaper to one side and spread out the American paper. It had yesterday's date. At the bottom of the first page I spotted a small article with the title "The war that doesn't want to end". My eyes quickly scanned:

*The armed clashes that took place yesterday in West Beirut offer a highly indicative picture of the state of affairs in Lebanon since the civil war broke out in 1975 among the people of this beautiful country. (Its 3 million inhabitants before the war have been reduced to 2.5 million now.)*

*Officially, this war ended in 1977, once Arab peacekeeping*

7

forces, primarily made up of Syrian troops, assumed control. But the various conflicts between the two sides have not definitively come to an end. Mostly that is because recently these clashes have centered on internecine fights within each side, reminiscent of Chicago's gang wars in the 1920s and 30s, or bloody fights between Mafia families.

This past July 7, Bashir Gemayel *(age 33)*, the young military leader of the Maronite Phalangist militia, and de facto ruler of East Beirut, led a campaign of elimination against the strongholds of his partner in the Maronite front, Camille Chamoun. *He cynically called it the "corrective movement" and in a few hours killed more than 500 men from the "Tigers" militia, who were followers of Chamoun. As a result, a submissive Chamoun agreed to participate in the meetings of the military council of "Lebanese forces" under the command of Bashir Gemayel, in exchange for his continuing to get his share of the profits from Dbaiyeh harbor, in addition to a million dollars cash.*

*Four months before the massacre of the Tigers, an explosive charge, operated by remote control, went off in Bashir Gemayel's car. It took the life of his daughter Maya (age 3), who had been born the night before another attack her father organized against the summer palace of the previous president* Suleiman Frangieh, *in the village of Ehden. Among the victims were Frangieh's oldest son Tony (age 36), his wife Vera (age 32) and their daughter Jihan (age 3).*

*These massacres accompanied the rise of Bashir Gemayel, and his ambition to impose his leadership on the Maronite front, or the "Lebanese front", as it calls itself. It is composed of the forces of* Pierre Gemayel *(the Phalangists), Chamoun (the Tigers), and Frangieh (the Giants), not to mention*

*Charbel Qassis (the Permanent Congress of Lebanese Monastic Orders) and Etienne Saqr (Guardians of the Cedars).*

*On the other side of the Green Line that separates the two halves of the Lebanese capital, similar battles take place between the various forces that make up the opposing front – sometimes called the Islamic front, and other times, the Nationalist, Progressive or Leftist front.*

*In addition to the Palestinian organizations, some of which have ties to Arab countries that are at each other's throats, such as Iraq, Syria, Saudi Arabia and Libya, this front is made up of Nasserist parties whose allegiance is divided among Iraq, Syria and Libya, and two Baathist organizations, one of which follows the Iraq line, while the other falls in behind Syrian leadership. Others are Communist groups that fly the flag of Marx and Lenin, a socialist party that is considered the liberal wing of the Druze sect, and scattered Islamist factions, some of which represent local leadership for Sunnis and Shia. These are semi-feudal leadership positions bound by firm ties to monarchies in the Arab world, whereas others represent new forms of leadership for these two religious communities, some of which enjoy the support of Khomeini, while others are in Gaddafi's good graces.*

*Discord can easily flare up among these widely-differing groups, as a reflection of existing struggles among Arab regimes, or because of struggles over spheres of influence, in the same way that the trivial dispute in the street could lead to a wide-ranging mêlée. Every individual, one way or another, follows an organization or a party. Tribal thinking holds sway: the parties he follows must leap to his aid, whether right or wrong, using one dominant idiom – that of the gun.*

\*   \*   \*

The newspaper concluded its editorial by stating: "The coming few hours will reveal whether it is possible to cordon off the clashes and impose order, or whether the country will continue its slide into a seemingly bottomless chasm."

The Saudi was reading his newspaper with interest as he nervously looked up at me from time to time, trying to get a fix on my reaction. I let my face stay frozen until I finished reading, then I turned to him.

"Obviously, we've arrived at just the right time," I said.

# 2

I took my passport from the bored passport officer, and put it in the bag hanging on my shoulder. Then I picked up my suitcase in my right hand, and the duty-free bag in my left, and crossed the passport control barrier to the small airport arrivals hall, without anyone bothering to inspect me, even from the customs area.

I walked to the bank window and exchanged fifty dollars at the rate of four lira per dollar. Then I headed to the airport exit, a few steps away. There was a row of taxis directly outside the door, overseen by a policeman carrying a notebook. I noticed the Saudi standing beside one of the taxis, and I heard him ask the driver to take him to East Beirut.

I went up to the next car and gave the driver my destination. He left his seat and walked around the car. I followed him and handed him the suitcase so he could put it in the trunk. Then I walked up to the policeman and asked him in a low voice how much the fare would be.

"Thirty lira," he replied.

From where he was standing by the car, the driver shouted, "Thirty isn't enough. Everyone pays forty."

The policeman gently rebuked him, indicating to me to get in.

The driver dug in his heels, shouting, "I don't want to go to West Beirut."

"Come on," the policeman said, chiding him. "Don't yell. Are you going to take him or should he take the next one?"

The driver gave in, shouting at me, "Hurry up, man. Get in."

I got into the back seat. The car took off, with the driver audibly muttering to himself as he made a fast turn that put us on the main road.

The airport road appeared more abandoned than I had expected. Earthworks and mounds of dirt extended on both sides. We approached a group of soldiers concealing themselves behind one of these mounds, standing around an armored car that bore the name *Arab Deterrent Force*.

"Now the Syrians are stopping us," the driver muttered.

Our car stopped in front of the soldiers. One of them examined the driver's papers, and then asked for my passport. After a close look inside the car, he let us continue on our way.

We reached the Bourj el-Barajneh camp, with its humble dwellings cheek by jowl, none of which were more than two stories high. We passed a group of armed men wearing the badges of the Palestinian Armed Struggle on their shoulders. They stood behind a barrier made up of a line of barrels. The driver slowed down in order to be ready to stop, but they waved at us to let us pass.

"Where in West Beirut?" the driver asked without taking his eyes from the road.

"*Hamra Street*," I said. "At the Piccadilly Cinema."

We reached the end of the camp, then we crossed a small

city square, and made our way alongside the Sabra camp. Three men wearing scruffy clothes blocked our path. The first of them had his head wrapped in a woolen headscarf, and the second held a big bundle of cloth in his hands. One of them addressed the driver: "Mazraa?"

The driver raised his chin, using the well-known Lebanese gesture that means "no". As they continued walking, the man with the headscarf asked him, "Where are you headed?"

"Hamra," he replied.

"Why can't you go by way of Mazraa?"

"I don't want to."

An old man, his face filled with wrinkles, interjected: "Please, driver. We're late – we'll pay what you want."

"Hey man," the driver yelled, "I can't take Mazraa. Those guys keep you held up."

"Look, it's right by the Abd al-Nasser Mosque. Why can't you go from here to the Cola intersection?"

The driver thought about it, then asked, "You're getting off at Cola?"

The three of them agreed, and the driver asked me to move up to the front seat so the three men could sit together in the back. I sat down beside him, putting my carry-on and bag of cigarettes and alcohol between us.

"That's just like you Palestinians. Always causing problems," he said as he started us moving again.

No one answered him. Silence descended over the car for the rest of the trip. From time to time, I would catch the eye of the old man in the rearview mirror as he looked nervously between me and the driver.

We emerged onto another city square. After a little while, we turned off to the left, and passed by a large building that showed extensive destruction. All that was left of its façade was a row of darkened crevices, one next to the other.

Scenes of destruction followed in succession as darkness quickly descended. Locked-up shops lined both sides of the street, which was empty of pedestrians. The driver turned into a side street, then stopped near a high bridge.

The three men got out of the car, and they collected among themselves several banknotes, which the old man handed to the driver, saying, "God be with you."

The driver examined the cash, then shouted, "Ten bills? That's not enough. Who do you think you're dealing with?"

The three men exchanged glances, and the youngest responded, "That's what we always pay."

A powerful searchlight suddenly fixed on us, and a military jeep approached. When it pulled up alongside us, we could see the emblem of the Palestinian Armed Struggle on its side.

The driver cursed under his breath and put the cash in his pocket. Then he stepped on the gas, and the car sped off.

We reached the edge of Hamra, and as he was about to stop, he said, "Here's Hamra."

"Not yet," I said. "I'll be getting out at the cinema."

He proceeded down the street. Its shops and cafés were locked up, even though there appeared to be a few people about. Then he turned down a side street. A distracted look appeared in his eyes, as though he were thinking over some problem.

"Where are you going?" I called out. "The cinema is on the main street."

"Now we'll see."

He leaned out the window and shouted at the driver of a passing taxi: "Save me a space, Abu Hasan!"

I asked him where he wanted to save a space. "The airport roundabout," he replied.

He began to drive aimlessly between the streets, so I told him, "We have to get onto Hamra Street itself. That's where the cinema is."

He didn't respond, but headed towards a street corner where several young men were gathered, armed with machine-guns. He stuck his head out the window and shouted, "Hello, guys! Which way to the Piccadilly Cinema?"

One of them came up to us and rested his gun on the edge of the window. He looked to me like a teenager with a mustache that had barely begun to appear on his lip. He looked me over carefully, then turned to the driver and explained to him which way to go.

"These streets all look alike," he said, as we took off.

"Obviously you don't know the streets of Beirut very well," I said, trying to imitate the Lebanese accent.

"We came from the south in '78, after the Israeli invasion."

We emerged onto Hamra Street. In a few moments, the cinema appeared, and I asked him to turn into the street next to it. I had a hard time recognizing the hotel I was heading for, since everything was dark.

I made him stop and I got out of the car. Then I turned around to take my carry-on and duty-free bags, and I found his hand exploring inside the carry-on. I wrenched the bag away from him, saying, "Shame on you!"

He left his seat in silence, and opened the trunk, then he took out my suitcase and put it on the ground.

I counted out thirty lira, then added five extra, and gave it to him. Silently, he put it in his pocket and drove off. I picked up my things and crossed the street.

Dim lights illuminated the hotel lobby. Several young men were scattered on worn-out leather chairs. Some of them were armed.

The employee at the reception desk dealt with me without much enthusiasm. I asked for the cheapest room with a bath, and he gave me one for forty lira per night. A young man sluggishly carried my suitcase and accompanied me in the elevator to the fourth floor. Then he walked ahead of me to an extremely narrow room with a torn carpet.

I gave him a lira and he took it with a show of indifference. I locked the door behind him, then I leaned over the suitcase and opened the lock. I raised the lid and laid it against the floor. I got down on my knees and with my fingers groped around the inner lining. Then I pulled out a delicate leather frame that went around the entire lid. The frame submitted to my fingers, and peeled off the lid like adhesive tape.

A slight crack appeared in the lid's inner lining. I stuck my fingers in it and pulled out three medium-sized yellow envelopes. I put the lid back in its place and locked the suitcase.

I took out the papers the three envelopes held, emptying them onto the bed, and arranged them according to how many sheets there were of each, then I gathered them all up in one envelope and put it in my carry-on.

I washed my hands and face and slung the bag over my shoulder, heading out of the room to go downstairs. I left the key at reception, then went outside. All of a sudden, one of the young men stopped me, calling out, "Where are you headed, sir?"

I looked up at him inquisitively, and he added, "Are you crazy? The streets are dangerous now."

I hesitated and looked around me. I noticed a payphone in a corner and headed towards it, as I pulled my notebook out of my pocket.

# 3

I met Wadia Masiha when I entered high school. We studied in the same class, but he sat far away from me. We all wore shorts, except for two or three of the oldest boys, and we got a hidden pleasure from our bare knees rubbing together. In some classes, we would change places for this purpose, and everyone would sit beside someone he took a liking to. In this contest, I would strive to sit next to Wadia. He had long legs, with thick calves and smooth knees.

We didn't visit each other's homes often. My mother didn't like him coming over, and his house stirred up feelings of aversion and terror in me. In broad daylight, it was dark, and stuffed with old furniture. Sounds didn't echo back there, and a distinctive smell wafted within it – a mixture of frying oil and decay resulting from the damp walls.

Once I told him he was a "*blue bone*" without understanding what that expression meant. Instantly, his face grew pale and he became angry, then he stopped being friends with me. Two weeks later, I happened to meet him after we were let out from school. Several of the biggest boys in our class surrounded him and made him repeat "*blue bone*". The look in his eyes terrified me. It spoke of a fear I had never seen before.

We renewed our friendship at the university, which we entered together some months after the outbreak of the Egyptian revolution. We found ourselves among a group of ardent youth: we would read Sartre, Gorky and Lefebvre; we would attack Taha Hussein in defense of socialist realism, and attack the government of "military men" in defense of democracy. We would cross the streets of Cairo on foot, in our shoes with holes in them. Then we were all arrested when *Gamal Abdel Nasser* tightened his iron fist in March 1954. After that, we went to prison together, during the climax of Nasser's battle with the left.

But Wadia left prison after only one week, while I stayed there until the general pardon was proclaimed in 1964. After a while, I found a job at a newspaper. I found him working there. He had become prominent in the government's political organization, the Arab Socialist Union, of which everyone was trying to become a member. So it was no surprise that our ideas and opinions were in accord. We both felt the same shock when the Israeli aggression in 1967 resulted in our defeat.

The next year, he was appointed to the newspaper's office in Beirut. At that time, traveling abroad was our collective dream: it was easier to pass through the proverbial eye of a needle. I wasn't able to do it until I had resigned from the newspaper and sought the help of several personal connections. I went to Beirut, where Wadia hosted me for several weeks. Then I left Lebanon, and didn't see him for many years. But I knew that he had gotten married to a female relative of his, and had become the director of the newspaper's bureau in the Lebanese capital. That didn't surprise me, since he was capable in his work and had the most solid relationships with key people from all the different parties and factions and maintained meticulous records of every piece of information.

The newspaper transferred him to its main headquarters in Cairo after the war in October 1973. But he kept trying until he got back his posting in Beirut in mid-1976. When he was recalled to Cairo after a year, he refused to return and resigned. Then he joined a newspaper funded by the Iraqis, and finally moved from there to a private press agency run by an enterprising Lebanese journalist named Nazar Baalbaki.

I didn't find it hard to get his home telephone number from the agency's headquarters. I waited for him in the hotel lobby until he arrived fifteen minutes later. We embraced each other warmly, each studying the changes time had wrought on the other. He commented on the color of my hair, while I found fault with the weight he had put on and the prescription glasses that covered half of his face. Then he led me outside, ignoring my talk about the warnings I had been given about dangers in the street, saying: "I've got different identity cards for different situations. And we won't be going far."

We entered an empty bar on a nearby street. "Will you be staying long?" he asked me as we sat down.

"Several days," I replied. "I don't have a lot of money."

"Are you going to publish something?"

"Yes. I have a book being published with Adnan Sabbagh."

"But he isn't in Beirut now, I think."

I looked nervously at him, and said, "But we made an appointment to meet here on Monday. Do you think the recent events could have canceled this meeting?"

"What happened is a normal occurrence – it happens every other day. The Lebanese have gotten used to that, and life now moves along naturally, no matter what. In fact, there is a helicopter company that transports people across districts that are fighting each other so their work won't get interrupted.'

The waiter brought us two glasses of whiskey. I looked around me and found that we were still the only patrons under the dim lights. The bartender was in the midst of a whispered conversation with two of his colleagues, and they looked over at the door from time to time.

Suddenly the staccato sound of bullets reached us from outside. The whispered conversation at the bar stopped. We all listened in fear. Several minutes passed, but the sound wasn't repeated, and hesitantly the whispering began again.

"Where are you working now?" Wadia asked me.

"Nowhere," I replied.

"So how do you make your living?"

"From writing."

"Is that possible?"

"Maybe. If you keep your needs within tight limits. And my wife was working."

"I heard that the two of you split up."

"Yes. We went different ways, in spite of ourselves."

"You should have done like I did. My wife and I only see each other in the summer. She spends the rest of the year with the children in Cairo."

"I don't understand why you insist on not going back to Cairo."

He tapped the ashes from his cigarette in the ashtray, and with the tip of it began drawing imaginary circles in the air, then said: "Whenever I pictured myself there, I felt like I was suffocating."

We were both lost in thought, and then he asked me, "Who are you meeting?"

"Just a few people," I replied. "I don't get around much anymore."

A crooked smile spread over his lips. "So you've quit your old friends?" he said.

"You know what keeping in contact is like now. Traveling to Beirut is easier than moving between neighborhoods in Cairo."

"And how are things generally? The situation as a whole?"

"Normalization with Israel is moving ahead. Prices are increasing and services are declining, too. Plundering is a growth industry, and the number of millionaires has grown to several hundred."

He looked me carefully in the eye, then asked, "Are you planning on meeting someone in particular? There are a lot of fugitive Egyptians here."

"I've come for one purpose only, and as soon as I'm done with it, I'll go back."

"Tell me about your book."

I made a vague gesture with my hand. "It's essentially a trip around the Arab world in a way that resembles the venerable *maqama* genre of rhymed prose. The hero turns up in every country, then he is kicked out, only to appear in another one, and so on."

He gave a slightly mocking smile, then added: "Is the hero a revolutionary or a Palestinian?"

"Not necessarily either one," I replied.

He looked at his watch, saying, "We should leave now, before the streets become totally unsafe."

He paid the bill. I put my bag over my shoulder and we left the bar.

"I'll get lost if you don't take me back to the hotel," I said.

"We'll go to my house now," he replied, "and in the morning we'll get your things from the hotel."

"There's no need for that," I said. "I brought with me the cash I need. And I'll be getting an advance from Adnan in a few days. He's agreed to publish the book."

"You're coming with me," he said decisively.

"I don't want to be a burden on you."

"I live by myself. My wife and kids are in Cairo now. There's an empty room you can have."

We crossed several dark streets without encountering anyone. At one intersection, two armed men came out towards us, aiming the muzzles of their machineguns at us. But they didn't block our path when we continued walking steadily.

Wadia took a deep breath after we had moved away, and in a muffled voice, said: "They belong to a new organization that took over this street two weeks ago. I don't know any of their men."

We crossed a city square dominated by a demolished building, and he continued in his normal voice, "Now we're in a neighborhood that belongs to the Mourabitoun. I have some ID that shows – I'm one of their members."

"Why don't you buy a car?" I asked.

"I have one, but I'm afraid to drive it."

We headed onto a street lined with buildings of modern construction. Wadia stopped in front of one, the entranceway of which was covered with a sturdy metal screen. He banged forcefully on it while calling in a loud voice, "Abu Shakir!"

In the farthest part of the entranceway there was a door that opened up to reveal an old man with a beard, wearing shabby clothes. In his hand he carried a key ring. When he approached, I noticed that he was girded with a military belt with a revolver hanging from it.

Abu Shakir opened the screen for us in silence, and we took the elevator to the third floor. Then I followed Wadia to a neat apartment of two bedrooms and a sizeable living room. Cushions from the Khan al-Khalili were spread out all over it, and a wooden desk sat in one corner.

"Nice apartment," I said. "How much do you pay for it?"

"Four thousand dollars a year," he replied. "The price is cheap because I got it a while ago."

I sat down on a comfortable couch near the entrance to the living room. Wadia brought a small table over and placed on it a bottle of whiskey, a bucket of ice cubes and two glasses.

"I brought you a bottle of whiskey."

"Liquor is cheap here," he said. "They sell it almost at duty-free prices."

He poured himself a glass, adding, "The different factions collect customs duties from the ports in their areas. The Maronites resort to lowering duties on cigarettes, liquor and television equipment in order to lure businessmen into dealing with their ports, and the others are forced to keep up with them."

My eyes wandered over the Pharaonic and Islamic antiquities arrayed on the shelves that covered one wall. Among them, I noticed a crucifix with a photo of Pope Shenouda dangling from one end.

I looked closely at it and Wadia's face turned deep red.

"My wife hung that up."

I poured a glass for myself and lay back, saying, "Do you remember the woman who regularly visited you in '68?"

"Who do you mean?"

"The woman who said she charged a fee of fifty lira a session, but because she liked you, she would make it forty."

He seemed to have forgotten all about it, or pretended that he had. At one point, he had asked me to stay away from the house on certain days of the week, claiming that he was hosting a married Lebanese woman. I noticed her once as I was going out, and her appearance roused my suspicions. When I pressed him, he said that she needed cash in order to replace her refrigerator. She reminded him that she charged a fee of fifty liras, but she liked him, and so she would give him a discount of forty. I expressed my willingness to pay the fifty lira, which he proposed to her, but she refused with disdain, and became angry with him. How could he behave like that when the two of them were in love?

"Are there Egyptian women here?" I asked him.

"Of course," he replied. "Women looking for adventure, dancers, and women looking to 'find themselves'. I know one of the female students who participated in the 1973 demonstrations. She settled in Beirut during the war. She came to me one day looking for a place to stay. My wife wasn't here."

He lapsed into silence, and I asked him, "And then what?"

"She warned me against taking advantage of the situation, and confidently declared that she would initiate things with me of her own accord if she wanted to."

"And did she?"

"Once. But I left her."

"Why?"

"I was afraid."

He stood up, saying, "This is the time of day when we have access to clean water. It comes early in the morning for two hours. The rest of the day it's shut off, except for the two hours before midnight. I'll fill several bottles."

"You're luckier than we are in Cairo," I said as I followed him into the kitchen. "We don't get a single minute of clean water. Not to mention that our polluted water is shut off for most of the day."

# 4

Wadia gave me his children's room, and some loose-fitting pajamas, which I declined to use. But despite the overpowering exhaustion I was feeling, I turned over in bed for a long time, unable to fall asleep. I finally dozed off after what I imagined to be the sound of a distant explosion came to an end. But I only slept a few hours, and woke up as soon as sunlight made its way into the room.

I tried to go back to sleep, but to no avail, so I got out of bed. I put on my shirt and pants and went out into the living room. I came upon Wadia reading a newspaper. He was not wearing glasses, so he was holding it up close to his eyes. I said good morning to him and headed toward the bathroom. The water was cold, and there was no trace of heating equipment, despite the presence of two faucets in the sink.

I opened the bathroom door and called out: "How can you live in the 'Paris of the East' without hot water?"

"The water heater is centralized, genius. Turn on the left faucet."

I took a quick bath, then put on my clothes and combed my hair. I walked into the living room. Wadia handed me the paper, saying, "Bad news."

He read me a headline about new Israeli attacks, using Phantom and Skyhawk planes, against the cities of Tyre and

Nabatiya in the south. The victims came to thirty-three injured and killed, with sixteen homes destroyed. Below that was another headline about the return of normal life to West Beirut.

I looked at him inquisitively. He pointed to the lower half of the newspaper, then walked into the kitchen.

There was a report about the arrival of an Egyptian military delegation to Saudi Arabia on a secret visit for shared military planning with the United States. And another report about a memorial service that would take place that afternoon in one of the churches of Hamra, following the funerals of Bashir Ubayd and Kamal Kheir Bek. Buried in the back pages of the newspaper, I found what was causing Wadia concern, under the headline "Loud explosion at dawn".

The report was terse, but the gist of it was that an explosive charge had been set off at dawn at a publishing house owned by Adnan al-Sabbagh. It caused enormous damage, but no one was hurt.

I sat down on the closest chair and reread the article, then looked up at Wadia, who was setting out a tray with breakfast on the table.

"Who do you suppose did it?" I asked.

He shrugged his shoulders. "Anyone," he replied. "You've got the Iraqis, the Syrians, the Jordanians, the Shia, the Israelis and the Libyans, etc, etc."

"Is Adnan linked to a particular faction?"

"It's hard to say. It's no longer the case that people have ties to a specific faction. Nowadays everyone has ties to multiple groups in order to avoid surprises."

"But why did they blow up the publishing house when they knew for certain he wouldn't be there?"

"Maybe the idea was to punish him or to send him a message," he said, pouring tea from a colored ceramic teapot.

I contemplated the breakfast tray which presented, in the Lebanese style, an assortment of various types of foods, from boiled eggs to green and black olives, *lebneh*, jam, and *zaatar* mixed with olive oil.

"In any case," he went on, "he's luckier than Salim al-Lawzi, who was kidnapped by the Syrians. They burned his hands before they killed him."

"I wonder how he'll react when he sees what happened to his publishing house."

"I don't think he'd dare show his face in Beirut now."

He dove enthusiastically into the food, and when he saw that I was holding back, he said, "Don't be upset. Maybe you can contact him in Europe through his wife. She's the one who oversees the publishing house when he's away. You can be sure that what just happened won't have any effect on his work. In fact, it may have helped him get new sources of support. And there are dozens of publishers besides him. Did you bring a copy of the manuscript with you?"

"Fortunately, yes."

"Then we'll make copies of it and show it to a number of publishers."

"But that will take time."

"A week at the most."

"I was hoping to work with Adnan," I said, giving in. "He has a good reputation."

"Don't be naive," he said. "They're all the same."

I ate a little, and examined the rest of the newspaper. Then I volunteered to make the coffee. I wanted to clean up the remains of breakfast, but he insisted that I leave everything as it was, saying, "There's a woman who comes twice a week to clean. Today's her day."

I went to the bedroom, pulled out the thick yellow envelope from my shoulder bag, and brought it to the living room. Wadia had gone into his room, so I followed him there. I found him putting on his clothes. I noticed that his body, which had been slim when he was young, was now layered in fat in several places.

"Maybe we can make some arrangements today?" I asked as I brandished the envelope.

"Is this the manuscript? Today is Saturday. Everyone is heading out for the weekend. We won't be able to do anything with it before Monday. The only thing we can do now is photocopy it."

I happened to glance at the side table next to the bed, and noticed a gun on it. He saw where I was looking and laughed, saying, "It's only for show. I don't know how to use it."

He pointed to the window. He had replaced the glass with a sheet of cardboard.

"Can you imagine that two seconds were all that came between me and death? I was standing here, just the way you are now. It occurred to me to make a phone call, so I left the room. At that moment I heard the sound of glass shattering, and of something moving violently in the room and striking the wall. After that, I stumbled onto what was left of a rocket missile."

We shared our ride down in the elevator with an elegant Lebanese man in a suit of white silk the same color as the hair on his head, which he had combed with considerable care. He was accompanied by a blonde woman in her fifties wearing tight black pants that ended at her knees, and which were held up by thin suspenders over her shoulders that revealed her chest.

We walked in the opposite direction from the way we had come yesterday, passing a group of armed men under a balcony, over which had been raised the banner of the Mourabitoun. Sitting on the balcony was a tall young man with a vicious-looking face, wearing military fatigues. He had propped his machinegun against the balcony railing, and was engrossed in cleaning a long bandolier of gleaming brass cartridges. Several steps away stood an armored car bearing the emblem of the Deterrent Forces, next to a car rental office. Opposite the armored car – on the other sidewalk – a vendor had set out quantities of cigarettes, liquor, chocolate and condoms on top of cardboard boxes underneath a wooden umbrella.

We made our way through several quiet streets. Sandbags blocked the entrances of the houses, and empty cars lined the sides. Wadia pulled me by the arm far away from the edge of the sidewalk, saying: "Any one of these cars could be booby-trapped and explode without warning."

We walked down a street crowded with more Deterrent Forces armored cars. Perched on top of them were soldiers wearing steel helmets. The armored cars were standing in front of a building over which one of the flags was raised, and traces of damage appeared on the closed-up shops on the building's ground-floor level.

We emerged onto a city square, on one side of which stood a military truck. A machinegun was mounted over the driver's cab, with a bare-headed soldier standing behind it. Behind the truck a locked-up storefront could be seen; above it was a torn sign, where the only remaining word was the Syrian-Lebanese *Malhama*, derived from the Arabic word *lahm*, meaning "meat". And along the stretch of the street we were coming from, the remnants of another sign flapped in the breeze, this one with European letters on which the word "Bar" stood out.

Several military cars passed by us, carrying the emblem of the Palestinian Armed Struggle. We walked in front of a hotel whose façade had been destroyed, and several young men were busy clearing the rubble. Beside it was a shop whose front window was bare of glass, revealing an elegant-looking man surrounded by modern display lamps made of two short, gleaming metal rods with round black ends. The man was collecting shards of glass with a straw broom and piling them up to one side.

We reached my hotel, where I paid the bill for the night before and got my suitcase and passport. We headed out, walking on foot, towards Hamra. Gazing down at us were portraits of Saddam Hussein on a cluster of neighboring buildings, which turned out to house Iraq's Rafidain Bank. A few steps beyond, the walls were covered with portraits of Hafez al-Assad, Khomeini and Gaddafi. A traffic light blocked our way in front of a building covered with Palestinian flags, along with portraits of Yasser Arafat and martyred victims of battles, hostilities and ambushes.

I was instantly reminded of Cairo's streets when we reached Hamra. The main thoroughfare, where traffic was one-way, coming from East Beirut and heading toward the sea, was crammed with four lanes of cars slowly moving bumper-to-bumper. The sidewalk was crowded with vendors, pedestrians, movie-theater patrons, and customers of sandwich, *shwarma* and drink stands.

I noticed there were few women out on the streets, and the distinct difference between how women looked now and how they looked at the beginning of the decade. Gone were the imported chic and glamor that marked the 1960s and the beginning of the '70s. But the elegant cafés still kept their wide glass-front windows. The luxury shops selling watches, jewelry, silverware and clothing were as crowded as ever.

We slowed down in front of a book and magazine vendor who had spread out his goods on the sidewalk. I bought a copy of the Arabic translation of Miles Copeland's *Game of Nations*, which revealed the secret of the well-known "game room" inside the Pentagon. Likewise, I bought several books that were banned in Egypt, among them one on the October 6 War and the Camp David Agreement. There were several porn magazines, including one that was new in Arabic. I flipped through its pages, and then bought it.

Wadia pointed out a book by Naguib Mahfouz in an unusual format, and another by Jurji Zaydan in a cheap binding with faded colors.

"Those two books are pirated," he said.

My face registered surprise.

"They are photocopied from the original edition. Publishing here isn't subject to rules and has no standards. Most publishers are thieves. They make an agreement with you to print, say, three thousand copies of the book, but they secretly print five thousand. Then they get out of paying what's owed to you, making the excuse that only a limited number of your books were distributed."

We continued walking, then moved off onto side streets. We entered a modern building and took the elevator up

to the second floor. I followed Wadia into an open apartment. On the door hung a sign for the Nazar Baalbaki
Agency.

Wadia's office contained two desks that faced each other,
a metal shelving unit for books and folders, and a television.
The furnishings were obviously new and chic.

"Does Nazar have money, or is someone else backing him?"
I asked, as I put my suitcase next to the wall.

He sat down at one of the two desks, pulled out a pile of
newspapers and magazines, and began flipping through them.
Then he said, "A group of rich people from the Gulf, so he
says."

"But in reality?"

"Libya, mostly."

I tossed my shoulder bag on the other desk, and sat down
at it. I pulled out the envelope that contained my manuscript,
and set it to one side. I picked up one of the magazines.

A young man brought us some cups of coffee, and Wadia
gave him the manuscript, asking him to take it to the archive
so they could make three copies of it. Then he made several
phone calls, the upshot of which was that he managed to
get the phone number of Adnan Sabbagh. He dialed the
number several times without getting an answer.

Wadia was engrossed in his writing, while I made use
of the books on the shelving unit to look up the addresses
and phone numbers of several publishing houses. An hour
later, the photocopies came back to us, and I busied myself
going over them. After another hour, Wadia finished writing, and left the room. He returned after a few minutes
and tried calling Adnan's house once again, but with no
success.

He carried my suitcase for me, and we left the office. We took a taxi to his house. I went up to his apartment while he stopped off at a nearby grilled-meat shop.

The refrigerator was filled with beer cans. I took out two and carried them into the living room. A few moments later, Wadia arrived, and we sat down to drink our beers while he turned the radio dial to search for the news.

"There are at least seven Lebanese radio stations broadcasting from now until 10 pm," he said. "One belongs to the Phalangists, and another to Suleiman Frangieh, and a third is run by American churches and speaks in the name of Saad *Haddad*'s mini-state in the south. The fourth one is Nasserist – it broadcasts songs by Umm Kulthoum, Abd al-Halim Hafez and Shaykh Imam, and is run by the Mourabitoun. And on top of that, there's the official station."

*Fairuz*'s voice reached our ears, and I asked him whose station that was.

"All the stations play Fairuz's songs," he replied. "Even though she's a Maronite."

The news was calm: the morning funeral service had passed uneventfully. The parties and organizations had offered each other condolences and announced a desire to stabilize the security situation. The Mourabitoun station said that Bashir Gemayel, the military leader for the Phalangists, was making ready to announce a Maronite state in the eastern district on the anniversary of Lebanese independence, which would take place in two weeks' time. As for the official station, it was interested in news reports of accidents and miscellaneous crimes – the most important of which was a crime that took place in Jbail province (a Christian area, apparently). Elias al-Shami had raped a woman named Mariam in the village of Ayn al-Quwayni, and when she became pregnant, he abandoned her. It was a huge scandal in the village, and a doctor agreed to give the woman an abortion. Then pressure was put on Elias, until – against his will – he agreed to marry her. Not long after that, he killed her with pesticides and then turned himself in to the Phalangists.

I drank my beer before the food we'd ordered arrived on a big tray covered with clean linen. Removing the cover revealed paper plates filled with small pieces of grilled meat, and several plates of green salad and mezze, one of which was hummus with tahini, and another was green mint, a third was garlic mashed with potatoes, a fourth was pickled cucumber, and a fifth was pickled eggplant stuffed with garlic and green cilantro. There was a fork and spoon wrapped in thin paper. Everything was clean, neat and mouthwatering.

We ate, dividing our attention between the radio and the television, which capped off the midday period with an episode from an American TV series. We both took refuge in our beds for a nap. But I couldn't doze off. I got up, went to the kitchen and made a cup of tea. Then I made some coffee for myself and for Wadia when he woke up. I put a bottle of whiskey and a container of ice on the table. We began switching between the television channels, moving between an American cop show and an Egyptian one with the title *Loyalty Without End*, and then the news in French. From the choice of evening programs, we selected an American film about the Beatles. We switched to Channel 5, and patiently waited while a long string of ads made their way through the expected roster of perfumes, cigarettes and foreign toothpastes, not to mention the Toshiba fan, featuring four blades and a nightlight, and the radical changes coming in the Arab region, as predicted by the Jordanian monarch in an exhaustive magazine interview.

Finally, the film began, so I filled my glass and Wadia reluctantly agreed to drink also. By the time we got halfway through the film, we had had several glasses, and we gradually returned to the 1960s: prison, Vietnam, Gamal Abdel Nasser, '67, the students' uprising, Che Guevara, and Brigitte Bardot. It wasn't long before we were overcome by a violent feeling of depression.

## 5

The Sunday papers made much of reports of the security détente. *Al-Safeer* announced that the next twenty-four hours would be decisive with regards to the security situation in West Beirut, and the final and radical handling of what it termed "transgressions against personal security, dignity and property, and activities involving extortion and threats, protection money and robbery, not to mention entanglements between individuals and organizations, as well as undisciplined elements that frighten peaceful citizens and rob them of their dwindling insistence on clinging to their land, nation or cause".

The newspaper had a spread of photos of the meetings between the leaders of the different organizations and parties in West Beirut and the leaders of all the warring sides. One of the photos had them all together, with Yasser Arafat in the middle. Likewise, there were photos of the memorial service for Bashir Ubayd and Khayr Bek in a church, and photos of the funeral procession, at the head of which was a beautiful young woman in her twenties: Nahiya Bijani.

The newspapers' tone encouraged us to go outside in the afternoon, and we went to an exhibit of photographic portraits in a gallery in front of the American University. The photos were all old, the kind that hang on living-room walls, or that are kept in thick, leather-bound albums. The photos of the first type retained their antique frames, decorated with ornamentation and gold leaf. The second type had been placed in simple, modern frames. Both were gathered under one title: "Lebanon Long Ago".

Occupying the place of honor was a traditional photograph of a large family: the grandfather in the center wearing Ottoman-style clothes, and with a thick mustache and a long beard that hung down over his chest. Beside him was the oldest son who threw his head back with an arrogance befitting his family's prominence, with his fez moved to the back of his head. The firm edge of a stand-up collar drove into his chin, and was encircled by a thin ribbon affixed to a wide necktie. He was wearing a jacket and vest of colored checkered cloth, and striped pants that disappeared at the knee inside the high tops of his boots.

To the left of the grandfather sat his wife or oldest daughter, and then the second son who was distinguished by the jacketed book he was carrying in his left hand, and by his ordinary pants and shoes. Behind the four seated people there was a row of three young men and three girls, all of whom resembled each other. The last girl in the row had placed her hand with special affection on the one holding the book. At the grandfather's feet, two small boys sat on the ground; next to one of them was a straw hat. The picture seemed to have been taken outside, since its background consisted of a curtain or sheet that failed to conceal a stone wall.

There were no captions next to the photograph or in the catalogue we got from a girl at the entrance who wore extremely tight jeans. Wadia volunteered some explanations: these were the clothes of the Druze, and these people were

Shia or inhabitants of Mount Lebanon, and this woman was the old man's third or fourth wife.

He pointed to an old man in a long robe with a half-collar and an extremely short fez that revealed two white temples. Beside him was a woman who could be his daughter's or granddaughter's age wearing black clothes consisting of a loose-fitting outer robe, a vest and a veil. Between them stood a six-year-old child wearing a full suit and short-topped shoes. The old man had another child on his knees who was giving the camera a fatuously serious look. As for the woman, she was on the verge of smiling. In grief? Or in amusement? Or in compliance with the photographer's wishes?

I followed Wadia to a photograph of several young men with thin, delicate mustaches that barely reached the sides of their mouths, wearing tall fezzes leaning to the left or back, and dark *sarwal* trousers, as well as jackets that revealed white shirts without neckties, worn over robes or puffy *sarwals*. They were standing around a young man who sat on a wooden chair with a straw seat, like the chairs in lower-class cafés. Two of them were resting their hands on his shoulders. He was wearing a full set of European clothes, with a fez that was not as tall and leaned more toward the front and right, as well as a small-knotted necktie that almost concealed the bottom of the shirt collar, and a small Hitler-style mustache. He was gazing confidently at the photographer, with his left leg crossed over his right. His hand clutched a thin cane that was balanced on the side of his shoe.

"Antara on a brief visit to his village."

It seemed that the corner where we were standing was devoted to photos of the countryside and of Mount Lebanon:

a handsome young man whose mustache almost reached his ears, with a dagger sticking out from an opening in his embroidered vest. A mother clothed in black from the top of her head to a few centimeters above her feet – only her eyebrows, eyes and the tip of her nose could be seen – with a barefoot child beside her. Ten men, most of whom were wearing a shirt, pants and a fez at an angle: they sat around two wooden tables set out in the open air, laden with mezze dishes and small glasses of arak. One of them poured the drink from a flask the size of a fist, while another one puffed on a narghile, and a third leaned back, giving the photographer a heroic look, with a cigarette showing behind his left ear. Behind them stood a man with European features: he might have been the Armenian owner of the place.

We moved to another gallery, and it was as though we had crossed a divide separating two worlds. I stood for a long time in front of a photograph of the entranceway to a bourgeois residence in the city: the solemn wooden door composed of two panels, the lower halves of which were covered with engraved ornamentation, while the upper halves consisted of two glass windows encased in iron gridwork of symmetrical designs. The pots for houseplants. The familiar, colorful rocking-horse ridden by a child in a sailor suit. Standing next to him, in Napoleonic style, was another child wearing the same clothes.

The next photo had only a girl with delicate features in a silk dress that flowed down to her feet. Its narrow sleeves reached her fingertips, which she used to support herself on the ornate brass edge of the couch. Her hair was done up in a chignon, held in place with the rubber bar that was used for that style in the past. In a corner of the photograph, I noticed a signature in Roman letters, from which I could make out the name "Mary".

In one of the photos, there was a date: 1918. The era of the Arab revolt against Turkish rule, two years before the defeat of the Arab Army at the hands of the French at the battle of Maysalun, which was followed by the imposition of the French mandate over Syria and Lebanon. It was one year before the great Egyptian revolution against British occupation. The photograph was of a stern-faced mother with light-colored eyes. She was sitting beside her older daughter, while the younger daughter stood behind their chairs. The three of them were bareheaded, and they wore long garments that were notable for their many folds and ornamentations. But only the two girls stood out with light colors and lace sleeves that ended just below the elbow.

In another oval-shaped portrait, two girls had their heads so close that their cheeks touched. One of them was looking at the photographer with a confidence that clearly reflected the force of her personality. As for the other one who supported herself with her cheek against the first, she stared off into space with a foolish grin.

Instead of arak drinking-sessions, cafés and large extended families, individual portraits of elegant young men looked out at me. One of them had his hair parted on the left, with a slim lock of it hanging down over his forehead. He had bent the stiff collar of his shirt along its edges, so that its rim stood over his wide necktie. His right forearm was bent to clutch a chain that hung from his waistcoat pocket.

Another one had swept his hair back, and wore a shirt with a double collar and a bowtie, underneath a narrow suit with two rows of buttons. In his left hand, he carried a pair of gloves, while supporting himself with his right elbow against a wooden fence, gazing into the camera in contemplation. A third one wore a fez of medium height that leaned to the left, a high stiff collar, and a jacket with one row of buttons. Prayer beads dangled from his hand, while the tapered ends of his mustache pointed up toward his cheeks.

I couldn't keep from smiling when I saw a portrait of a bareheaded young man wearing evening clothes with a high stiff collar and bowtie. He was sitting at a table with playing cards scattered on it, leaning his head over the left hand of an elegant girl. He was raising her hand to his lips with his index finger to plant a giddy kiss on it. His eyes were lowered, while the girl was looking at him with a smile.

There was a dignified bearing mixed with apprehension in the wedding photographs. Or at least in the two photos I managed to look at before closing time. In the first one stood a bareheaded young man with a wispy mustache, wearing a pleated collar with two long edges that nearly touched, and the small knot of a striped necktie in between them. He carried white gloves in his right hand, behind the seated bride, who was arrayed in a lace dress that left her arms bare to the shoulder and almost came up to her knees. She was adorned with masses of jewelry: two rows of pearls above her forehead, necklaces around her throat, armlets on her arms halfway between the shoulder and elbow, and a bracelet of pearls around her wrist, along with the rings on the ring and pinky fingers of her visible hand that had settled in her lap.

In the second photograph, the groom wore a low fez that was leaning so heavily to the right that its edge touched his eyebrow. He had grown out a thick mustache with pointed ends in a straight line over his lips, and his jacket hung down below his knees, while his hands were concealed in white gloves.

The bride stood to his right, winding her gloved hand around his arm. The wedding dress covered her from head to toe.

We were the last of the few visitors there to leave the gallery. We walked along the sidewalk opposite the American University, which seemed like a dark mass. I smelled with longing the scent of damp trees looking down from behind the university walls. My eyes followed along the old trolley tracks that extended along the walls and gleamed in the dazzling light cast by the movie theater that was showing an erotic film.

We walked slowly in front of a building from which a dim light emanated. I followed Wadia up a few steps and through a glass door, to an elegant room with tables spread out along its sides. Its wooden walls were covered with paintings.

We chose a table beside the glass façade looking out over the street, and sat down across from each other. Wadia had his back to the room.

"This is one of the unique places in Beirut," he said, looking out over my shoulder onto the street. "Its owner is half-artist, half-politician. He offers light dishes, drinks, news and art exhibits. Café revolutionaries come here, as do thieves, exiles, lovers, pimps, gays, lesbians and spies."

The waiter brought us two glasses of whiskey, a bowl of peanuts (or "slaves' pistachios", as the Levantines call them), and another one of French fries. Presently, the owner joined us, welcoming Wadia. He looked about forty to me, with dark bluish eyes and a sensuous mouth.

He and Wadia traded the latest news and jokes. I turned away to observe the paintings hanging on the walls. They were by modern Lebanese painters of different schools and styles. I noticed that their names alternated among Armenian, Muslim and Christian. The Christians were of two kinds: those with Arab names, like Ilyas and Saliba, and those with European names, like Yvette and Helene. The subjects of the paintings were similarly divided: some had a distinct European feel, but a minority of them had a local character.

I was struck by two paintings next to each other by the same artist. They were distinguished by their rich colors, and the aesthetic unity of their folk origins. One of them, in which purple colors predominated, represented two horsemen facing each other, in the manner of popular images of al-Khidr and Dhul-Qarnayn. As for the second painting, it derived its topic from the shape of the cross which contained the Virgin Mary in the form of a blazing candle.

I noticed a young man and woman sitting in a corner, clinging to each other. In front of them were two martini glasses. The young man was continually whispering in his companion's ear. I sensed the café owner leaving our table, and I followed him with my eyes as he cut a path between the diners, directing an amusing remark at a heavy-set lady wearing black clothes. She was by herself at one of the tables, with her back to me.

"Did you hear what he said?" Wadia asked me. "He thinks it was the *Deuxième Bureau* that planned the explosion at Adnan's publishing house. Apparently, it also had a hand in what happened to Bashir Ubayd."

"How so?"

"Bashir Ubayd was a Maronite Christian. He was just about the only Maronite among the leading bodies of the Lebanese National Movement. Getting rid of him serves the purposes of the Phalangists, who want to be the only ones that represent the Maronites."

"But wasn't it the Mourabitoun that killed him?"

He shrugged his shoulders. "That doesn't mean it didn't happen with the planning of the Deuxième Bureau for the benefit of the Phalangists."

"What is the Deuxième Bureau exactly?"

"The intelligence agency. The way it's structured is a reflection of the current situation. You can find agents there working for all the political movements, not to mention international spy agencies."

I happened to look at the woman in black, and found that she was no longer by herself. Sitting across from her was another woman, in her early thirties, with a beautiful face, and wearing a light-blue sleeveless blouse that exposed her delicate arms.

"And what about Adnan?" I asked Wadia.

"Who knows? Maybe he was an operative for the Deuxième Bureau who turned against them, and so they wanted to teach him a lesson. Maybe they did the whole thing for a fee to benefit some party."

As I listened to him, I observed the woman with the blue blouse. Before me was an elongated face with radiant skin, a straight nose and full lips. Her long coal-black hair came down over her back.

"For the last ten years," Wadia continued, "Adnan hasn't held a steady job for more than a month or two before being let go. He had revolutionary ideas; then he married Lamia. She is from an old, respectable family, although she wasn't very wealthy. The two of them succeeded in amassing an immense fortune worth millions of lira."

46

The woman with the blue blouse crossed her legs, and her skirt revealed her attractive curves, and a side view of her firm thighs. She was talking non-stop and her companion was listening attentively. Then she stopped talking and I turned my attention to her hand spread out on the table. I noticed her companion's hand resting on it in a gesture of reassurance and affection.

I became aware of Wadia's voice: "What made Adnan's fortune was petroleum. It made it possible for him to move from books to printing presses, movies and tapes. But he had talent, too."

The woman stood up, revealing a slender figure topped by a long neck. She had a long-sleeved jacket thrown over her shoulders, letting it hang down over her bare forearms. She crossed the room with firm steps and an unintended haughtiness. Her friend, who seemed older than her, followed. Her face was attractive despite its masculine features that were emphasized by the lack of any trace of makeup.

Wadia followed the direction of my eyes, and suddenly he put his hand on mine, saying quietly to me: "There's a Lebanese expression that says, 'If you walk on the wolf path, bring a stick.' Lamia."

I gave him a puzzled look.

"Lamia al-Sabbagh. Adnan's wife," he added.

"The one wearing black?"

"No, the first woman – the tall one."

"So talk to her," I said, getting ready to stand up.

He didn't move, but shook his head, saying, "You don't talk to someone like Lamia in the street like that. You have to call her first. First thing in the morning."

# 6

The morning revealed that the armed displays in front of the house had vanished. When I went out into the street, I found no trace of the Mourabitoun flag.

I rode in one of the service vans heading toward the sea. I sat beside a young man with a beard. The scent of hashish wafted from his cigarette, and he was absorbed in reading a newspaper. From over his shoulder I noticed the photo that most of the papers had published, showing the naked bodies of three young Christian men that had been pulled out of a well in the town of Hammana.

We passed through the chic Raouché district, with its tall modern buildings, its entertainment palaces that never sleep, its cafés and expensive restaurants. We emerged onto the waterfront near the famous rock that the heartbroken are fond of throwing themselves off. I saw it was occupied by carts selling coffee, cold drinks, open-air tables with clothes, shoes, household appliances and vegetables.

On the other side, I noticed the façade of the Dolce Vita café, which was a symbol of Beirut's "sweet life" in the 1960s and beginning of the '70s. It had an air of neglect and decrepitude, just like the ruined buildings around it.

We left the coast road, and headed down the Corniche al-Mazraa. I paid a lira and got out near the Soviet Embassy.

I crossed to the other side of the street, walking in front of a large supermarket and different modern-looking businesses, as I gazed at the signboards hanging over building entrances and on different floors, until I stumbled on what I was looking for.

The director of Progress Publishing welcomed me in an office presided over by an enormous color photo of Lenin. He stood out as having an extremely calm disposition, made possible by a soft, settled existence, and he reinforced this impression with his plump body and his excessive elegance.

I gave him a letter from one of my friends in which he demanded the remainder of what was owed him from one of his books. He read it carefully, then pressed a buzzer. He started assiduously examining his fingernails, until one of the young men in the office responded to the call. He asked him to bring him the file on my friend, and ordered a cup of coffee for me.

The young man brought the requested file and he looked at it for a moment. Before I could say a word, he jumped in: "So far, your friend's book has only sold nine hundred and ninety copies, and he isn't entitled to another royalty payment until we get a thousand out."

"My understanding from him is that he didn't conclude an agreement with you over his share of the profits from distribution," I replied.

"Accounting was done on a ten percent basis," he said.

"I think he deserves fifteen percent," I countered.

"We don't pay authors more than ten percent. That's our policy."

I did a quick calculation of what I could get from publishing my book at that rate, and decided I wouldn't offer him the manuscript I was carrying. When I finished my coffee, I stood up, saying, "I will tell him what you told me."

There was another publishing house, by the name of Modern Publishing, near the Gamal Abd al-Nasser Mosque. It was founded at the beginning of the 1950s, and was famous for publishing translations of books that were popular in the West. But sales of those books didn't last long. At the same time, competing houses, very well supported by the oil-rich Arab countries, proliferated. This led to the house's decline at the beginning of the 1970s, until it ended up on the verge of finally leaving the publishing market. It would have done so, but for the fact that in the last few years it showed some surprising vitality, meaning that the publisher had stumbled on a good source of financial support.

I couldn't find the publisher in his office, so I left him a copy of the manuscript with a brief letter that included Wadia's phone number. I took a taxi to Hamra. I had no difficulty being directed to the headquarters of the publishing house that Safwan Malham had founded two years ago.

I was welcomed in by a petite olive-skinned young woman with wide eyes and severe facial features. Soon enough, Safwan came out to see me. We embraced, and I walked with him into his office.

We drank some coffee as we recalled the circumstances in which we had come to know each other at the end of the 1960s. At the time, he was an editor of little consequence at one of the Lebanese newspapers that was financed by the Egyptian Embassy.

I gave him a letter similar to the one I had given to the director of Progress Publishing, regarding another book by a friend; Safwan had published it for him when he had started up his operation. He took out a file from a cabinet behind him, and went through its contents. Then he wrote down some numbers on a piece of paper and presented it to me. He smiled apologetically, saying, "There's nothing for him. To date, we've only distributed nine hundred and ninety copies of his book. And taking into account the amount of money he's actually received, he's gotten all he's owed and more."

"Based on what royalty rate?" I asked him.

"Fifteen percent," he replied.

He got out of his chair and pulled me by the arm, so I followed him to a side room where stacks of books were piled up. With the apologetic smile still on his lips, he explained, "Distribution is the biggest problem of all. A book isn't successful unless a government buys a thousand copies of it. And of course, they pick books using extremely strict criteria. After that comes the job of dealing with the bureaucracy, and then lots of connections in high places. The upshot is that I'm continually in crisis."

I flipped through the books, and he asked me to take what I liked. I chose one about the role of the Saudi kingdom in supporting the global capitalist system, and another about the Iranian revolution, and a third about Israel's plans for the future of the region in the next decade.

We went out to the hall and I cast my eyes about looking for the olive-skinned girl, without finding her. We went back to his office.

"Perhaps you've brought something for me with you," he said as he sat down at the desk.

I pulled out my manuscript from my shoulder bag, and presented it to him, saying: "Unfortunately, I promised it to Adnan al-Sabbagh. But if he can't publish it, I will give it to you."

He picked up the manuscript. "Poor guy," he said. "He suffered a terrible loss. But he'll get back on his feet easily: he has a lot of sources of support."

"Such as?" I asked.

"His sources are well-known, my friend," he replied. "There's no need to mention them by name."

A woman of about forty joined us. She was wearing a green chamois jacket over an embroidered dress. In her hand she clutched a pair of prescription glasses. She had fair skin and light-colored hair, but I realized it was dyed.

Before Safwan could say a word, she declared: "I'm traveling tomorrow morning."

He introduced her to me, explaining that she was a Jordanian writer. She paid no attention to me, but instead directed her conversation to him:

"Did you prepare the contract?"

"It will be ready tonight," he replied.

"Then I'll be leaving now."

I gestured with my head toward the door as she went out. "What does she write?" I asked.

"Things in the style of Manfaluti's *In the Shade of the Jujube Tree* and *Wuthering Heights*. If it weren't for the fact that she pays for the cost of the paper and the hiring of the printing press, I wouldn't publish anything by her."

I stood up. "I will let you know in the next two days where Sabbagh stands about the book."

"How long do you plan to stay in Beirut?"

"Probably until the end of the week."

"You must come over to my place tonight."

"I don't know where you live. I'm afraid I might get lost."

"I'll come by to pick you up in my car, or I'll send one to you at seven."

I asked him for directions to Wadia's office, which was located on a nearby street, and he accompanied me to the front door. The olive-skinned woman was leaning over a book on her desk. She could feel my eyes on her, but didn't look up.

I found Wadia in his office listening to the radio. "What's the news?" I asked, as I threw myself into a chair.

"Sixty-eight kilograms of dynamite exploded in two car-bombs in East Beirut. The victims include nine killed and eighty wounded, in addition to the businesses, homes and cars that were damaged."

"Who did it?"

"Persons unknown, as usual. But we know what the result will be."

"What?"

"An act of revenge against West Beirut."

The young man brought me a cold can of beer which I sipped nervously.

"And you?" Wadia asked. "What have you been up to?"

I briefly mentioned to him the meetings I'd had. He commented on the story about the 990 copies, saying, "Did you really think you'd be getting anything out of them?"

After a moment, he asked, "Did you get in touch with Lamia?"

"I couldn't find her, but I left her my name and phone number."

"Obviously, you'll be staying with us for some time. That's great."

"Why?"

"I have some work for you."

"I'm not ready for anything. I'm overstressed and completely incapable of focusing."

"It's something that will certainly interest you."

"What is it?"

"Writing the voiceover commentary for a documentary about the civil war."

"But I don't understand anything about this war. I still don't know who's on whose side, and who's fighting who, and why."

"That's not a problem. You can easily figure out the whole story."

"Wouldn't it be better if a Lebanese writer did that, or at least someone who has lived through the war? There are lots of writers in Beirut."

"It's the director – she thinks it would be better if the writer of the voiceover came at the problem from the outside, so that his point of view is objective and fresh."

"It's a female director?"

"Yes. Antoinette Fakhuri."

"I've heard about her. Is she good-looking?"

"She's not bad."

"Who's the producer? Who's behind the film?"

"What does it matter to you?"

"I don't want to end up finding out I've been a shill for one of the organizations."

"So what?" he replied. "Do you remember your friend Abd al-Salam? He wrote a book about the life of the 'Guiding Leader' Saddam Hussein that had millions of copies printed. He made piles of money. It was his good luck that Saddam got rid of most of his longtime political allies who were mentioned in the book and then had the book pulled from the market. Abd al-Salam was commissioned to write a new book. That way, he was guaranteed never to be poor again. Then there was your other friend who made it known that he was Gaddafi's lapdog. In any case, the film has nothing to do with any government. It's being produced by a cooperative group of young Lebanese film-makers."

"And where are their political loyalties?"

"They're not related to any party or movement. But generally, they're leftists."

"Are you sure there's no one behind them?"

"I'm certain. The film is Antoinette's project. She's the kind known as a 'clean-hands progressive' – someone who's still mired in foolish idealism."

"Would they pay me, or would they see me as a partner with a share in future earnings?"

"They'll pay you, of course. Everything nowadays is done for pay."

"How much do you think it will be?"

"I don't know. But it will be a reasonable amount."

I thought for a bit. "I'd have to see the movie first," I said.

"*Bon*, as the Francophile Lebanese would say. We'll go see her in an hour and a half. She's using the studio that belongs to the PLO."

We ate some *shwarma* sandwiches, and I drank two cans of beer. Around three, we left the office, and we took a taxi to the Fakahani district that was teeming with people.

We walked by the tall building that housed the Palestinian Media Bureau, then we turned into a street packed with working-class coffee shops and restaurants. We stopped near a taxi stand, from which emanated a repeated call: *One seat left for Damascus!*

We went into a building guarded by two armed men. They took charge of inspecting us, after they confirmed by phone that we had an appointment. An elevator with a filthy floor carried us to the third story where Antoinette occupied a small office that had a desk, file cabinet and several chairs.

She was slim, of moderate height, in her late twenties, and was wearing a denim outfit. She stretched out to me a rough palm that she used to squeeze my hand with a force that betrayed her seriousness, while I gazed on two beautiful eyes that tended toward green, and a pale face that spoke of undernourishment, or stress and nervous tension.

She led us into a side room that was taken up by a table with a Moviola machine where the film editing was being done, saying, "Unfortunately, I haven't been able to reserve a screening room. But you'll be able to get some idea about the film from the Moviola."

There was a young man with long sideburns sitting at the table in front of a polished glass screen. The screen stood over a small projector surrounded by several reels, one of which held the black film tape, while another one had the brown audio tape.

Wadia and I sat down on a pair of chairs behind the young man. Antoinette leaned over him, following his hands as they spliced the two tapes together and affixed them to a double row of sprockets on the calibration machine.

She switched off the lights, and the room went dark, except for the thin light coming out from the table.

The young man touched one of the reels, and the two calibrated tapes started moving. A musical rattle made its way into our ears, while film frames followed each other in succession on the small screen.

The first frames were dark; they were followed by others defaced with scratch marks and circles. Then a large title card appeared in the middle of the frame with a scratch mark on it:

What happened to Lebanon?

Brief shots followed one after the other: of villages, of Beirut's streets in both rich and poor districts, of storefront windows, of posters on walls, of television ads and photos of leaders. Fairuz's enchanting voice wafted over them in several of her songs. Finally, the large title card appeared once again:

What happened to Lebanon?

Then Antoinette's name, identified as both writer and director, and the names of those who worked with her. And then, finally, the film began.

At first, I was able to follow the various events and keep track of some of the key individuals. I was helped in that regard because the film resorted to the silent-movie tradition of using title cards that filled the screen in order to explain some details. But soon enough, I found myself incapable of following events, which started to blend into each other, and I was no longer able to keep track of individuals or places.

The screening went on for an hour and fifteen minutes. And when the light went on in the room, Antoinette took off her glasses. She offered me a pack of American cigarettes, so I took one and lit hers.

"What do you think?" she asked, smiling nervously.

"The film certainly grabs the viewer," I replied. "And it has an obvious political value. But I would be lying to you if I told you that I understood everything."

The muscles on her face relaxed, and her eyes sparkled as she responded, "That's our problem. The only person who could absorb the film this way is someone who already knows Lebanon well. So from the beginning I resorted to using title cards. But clearly they haven't solved the problem; they just created a new problem with the film's balance. The solution I've reached is to replace the title cards and accompanying music with a voiceover commentary that closely follows the narrative, fills in all the gaps, and plays a part in supporting the dramatic structure of the film.

"Something that would tie the entire film together," she added, nervously waving her hand. I nodded my head to show I understood what she was saying, and she took that as my agreement to write the desired voiceover, saying: "*Bon.* I've put together some books, reports and newspaper clippings for you: they'll give you a clear idea about the Lebanese problem as a whole. Read them first, and then we'll talk."

Wadia helped me carry a number of tomes and folders to a car belonging to the media office. The car took us to the house, and then delivered Wadia to a bookstore.

It was nearly six o'clock, so I took a quick bath and changed my clothes. Then I poured a big glass of whiskey and sat down in the living room in front of the television. Around seven fifteen, the taxi that Safwan had promised me arrived.

At his place, I found the Jordanian writer from that morning, and the olive-skinned woman who worked in his office, along with two young Libyan men from the embassy. We congregated in a big room stuffed with pieces of expensive furniture, from two Louis XV chairs, each of which occupied one and a half square meters, to enormous carved tables covered with a sheet of black marble.

The two Libyans were sitting next to each other on the edge of one of the chairs, facing the two women. While the olive-skinned woman relaxed serenely in her seat, a glass of whiskey in her hand, the Jordanian woman perched on the edge of hers, holding a key chain as if she were getting ready to stand up at any moment.

I sat down near the Libyans, so that the olive-skinned woman was directly in front of me. Safwan brought me a glass of whiskey; then his wife appeared, carrying several dishes of food. She was taller and younger than he was, by a wide margin. She moved with a noticeable listlessness. When she shook hands with me, she gave me a smile that didn't radiate past her lips.

I heard them address the olive-skinned woman as Randa. I saw she had drained her glass and refilled it. The Jordanian woman refused to drink. She started shifting her gaze among the guests, and then she suddenly stood up, saying she had to leave, because she would be traveling early the next morning.

Safwan tried to dissuade her, but without success, so he said goodnight to her at the door. He sat down beside the Libyans after putting on a Fairuz tape. His wife didn't join us in eating or drinking, but she sat down where the Jordanian woman had been, grabbed a hookah pipe, and busied herself with smoking, letting her eyes wander. Randa was avidly, steadily downing her whiskey. I looked at her several times, but she pretended not to notice.

I suddenly moved over next to her, saying, "I'm impressed by the way you drink."

She laughed, but didn't say anything. Then she turned her attention to the conversation going on between Safwan and the young Libyans.

I filled my glass and heard her tell Safwan, "They'll take a thousand copies of each book."

"We haven't decided yet," interjected the older of the two Libyans.

The other one, who had a drunken look in his eyes, added, "The writer was the reason one woman left the party. Now he wants to drive the second one away."

"Calm down," said Randa. "That won't happen."

She got up from where she was sitting beside me, and walked around the tables until she stood in front of the two young men, saying, "Make room for me between you."

The two gladly obeyed. Safwan got up and sat next to me. He clinked his glass against mine.

"The Iran–Iraq war struck me a mortal blow," he said. "When the Iranian revolution began I published several books about it, and the result was that the Iraqis boycotted all my books; in fact, they refused to pay me what they owed me."

We were joined by a young Lebanese man. He was elegantly dressed, with an animated face, and carried a Samsonite briefcase. Safwan's wife beamed with joy when she saw him. He looked a lot like Safwan, even if he was younger than him. Safwan introduced him to me as his brother.

Safwan's wife left her hookah, getting up to bring the young man a glass of gin and a plate of mezze.

I asked him if he worked in publishing too, but his sister-in-law jumped in: "One brother is enough for that wretched profession."

The young man said he worked in the music industry, making tapes.

"He makes in one day what I make in an entire year," Safwan added.

His wife sneered and asked him, "So where is the money you've made in the last year?"

Safwan kept silent and stared into his glass. Then he turned to me.

"You haven't told me about the situation in Egypt," he said. "You know it's been ten years since I was last there."

"You wouldn't recognize it if you saw it now. Everything's changed in these last ten years. The air itself has changed, in some people's view."

"How so?"

"The streets have grown crowded with expensive cars and luxury buildings, and with potholes, dirt, rubbish, and foreigners. The stores are filled with imported goods and rotten foods. The newspapers are filled with lies, and drinking water with live worms."

"What about the people? How can they stay silent about all that?"

"People are desperate for bread, cigarettes and chickens, and put up with epidemics, noise and hypocrisy. Every morning, an Egyptian is flung about into several hundred pieces and he is unable to put himself back together again in the evening. Even national dignity no longer means anything to them. But what do you expect? Nasser killed off in them any capacity for working for a common cause."

The Libyans stood up, expressing their desire to leave. Randa got up with them and turned to escort them out.

I announced my desire to leave as well, but Safwan begged me to stay. He wanted to fill my glass, but I objected.

"I have to work in the morning," I explained.

He addressed his wife: "Can you drive him home? I don't think I can drive after all I've had to drink."

"Why do you drink when you have someone you want to drive home?"

"I'll drive him," the brother interjected.

I got up, and everyone stood. Safwan's wife approached his brother and put her hand on his shoulder.

"It's still early. Stay the night at our place."

"I can take a taxi," I offered.

"At this time of night?" the brother asked. "I have to be leaving now because I'm traveling to Damascus early tomorrow morning. Lead the way."

I walked ahead of him toward the door. Safwan and his wife followed us in silence.

# 7

I stayed at the house for the next two days, devoting all my time to the books and documents that Antoinette had supplied me with. At first, I found that I was lost among the meanings of events, and the significance of names and places. The various points of view, and their contradictory nature, multiplied my confusion as I read. Likewise, they were all armed with an arsenal of decisive proof and justifications. But soon the benefit of that became clear when I managed to take a comparative approach among different opinions. Wadia helped me with his memories and observations, and soon I was making my way with some – by no means easy – effort.

Previously, I had had a foggy idea about the Lebanese Civil War, the gist of which was that it was a war between progressives and reactionaries set in motion by colonialism, and that the majority of progressives were Muslims, just as the majority of reactionaries were Christians. But I realized now that the matter went much deeper than that. The Lebanese problem seemed like an enormous quilt of multicolored strands that were entangled with each other, so that separating them out became an impossible task.

Whenever I followed one of the threads, it brought me to the complete sectarian divide that made Lebanon unique among Arab countries. The Lebanese, whose population has never grown beyond 3 million, are divided into nearly twenty sects, beginning with the Shiites, Sunnis and Druze, then the Maronites, Catholics and Greek Orthodox, and the Armenians and Syriacs (Catholic and Orthodox), then the Protestants, Assyrians and Jews. Dominating these sects is a limited group of clans and families whose influence is handed down generation after generation. It's as though Lebanon were a country frozen in the Middle Ages.

Seen in the light of history, the civil war – which flared up in April 1975, and in which 75,000 have been killed and 140,000 wounded (not one of them carrying the name of one of the families that started the fight and that profits from the victims) – seemed like one link in a long series of conflicts and wars. As for how the war began, it had two origins: the moment the extended clans in the region fighting each other discovered that Mount Lebanon made an ideal refuge that could protect them from their enemies, and the moment that the ships of the invading Crusaders dropped anchor at the foot of the venerable mountain.

These first colonizers, who came from Europe raising aloft the holy banners of Christ, strove to establish special relationships with some of the religious minorities in the region. And they achieved their aim in an eastern Christian community that traced its founding to Saint Mar Maron. This community lived in relative comfort as a result of its monopoly on silk production. For its part, the Maronite community saw in European support protection for, and consolidation of, their economic interests.

The Turks applied the same policy when they occupied the Levant in the year 1516 in the name of Islam. They proceeded to embrace the Sunni Muslim community at the expense of the rest of the Muslim and Christian minorities. The Egyptians that *Muhammad Ali* sent to the Levant after 1833 abolished all the public dress and other symbols the Turks imposed on Christians to distinguish them by their clothing, and opened up government positions to them. The entire eastern Arab world seemed to be poised on the threshold of a new period that would bring it from the darkness of the Middle Ages to the broad horizons of the modern era.

But colonial forces were lying in wait for Muhammad Ali: the struggle between the French and British in the region ignited the well-known strife in the year 1840 between the Druze and Maronites. The former – Muslims who consider the Shiite Fatimid caliph al-Hakim bi-amr Allah divine – followed the example of the Maronites and established a special relationship with Great Britain, as a counterweight to the Maronites' special relationship with France.

Five years later, the conflict widened when the Orthodox, Sunnis and Shia joined the side of the Druze. Conflict broke out again in 1860 when the Maronite peasants rose up against their feudal lords. Just as the attempts at an agreement were on the verge of succeeding, a band of Christians from the Matn region attacked Druze villages, and the Druze raided Maronite villages. The affair turned into a war between Muslims and Christians, and ended with the intervention of European nations, and the entry of the French Army into Beirut.

Historians attribute to Napoleon III a role in provoking this strife. During his reign, France had entered into a new era of rising expectations, and the emperor wanted to be seen as the defender of the rights of Christians in the Orient.

But France's hopes were realized only after the fall of the Ottoman Empire at the end of World War One. The British and French divided the eastern half of the Arab world between themselves, and defeated the forces of the *Emir Feisal*, who was on the way to founding a unified Arab state out of Jordan, Syria, Lebanon and Palestine.

France was entrusted with mandate authority over the regions of Syria and Lebanon; it preserved the confessional system and buttressed the position of the Maronites by giving them a number of special privileges and bestowing French culture on their children – something that gave them social opportunities unavailable to others.

The hope of a united Arab state emerged again in 1925, with the breakout of an uprising that had been started by the Druze under the leadership of *Sultan Pasha al-Atrash*, calling for the unification of Syrian territories (Jordan, Syria, Lebanon and Palestine), and their independence. But the French suppressed the Syrian uprising militarily, and they doused the torch of Arab unity by establishing a separate nation for Mount Lebanon.

In 1926, France announced the establishment of the Lebanese Republic, giving it a flag identical to the French flag but with the addition of a cedar tree. Some Maronites dubbed the new nation "Little France".

After eighteen years, the French mandate over Lebanon came to an end, and it became an independent republic. With that, the Maronites realized that the era of the French empire had passed, so they gravitated towards making alliances with the British. Along with elements from the Sunni, Shia and Druze, it formed what was known in Lebanon's political history as "the Constitutional Bloc".

The entity known as Lebanon was effectively born in the embrace of the English in 1943, according to a formula agreed upon between Bishara al-Khouri (Maronite Christian) and Riad al-Solh (Sunni Muslim) that specified that Christians would relinquish their desire to seek protection from "the merciful mother" – as they called France – and emerge from their isolation in order to enter the Arab League. In return, the Muslims would relinquish their aspiration for annexation to Syria or any larger Arab unity.

And according to this unwritten covenant, it was agreed that the chief state positions would be distributed equitably by religious community, and that there would be a ratio of six Christians in parliament to five Muslims. This agreement guaranteed that the president of the republic would be a Maronite Christian, the prime minister would be a Sunni Muslim, and the leader of parliament would be a Shiite Muslim. This arrangement was given the name "the Lebanese equilibrium".

However, from the beginning, the agreement carried within it the potential for an explosion. For one thing, it wasn't only a balance of religious communities; at the same time, it was a regional equilibrium, a balancing act among large families, clans and institutions. For another thing, the prominent position the French gave to the Maronites allowed them to flourish. With the arrival of the agreement, it gave them the nation's five main official positions: president of the republic, head of the army, president of the Deuxième Bureau intelligence office, director general of the National Bank of Lebanon, and director of public security.

Naturally, the upper social classes from the other religious communities, Muslim and Christian, felt cheated, especially the Sunnis, who formed the majority of the population of Beirut, and who from ancient times had worked in business. After their numbers noticeably increased, they also began to sense that they were no longer in the minority.

Thus, the confessional balancing was not a stage on the way to nationhood, but instead was a postponement of it. The nation had become the religious community, or to be more specific, the struggle between religious communities.

Personal status laws proliferated as a result of this situation, until most matters pertaining to the individual came to fall under the jurisdiction of the religious community. Every religious community became a nation within the nation, enjoying a legally recognized status and the right to legislate and to rule on questions of personal status for its members. If an individual wasn't classified in one of the religious communities, he was deprived of the right to live within the personal status system, and was consequently forbidden from getting married on Lebanese soil.

In this way, Lebanon acquired the character it is known for. Its economic structure has never been based on the foundation of a production economy in the true sense of the word, with the exception of hashish and opium farms. Rather, it is based on a service economy, which represents 70 percent of the national income. Lebanon is known as the ideal market for low-price European products.

Arab oil money flooded Lebanon's banks, invigorating the finance and banking markets, which consist of foreign and partly-Lebanese-owned banks whose function is to move Arab funds to international markets. A new class of bankers, businessmen, managers, administrators and accountants appeared, suited to work for the oil companies of Arab countries whose main offices were located in Beirut.

This led to a tourism boom, and Beirut became a center for services of all kinds, including leisure services. Getting rich quick – in any way, shape or form – became the goal, even if it was done at the expense of moral values, or even national ones. Beirut turned into a center for political conspiracy and espionage, and a haven for the white slave trade.

By virtue of the confessional system, by which positions of political leadership and government posts, along with wealth, moved from fathers to sons, fortunes in real estate – built-on, unbuilt, industrial and commercial – piled up in the hands of a few, who profited from a weak central authority and the poverty of the majority of the citizens. Half of the population ended up earning 18 percent of the gross national income, while the other half earned 82 percent. The greatest share of that 82 percent went to the top 5 percent of the population.

Thus a new component – the social component – was added to the religious-confessional struggle which was about to develop into a national struggle over Lebanese identity. But just as the nationalist struggle continued to be dominated by sectarianism, the social struggle also remained within this framework. Coalitions and political parties – however much they assumed the guise of political or social ideologies – continued to be façades for religious communities, and sometimes for families and clans.

The spread of nationalism that swept over the Arab peoples at the beginning of the 1950s, under the twin banners of complete independence from colonialism and Arab unity, had the effect of stoking the fires of the nationalist struggle over Lebanese identity. The Arab nationalist movement reached its peak with the outbreak of the Algerian Revolution, and the nationalization of the Suez Canal by Gamal Abdel Nasser. When Great Britain, France and Israel attacked Egypt in 1956, the Maronites and Camille Chamoun, president of the Republic of Lebanon, didn't conceal their sympathy for the attack; the Phalangist Party newspaper applauded it.

Naturally, the victory of the Arab nationalist movement, with the failure of the tripartite aggression, led to a strengthening of the position of the front hostile to the Maronites. It also led to the United States playing a primary role on the Arab stage.

According to Jonathan Randal, a reporter for the *Washington Post*, "A former American ambassador years later remarked of that period [the 1950s], 'We were buying people wholesale. I would not be surprised to discover that everyone important in Lebanon was on the CIA payroll . . .'"

And so, no sooner had the United States launched its operation to take the place of Great Britain and France in the Arab Middle East, via the Eisenhower Doctrine in 1957, than Lebanon became the only Arab country that ventured to make public its acceptance of it.

But Arab nationalism continued to spread: Jordan cancelled its treaty with Great Britain, in February 1958 the union of Egypt and Syria was announced, and collectively, Arab emotions ran high. Thousands of Lebanese poured into Damascus to catch a glimpse of "their Nasser".

Taking a cue from Gamal Abdel Nasser and Arab nationalism, Sunni and Shiite leaders – chief of whom were the two Sunnis Saeb Salam (the Saudis' top man in Lebanon) and

*Rashid Karami*, and the Shiite *Kamil al-As'ad* (also with ties to Saudi Arabia) – found that the time was right to take a bigger slice of the pie, of which the Maronites had taken the lion's share, in response to the secret assassination squads formed by Camille Chamoun (who in the early 1970s was exposed as having been in the pay of the British intelligence service). So, in cooperation with *Kamal Jumblatt*, the leader of the Druze, Chamoun's former ally and his rival for the leadership of the Chouf district, they ignited what was later known as the "revolt" of 1958, relying on the nationalist enthusiasm of the Arab street. The Muslims resorted to arms, raising aloft photos of Gamal Abdel Nasser.

July 14, 1958 was the high-water mark for Arab nationalism, when the monarchy fell in Iraq, and in seconds, the Baghdad Pact collapsed. Full Arab unity appeared to be on the horizon. Nasser flew across the Mediterranean to Moscow, in preparation for a full confrontation with colonial powers old and new. At this point, Chamoun sought the help of the American, British and French ambassadors. The response from Washington reached him in the early hours of the following day, and at 3 pm that same day – July 15 – around 2,000 khaki-clad US marines landed, about 5 miles south of Beirut, ostensibly to protect Lebanon from Gamal Abdel Nasser. In the following days, the total number of American forces in Lebanon reached around 15,000 combatants.

The "revolt" ended with an Egyptian–American agreement to choose General Fu'ad Chehab as a new president for the Republic. As a result, the US marines withdrew. But the Phalangist Party rebelled against the agreement. The Phalangist Party was founded by the Maronite leader Pierre Gemayel in 1939 on the model of (and taking its name from) the

Spanish fascist Falange Party, following Gemayel's participation in the notorious 1936 Berlin Olympics. He bestowed on it the meaningful motto: "God, the nation, and the family". Members of the party began kidnapping allies of Saeb Salam and branding their bodies with the mark of a cross. Salam's allies, in turn, responded in kind. The discord only came to an end once Pierre Gemayel joined the new government as a minister.

With Gemayel's ascension to the ministry the bloody phase began, which his family started in order to keep their monopoly on the leadership of the Maronite community and maintain their seizure of power. In reality, until that time, the Lebanese hadn't taken seriously that athlete-pharmacist of erect bearing, with his white hair plastered to his skull, and his ridiculous militias. They derisively called him "Pierre Condom", a nickname given to him because he ran a pharmacy in *Martyrs' Square*, a few steps from Beirut's red-light district.

But Gemayel's appointment to the ministry meant something equally significant: it was tantamount to the adoption of the slogan coined by the Havana-cigar-smoking Muslim leader Saeb al-Salam, the underlying idea of which was: "No winner and no loser." That meant that all the violence and victims no longer mattered. The past had to be forgotten, and everything should go back to what it was before, on the premise that neither side gained a victory over the other, and consequentially, neither one obtained any special privileges. This slogan became the basis for what is now happening in Lebanon.

The following years marked the apogee of Lebanon's prosperity. Society's "socialist" orientation, achieved by the Arab nationalist movement in the wake of Nasser's well-known nationalization programs, caused the rich in various Arab countries to quake in fear of their own people, and they deposited their wealth in Lebanon's banks, or invested in its public projects.

On the other hand, the authoritarian, military character that colored governments, both Arab nationalist and reactionary alike, made Beirut the sole free space for political refugees and opponents of different governments, as well as a public arena for conflicts between these regimes, conflicts between them and Israel, and internal conflicts within Israel itself.

With their traditional business acumen, the Lebanese realized that they could benefit enormously from this state of affairs. A black market in all kinds of goods flourished, from books to prostitution, and all of Lebanon became an open marketplace for ideas and commodities. Dozens of newspapers were published, financed by different factions – or rather, political parties and organizations were formed, financed by the different factions.

The average Lebanese citizen assumed the character of a middleman. All he needed was to wear – even if it was borrowed – the most splendid clothes and latest fashions, and use the latest gadgets, in order to succeed in selling the goods he had imported from the West and sought to re-export to Arabs. Members of parliament came to pride themselves on the foreign embassy that backed them. It was common knowledge that anyone who wasn't being paid by some source was a failure, and unworthy of respect.

As for the Arab forces of reaction and the colonial powers, they began to promote the idea of "prosperity, economic freedom and democracy" as successful Lebanese products. But the glittering façade of Hamra Street could not conceal the country's different reality. Along with the luxury buildings that went up in downtown Beirut and in the aristocratic neighborhoods was a belt of tin-sheet shacks around the city. And in Akkar, Jabal Amil and the Bekaa (regions where the majority of the inhabitants were Shiites) peasants lived in a disgraceful condition of servitude. Anyone who dared to rebel against the landowning nobility was forbidden from being appointed to the police, and his children were prevented from attending government schools. If he was a tobacco farmer, he was not allowed seeds, and for his harvest, he only received the lowest prices. The state recruited for government service from a group of longstanding Maronite, Sunni and Shiite families that held a monopoly on the country's affairs and wealth.

In the meantime, the number of Muslims steadily grew, until they came to form the majority of inhabitants. The Maronites – as the British magazine *The Economist* acknowledged – no longer made up more than 20 percent of all Lebanese. This increase in the number of Muslims was due to none other than the Shiites, who now – according to the same magazine – represented a quarter of the population. The end of the 1960s witnessed the beginning of their ascent under the strong leadership of the ambitious *Imam Musa al-Sadr*, who succeeded in uniting the Shiite masses around him in the *Movement of the Dispossessed*, before his disappearance in Libya in 1978.

But the 1960s also ended with the death of Gamal Abdel Nasser, the powerful champion of the Arab nationalist street in Lebanon, and the bulwark to whom Muslim leaders turned for protection as they demanded a redistribution of power. Everyone looked around, searching for a new champion, and they soon found one in the Palestinian resistance.

The link between the situations in Palestine and Lebanon dates back to the beginning of the British incursion into the region. The same year that the British occupied Egypt (1882), Jewish settlers were building their first settlements on the heights overlooking the Litani River. Later, British communications with Arab leaders would always insist on the "special circumstances" of both the Jews in Palestine and the Maronites in Lebanon.

It was an irony of fate that Lebanon owed its flourishing growth to the Palestinian problem. The vast wealth that the ruling families accumulated arose thanks to the Arab–Israeli struggle, and the defeats and victories equally that befell the Arabs over the course of it.

As a result of the defeat of the Arab armies and the founding of the state of Israel in 1948, the center of economic activity moved from Palestine to Lebanon, and especially the role as broker which Palestine had previously held in the fields of business, transportation and tourism. Palestinian refugees took part in the development of the service industry, and the "economic miracle" was supported by the Arab boycott of Israel and the Arab consensus to remove Lebanon from the group of states maintaining an armed struggle with Israel which consequently exempted it from armaments expenditures. On the other hand, the Arab victory in October 1973 led to a doubling of oil profits and an influx of capital into Lebanon. The exchange value of the Lebanese lira against the dollar increased to 2.3 from 3.25 at the beginning of 1970.

As far as Israel was concerned, it didn't hide its ambitions in Lebanon for a moment. In February 1954, Ben Gurion wrote to Moshe Sharett, saying, "It is clear that Lebanon is the weakest link in the Arab Union. Other minorities in Arab countries are all Muslim, with the exception of Egypt's Copts. But Egypt is the most harmonious and cohesive of all the Arab countries . . . The creation of a Christian state in Lebanon can be considered a natural course of action with historical roots . . . Achieving something like that in normal times is next to impossible . . . but in times of confusion or revolution or civil war, things can take a different turn."

On the eve of the Israeli attack on Egypt, Syria and Jordan in 1967, Levi Eshkol, the Israeli prime minister, declared to the correspondent of the French newspaper *Le Monde* that "a thirsty Israel cannot stand by with its hands tied while watching the waters of the Litani flow uselessly into the sea".

Faced with that, Lebanese governments took on the role of Israel's enforcer within Lebanon. Following Israel's founding, 100,000 Palestinians migrated to Lebanon. The Lebanese government granted citizenship to 40,000 Christians among them, and imposed on the rest a life fit for dogs in refugee camps ruled by security officers.

A new Palestinian influx occurred following Israel's seizure of the West Bank up to the Jordan River, as well as the Gaza strip in 1967. Several thousands more settled into the refugee camps in southern Lebanon and in the areas around Beirut.

Lebanese authorities imposed a blockade on the Palestinian camps, and prevented Palestinians from moving from one camp to another, or to the city, except by prior permission. They forbade them from establishing political organizations or communicating with them. They pursued and killed all who tried to slip back into Israel. Similarly, they forbade Palestinian workers from enjoying government benefits. The latter found themselves forced to take onerous, marginal jobs, and at wages lower than what their Lebanese peers earned. As one writer put it, misery, poverty and displacement were smoldering embers in the alleyways of the camps and within the tin-sheet houses.

But the defeat of nationalist Arab leaders in 1967 made it possible for the Palestinians to organize themselves in armed federations. In 1969, when Lebanese authorities attempted to curtail *fedayeen* operations in southern Lebanon during an Israeli attack on Beirut's airport, in the course of which thirteen Lebanese civilian planes were destroyed with no interference from the army, the first major clash between the two sides occurred. It ended with the involvement of Gamal Abdel Nasser as mediator and the signing of the secret Cairo Agreement in November of the same year. This gave Palestinians the right to work, live and move freely in Lebanon, to have supervision over the refugee camps, and to establish stationhouses for the armed struggle (the military police) within them.

With this agreement, the clash between the Palestinian resistance and the forces opposed to them was delayed for a time. But it began to escalate again after King Hussein began liquidating Palestinian resistance forces in Jordan in 1970. As a consequence, thousands more Palestinians were displaced to Lebanon, which also became the primary point of access to the occupied territories.

Meanwhile, the Muslim and Arab nationalist street found a strong ally in the Palestinian resistance, while the Palestinian organizations belonged to this same street by virtue of their makeup and aims. They had to protect their existence in Lebanon by making the widest possible array of alliances.

Israel played its role by elevating the tension in coordination with the Maronites, and with the Phalangist Party specifically. It launched a military attack on the Bared and Badawi camps in 1973, throwing in for good measure a commando raid in the heart of Beirut, in which it killed three PLO leaders and a number of civilians, without the Lebanese Army lifting a finger.

The situation exploded in a way it never had before: demonstrations and strikes were called by Arab nationalist forces, criticizing the government's failure to protect the country. Right-wing forces, for their part, demanded that the Palestinian camps be moved away from the outskirts of Beirut. It was no secret that the monasteries that owned a large part of the territory on which the camps were located were making an effort to get it back, after its value had gone up in the previous few years. The president of the republic, Suleiman Frangieh, took it upon himself to carry out this task.

The life of Suleiman Frangieh would make a suitable subject for a thrilling gangster movie; at the same time, it offers an accurate picture of the nature of politics in Lebanon's celebrated democracy. He began his professional life in the 1940s, under the wing of his older brother, Hamid Frangieh, who was leader of the Maronite community in the town of Zgharta, and its representative in parliament and the government. In addition to electoral advertising for his brother, Suleiman's assignments included organizing the murder of a Muslim from the city of Tripoli each month, as a kind of repeated warning to the inhabitants of the neighboring Sunni-majority city.

On the eve of the presidential election in 1958, Hamid Frangieh emerged as a likely candidate. Camille Chamoun was eager to retain his position as president of the republic, and he pulled off a cunning maneuver to remove his Maronite opponent, by stirring up trouble between the Frangieh and Duwaihi families. As Chamoun guessed, the discord escalated to a confrontation between the two families at a mass in a church in the village of Miziara, when Suleiman Frangieh opened fire on his rivals, killing twenty of them. Chamoun immediately issued an order to arrest the killer who fled to Syria and stayed as a guest of the Syrian government at a hotel in Latakia, where he made the acquaintance of the military officers Hafez al-Assad and Rifaat Assad, who partnered with the Frangieh family in a number of profitable black-market deals – both business and political.

Less than a year and a half later, he was granted amnesty. Meanwhile, his brother had been paralyzed by a stroke, and Suleiman returned to enter parliament in his place. He became a respected leader of his family and clan, thanks to his high body count (with the passage of years, the total number of his murders climbed to 700).

When new presidential elections were held in 1970, complex local consultations took place among the ruling families – *Eddé*, Gemayel, Chamoun, Jumblatt, Salam, Solh, Hammada, Karami, etc. – to look for a candidate that would satisfy everyone. In the office of Ghassan Tuini, on the ninth floor of the *Al-Nahar* newspaper building, which he owned, an agreement was made to nominate Suleiman Frangieh.

On August 17, 5,000 armed men belonging to Frangieh descended from Zgharta onto Beirut and surrounded the parliament building to ensure the election of their leader. The third round of voting ended with fifty votes for him against forty-nine for his opponent Elias Sarkis. When Sabry

Hammada, the speaker of parliament, announced that it was necessary to hold a fourth round, Frangieh's allies outside fired shots in the air to declare their man had won. Drawing his gun, Frangieh rushed over to Hammada, shouting, while his sons came to blows with the Duwaihi patriarch (who subsequently became one of Frangieh's allies). Hammada's bodyguards advanced to protect him, raising their machine-guns, while Frangieh's men, who had succeeded in making their way into the building ahead of the voting, took out their weapons.

Hammada retreated to his office, and called the president, Charles Helou, to ask for advice. Helou told him, "From what I've heard, I can tell you that if you resist, no one in the parliament building will survive."

Three years later, in May 1973, Suleiman Frangieh used the slogan "Whatever is necessary to prevent the destruction of the country" to justify the command he issued to the head of the army to attack the camps surrounding Beirut in order to put an end to the control the Palestinian resistance had over them. An American diplomat described this attack, which involved the use of airpower, thus: "It was the first time I saw the Lebanese Army move effectively."

But the Lebanese Army failed in its mission, and the Maronite parties began to strengthen their armed militias so they could carry out what the army had proven incapable of doing. The "Kaslik" society – a group of Maronite monks and educated people – took upon themselves the greatest burden, in collecting donations towards this goal; it was able to collect 56 million lira (worth 21 million dollars in 1973–4). Also for this purpose Pierre Gemayel visited Saudi Arabia on April 1, 1974, in a private Saudi plane. Plans were made to train the Phalangist militia in West Germany, Israel and Jordan. Iskandar Ghanem left his post as head of the army in order to assume leadership of the militia.

In his book *The Arms Bazaar*, which was published in the middle of 1977, Anthony Sampson mentioned that the Maronite front purchased a quantity of weapons at a price varying between 200 and 600 million dollars, which came – according to him – from banks that the Maronite militias had plundered in Lebanon, and from the CIA, Israel, West Germany, the Vatican, the Shah of Iran and conservative Muslim Arab countries.

Naturally, the other side – starting with the Palestinian resistance, and continuing to the local religious communities hostile to the Maronites, to the advocates of "progressive" social and economic programs – would not stand by in the face of this enormous campaign of armament. Its leaders found an endless supply available to them in Baghdad, Libya and Saudi Arabia as well. Kamal Jumblatt armed his Druze, and the Imam al-Sadr formed a military apparatus for the Shiite Movement of the Dispossessed. Young Sunnis assembled in the armed Nasserist organization, the Mourabitoun, and the Communists and Baathists formed their own armed militias.

War was now inevitable.

# 8

A number of aspects remained hazy in my view. But time was tight. From experience, I knew that things would become clear during the work itself.

I called Antoinette, and made an appointment to meet with her. As soon as I put down the receiver, it rang. I lifted it to my ear again.

It was a soft female voice: "Hello . . . ?"

"*Who is speaking?*" I asked, imitating the Lebanese dialect.

"Please – do speak in Egyptian."

"Yes, ma'am," I replied, laughing.

"I'm Lamia – Lamia Sabbagh."

"Oh, hello. I tried calling you several times."

"I know. But I was at the country house, and then I was busy repairing the damage."

"Ah yes . . . Terrible."

"No matter. Those kinds of things have become normal here. My husband spoke with me today from Paris."

"Will he be coming to Beirut?"

"I don't think he will now . . . The important thing is: something stupid happened. He told me that your manuscript got lost before he'd had a chance to read it."

I stayed silent, not saying a word.

"Hello . . ." she said, with some hesitation. "I wonder if you happen to have another copy of it?"

"I have one with me."

"Would you be so kind as to bring it to me?"

"So you can send it to him?"

"Of course."

"I was hoping to get this resolved quickly."

"How long will you be staying in Beirut?"

"Another week, perhaps."

"Alright, then we'll see. When will I see you?"

"Whenever is good for you . . . tomorrow morning, for example. At ten?"

"*Okay*," she said in English. "I will be waiting for you. Do you know where the publishing house is?"

"Wasn't it destroyed?" I asked, confused.

She laughed. "The explosion was on the ground floor," she explained, "where the warehouse was. The offices themselves didn't get much damage. We've repaired them and they are back to what they were."

"That quickly? I will find out how to get there."

"At ten o'clock, then," she added.

I put back the receiver and lit a cigarette. It was still early in the day, but I felt like I needed a little drink, so I poured myself a glass of gin. I sat down and flipped through a large volume about the Lebanese Civil War.

Around noon Wadia called me to say that he would be dining with one of his friends. He told me to help myself to the contents of the refrigerator to make my own lunch.

I fried an egg and ate it with some olives and salad, as I scanned an ad in yesterday's paper inviting Arab citizens to join armed groups in Libya, "the revolutionary core of the united Arab nation", in order to confront "the vicious assault the Arab nation faces from imperialism, Zionism and Arab reactionary forces". Next to the ad, I discovered a small news item about the widening scope of Libyan involvement in Chad on the side of Chad's head of state, Oueddei, against his rival, Habré, who was supported by the United States. There was also an allusion to an editorial in the Cairo-based *al-Ahram* newspaper, demanding that America "regain its prestige and standing, and shoulder its responsibilities to preserve peace, confront aggression, and stop the escalation of conflict, the rejection of authority, and the terrorization of populations through incursions and outside interference".

After eating, I felt a desire to rest a little. But I roused myself, got dressed, and left the house.

A taxi took me to Antoinette's building. An armed man walked me to her office. I found her with a stocky man around fifty years old. He occupied a chair next to her desk.

She brought me over to him, saying, "Abu Nadir. The head of the PLO film office. Perhaps you've heard of him."

I shook hands with him warmly, saying, "Who hasn't heard of him?"

The guerilla operation he had led in downtown Tel Aviv was legendary. The Israelis had arrested him afterward and condemned him to death. He had been critically wounded, which kept him immobile for a long time, but afterwards was able to escape.

I sat down opposite him as he continued his conversation with Antoinette. "Movement in the playing field is limited now. Tomorrow's events will prove to you I'm right. You know how my predictions come true. It's something like a hunch. Did I tell you about the Tel Aviv operation?"

She bowed her head, but he went on talking, turning toward me: "There was an Israeli soldier in front of us carrying a machinegun. His finger was on the trigger, preparing to open fire at any second. But I got the feeling he wouldn't do it, and I confidently headed toward him, until the mouth of his gun touched my chest. Then I put out my hand and took the gun."

He changed the subject, suddenly. "How is Egypt?" he asked me. "I visited it once in '68, and met Gamal Abdel Nasser. I should have gone again in 1970 if it weren't for the Russians."

"How?" I asked, confused. "I mean, why?"

He smiled. "In my first commando operation, we snuck into the occupied territories from Jordan," he said. "Do you know who opened fire on us? The Jordanians. At the time, I told my comrades: 'Our misfortunes always come from our friends, not our enemies.'"

". . . but the Russians . . ." I stammered.

He cut me off. "I know what you're going to say. Believe me, all we get from them is a lot of hot air."

Antoinette jumped into the conversation, adding, "Sadat says the same thing. As though they should be taking up arms instead of us."

"We're just pawns in the game between the Russians and the Americans."

"If Begin heard you, he'd jump for joy," she snapped at him. His smile widened.

"When they arrested me," he went on, "they asked me about my position on the Russians, so I told them the truth. That didn't stop them from condemning me to death. But enough about me: Antoinette tells me you like the film?"

"I really do," I replied.

"Do you think it would be a success if it were shown in Egypt?"

"Generally, documentary films aren't popular in Egypt. Plus, Sadat's media has succeeded in killing off people's interest in Arab causes."

He turned to address Antoinette.

"Didn't I tell you that books are better than movies?"

He turned back to me, adding, "Do you know that I wrote a major novel? Everyone who read it was astonished by it and told me I missed my calling."

He looked back and forth between the two of us, then stood up.

"I'll be going now," he said, "and let you get to work."

After he left, Antoinette told me, "Abu Nadir is an exceptional person, even if he has his opinions. Did you find the material I gave you helpful?"

"Very. But I want to see the film again."

"Of course. I reserved the screening room for you today."

She stood up while gathering some papers on her desk. She was wearing the jeans I had seen her in the first time, but she had traded her jacket for a light floral-design blouse with half-length sleeves.

She walked out of the room ahead of me, and we went upstairs to the top floor. We entered a screening room the size of a living room. It had several rows of cushioned seats, in the middle of which was a small table with two ashtrays. The seats were two steps away from the screen, which covered one wall completely.

I took a seat in the front row and lit a cigarette. Antoinette walked over to the projection booth and spoke to the projectionist. Then she turned off the light and sat down in the seat next to me.

The show started immediately. I found myself better able to follow the film's shots than I had been the last time.

The air was warm, so I took off my jacket, and tossed it on the seat next to me. I rested my right arm on the armrest of my seat. I was wearing a short-sleeved shirt. I could feel her bare arm near me. At the first movement from her, our arms touched.

Our arms stayed that way for a few moments, and then she gently pulled her arm away.

I focused my attention on the film, and it wasn't long before I became absorbed in its images. I wasn't aware of the passage of time until I read the words "The End".

Antoinette got up and turned on the light. She put her hands in her pants' pockets as she turned around and walked toward me. She stood in front of me, bending one of her knees as she rested it on the edge of the seat she had just occupied. I noticed that her pale face was now a little flushed.

I offered her a cigarette and she took it. She pulled out a gold lighter from her pocket and held it up to me. I lit my cigarette, saying: "There are a lot of title cards: they should be incorporated into the voiceover. I'll have to work with the scenes playing in front of me."

"You can work on the Moviola," she suggested.

"No. The problem is that I wouldn't be able to work anywhere or at any time. Don't you have a screenplay?"

"It's just general outlines. Everything else is here," she said, pointing to her head.

"Not even a list of shots?"

"I have one that won't be of any use to you. It consists of numbers and symbols."

"The only option left then is for me to make a list for myself. I'll write down what is in each shot using the Moviola."

"But the film has six sections plus the introduction."

"It will be a nuisance, for sure, and it will take some time. But it will put me completely inside the film. But I only have one condition."

"What is it?"

"That nothing I write will be modified except with my agreement. I understand the demands that cinema imposes, and I will try to conform to them as much as I can. But I won't accept any attempt to distort what I write for the benefit of one faction or another."

"That is your right. When can you begin?"

I looked at my watch, then said: "Now. We'll try it with the introduction."

I put on my jacket and we went down to her office. The projectionist followed us, carrying the metal canisters containing the film, and we helped move them to the editing room. With skilled fingers, Antoinette took care of fixing the sound and film reels in place. Then she handed me some blank sheets of paper, and after putting on her glasses, she turned out the light. I pulled up a seat beside her, then took my pen out of my pocket.

The first dark, distorted shots followed one after the other. The title of the film appeared and I put pen to paper without taking my eyes off the small screen. I started recording what I saw.

General nature scenes. Snow covers the peak of Mount Lebanon. Cedar trees stick out from the melting snow. The foot of the mountain is covered with abundant green.

Mulberry, fig and orange trees. A stream of water beneath a walnut tree. The sun's rays sparkle on the surface of the water. Small green tobacco shrubs. Brown tobacco leaves on pieces of cloth along the edge of the road. Beside them, farmers in white clothes and baggy pants. Goatherds. A transistor radio on a donkey. Fairuz sings: *O bee-eater bird!*

The road stretches out, ascending to a large palace perched upon a hill. On a wide balcony sits the *bey* in rustic clothes, with a short *tarbush* at an angle on his head. Nearby are a number of his enforcers awaiting his orders.

The road cuts through a village. Dusty chalk and low houses. In front of one of them an old man sits cross-legged on a stone bench, smoking a nargile. A shop with a number of wooden tables, around which several young men are playing a game like table football.

The village at night. Youths in shirts and pants make their way along its streets carrying torches and shouting: "We want union, union now! Nasser, Nasser, show us how!"

Fairuz sings: *I loved you in the summer, I loved you in the winter . . .*

Fairuz sings another song notable for its fast, Western beat.

The song was in Lebanese dialect, and I couldn't make out what she was saying. I indicated to Antoinette to replay it, and she stopped the reel. She put her hand out to a wheel connected to the Moviola spool, and slowly moved it. The film played in reverse.

The song seemed familiar to me, but I still couldn't make out the words. After a moment, I realized why it had caught my attention. The melody was from a popular Western song. The mix of Lebanese dialect and Western dance music seemed strange.

"The song is called 'Days Gone By'," explained Antoinette. I nodded. The film rolled, and I began recording again.

Hamra Street in Beirut. Chic glass-window displays. Signs sticking out over the sidewalk. Slick fast cars. Glittering lights. Jewelry stores and pinball arcades. Mink coats. Luxury movie theaters. Mini- , midi- and maxi-skirts. Dim red lights on the side streets. La Dolce Vita café. Cafés scattered along the waterfront up to Pigeons' Rock. Unbelievable crowds. The *ghutra* headcloths of Gulf Arabs and white *gallabeyas*. Half-naked blonde girls parading on a stage.

A poster with these words fills the empty screen:

*Lebanon Tourist Casino*
*Presents Every Evening*
*The Finest Mezzes and Best Oriental Dishes*
*Fully Prepared to Cater to All Special Requests*

And another poster:

*Lebanon, Oasis of Freedom*

Fairuz's angelic voice: *Visit me once every year; you must never forget all about me.*

Beirut Airport. A plane coming from Africa, with a mix of Africans and Lebanese disembarking. A stout Lebanese man in a white suit with a bald head. His belly bulges out over his pants inside a white silk shirt. His sideburns reach the middle of his cheeks. He is carrying a Samsonite briefcase. Nervously, he follows the progress of a big cardboard box being carried out of the airport.

A metal dais rises nearly a meter off the ground. It spins around, carrying large electrical appliances: a Westinghouse refrigerator, a Moulinex blender, a Hoover vacuum.

An empty modern car spins around on the dais.

A man's voice in a theatrical tone and a rapid delivery: "Enjoy the good life with the new sports car. Five speeds. Computer-guided steering, fuel consumption and engine testing. With a digital radio, sun roof and cassette-deck radio."

A young man in modern European clothes. His hair wavy and soft, carefully coiffed. He looks like a young European in every way. He sits on the same circular dais, and it turns around quickly, with him on it. The dais stops suddenly, causing the young man to face the camera. He puts his hand up to his jacket collar to show us the tag as he beams with pride.

The façade of a furniture showroom. A middle-aged woman in a modest coat. Her hair is covered with a colored scarf, its ends knotted under her chin. She has her face up to the glass to look at the objects on display. Her eyes move back and forth between the stainless-steel kitchen, the different kinds of pile carpets, and the Louis XIV sofas.

Other women like her rummage through piles of different clothes sitting on wooden carts in *Sahat al–Burj Square*.

Adjacent shacks made of tin sheets. The ground is filthy with traces of waste water. Children in scruffy clothes carry colored plastic tubs in their hands. The tubs are filled with water from a public faucet that supplies every shack.

A woman washes clothes in a puddle of water pouring from a broken water pipe.

Photos of Gamal Abdel Nasser on the walls of the shacks.

Fairuz's voice: *I waited for you in the summer, I waited for you in the winter . . .*

A magnificent palace surrounded by an expansive garden flooded with lights. Groups of men and women in evening clothes. The dance music that was used in Fairuz's song, "Days Gone By".

An advertisement fills the screen: *Lamb intestines are a dog's favorite food. We've prepared them for you in several ways to suit various tastes.*

Hamra Street at night. A girl in white jeans crosses the street. The camera focuses on her thighs, zooming in on them. Her pants are extremely tight. The camera zooms above her thighs. The details of her body are clearly shown: her curvy hips and cleavage.

The glass display of a clothes shop. Perfectly manufactured mannequins of women and girls in sheer and colored negligées. A number of young men stare at the displays. The young men are wearing embroidered shirts and platform shoes. Their sideburns are long. The general air about them reveals that they are working-class, or generally poor.

A color television screen showing an advertisement for men's underwear. The underwear is worn by young men with smooth, hairless bodies.

Another ad for a new men's skin cream. A title fills the screen: *Take care of your skin the way you take care of your car.*

A number of young men gather in a circle around books and magazines spread out on the sidewalk. A tabloid-size newspaper with a large photo of a half-naked girl. From the paper's headline the word "rape" appears.

Crooked alleys that pass through old Ottoman-era souqs. They also lead to the red-light district. Martyrs' Square. Taxi stands for Mercedes service cars heading to Tripoli, Amman and Aleppo. Sahat al-Burj Square in the evening. Crowds in front of the modest façades of clothing and shoe stores. Falafel restaurants and sweets shops. Piles of *mamul* and *baraziq* sesame cookies, and trays of baklava behind the glass windows. The crowd multiplies in front of the narrow entrance to a movie theater. A wide billboard carries the half-naked image of the American movie star Raquel Welch.

Inside the theater during the show. Thick clouds of cigarette smoke. Raquel Welch is on the screen in threadbare rags that reveal her legs. Shouts and whistles from the audience.

Part of the crimes and accidents news from a daily newspaper:

### Burj Hamoud Crime

*Badariyya Muhammad Taha had unmarried relations with an unidentified person. She sought refuge in the Good Shepherd monastery where she bore a child. A month and a half ago, her family took her back after pledging to the office of the prosecutor general that they would not repudiate her. Ten days ago, they married her to Kamil Karam Taha, a former employee of the municipality of Beirut. He brought her to the capital, and they resided at his home in the Burj Hamoud district. Five days later, she was found murdered: she had been shot not long before by two bullets to the head and chest, fired at a close distance. The husband vanished.*

93

*Assault on a Child*
*Wadia Z. (age 17) lured the child, Rajaa, to his private room*
*and tore off her clothes, then attempted to assault her.*

Hamra Street by day. The Wimpy Café. The Mövenpick. The Horseshoe. The Modka. Café de la Paix. In the middle of the street, a demonstration by young men in chic clothes. The demonstrators hold up placards in English and French, bearing leftist slogans in defense of the lower classes.

Fiery slogans and posters on the walls.

On a wall, a sketch done in oil paint of Gamal Abdel Nasser, and beneath it, his famous expression: "What was taken by force can only be restored by force."

A number of young men surround one of their own who is sitting at a table opposite the camera. He is wearing an open shirt that reveals thick chest hair and a gold chain. He is talking into a microphone in fiery tones: "The Zionist-imperialist movement in the Arab region has come to form a dangerous and direct threat to the gains made by the Arab revolution, its defiant masses, and its nationalist, socialist, democratic, progressive and pro-unification aspirations . . ."

Fairuz in the final, stirring section of the song "Jerusalem, Flower Among Cities":

> *The radiant wrath is coming*
> *The radiant wrath is coming, I believe with all my heart*
> *From every direction it is coming.*

A row of television, video and other equipment. An elegant young man smiles at the camera and points at the equipment:

"More than forty video games, all of them fun and exciting."

Another ad for similar technology above a television screen. A voice from behind the screen: "Now! A new world of three-color viewing. Watch and record five-hour video tapes! Search for the image you want, pause it, and be in control of the whole system from the comfort of your chair!"

A poster carrying these words above a background of snow-covered mountain peaks:

*Lebanon*
*Land of Welcome and Tolerance*
*Crossroads of Civilizations*

Young men in black military outfits and large caps of the same color march in unison on a street while shouting: "*Han duwa, han duwa*" ("One, two" in French as spoken on the Lebanese street).

Posters of different sizes with photographs of Lebanese leaders.

A title fills the screen:

The Commanders of Lebanon

Fairuz's voice in the song "Oh Me Oh My". Note to self: The song's melody is taken from a symphony by Mozart.

The camera flashes photos of Camille Chamoun, Suleiman Frangieh, Pierre Gemayel, Father Charbel Qassis, Patriarch Khuraysh, Raymond Eddé, Saeb Salam, Mufti Hasan Khalid, Kamel Assaad, Imam Musa al-Sadr, Rashid Karami, Elias Sarkis.

The camera paused on the image of Kamal Jumblatt.

Title card:

Kamal Jumblatt inherited from his father substantial religious and feudal authority among the Druze community.
But his wide-ranging cultural education and travels led him
to Gandhi and Marx. He became a devout Sufi who practiced yoga and became a vegetarian. That didn't prevent
him from actively participating in the game of Lebanese
politics and playing by its rules, such that he has been
described as a presidential kingmaker and head of shadow
governments. He has often complained that the Druze –
according to the confessional balancing agreement – don't
have the right to anything more than a ministerial post. He
formed the Socialist Progressive Party. Before he left his
position as minister of the interior in the early 1970s, he
allowed the Communist Party to operate openly. He won
the Lenin Peace Prize. In recent years, he has been a leader
of the urban poor against the scions of the major families.

A round table around which sit the leaders of the Nasserist,
Baathist and Communist organizations, at the center of
which is Kamal Jumblatt. Among those seated are George
Hawi, Muhsin Ibrahim, Ibrahim Qalilat, Bashir Obayd,
Inaam Raad and Kamal Shatila.

The French song "Coupable". The melody was borrowed
for Fairuz's famous song "I Loved You in the Summer".

The city of Nabatieh in the south. A religious festival in
commemoration of Ashura, celebrated every year by the Shia
on the 10th of the Islamic month of Muharram. A parade

of Mercedes cars and mopeds bearing aloft portraits of Khomeini and Musa al-Sadr. The latter's portrait carries these words: "My role is defined by God, my nation's history, my religion and my *umma*." On top of the lead car sit two young men, one of whom wears a white shirt saying "I am yours to command, Hussein". The other one wears a black shirt with *"Allahu Akbar"* painted on it. Both of them wear black headbands that nearly cover their eyes.

A public square in the middle of the city. Dozens of young men standing in circles beat their shaved heads with their hands. Some of them use the edges of swords instead of their hands, and continue striking their heads until blood flows. (The tradition is an expression of the Shias' remorse over their ancestors' stance more than 1,000 years ago, when they abandoned Hussein, the son of the Imam Ali, and let him be slaughtered at the hands of his enemies.)

Latin religious prayers.

Inside a deserted, dimly lit church. A priest ascends the pulpit and opens the Holy Book. He reads aloud: "Oh that I had in the desert a wayfarers' lodging place; that I might leave my people and go from them! For all of them are adulterers, an assembly of treacherous men."*

In the dock where the accused sits in a courtroom. A priest stands up. The judges sit below the Star of David.

Title card:

In August 1974, Israel arrested Archbishop *Capucci*, leader of the Christian community in Jerusalem, on charges of

---

* *Jeremiah 9:2. Translation: New American Standard Bible.*

belonging to the *Fatah* organization and smuggling weapons to the *fedayeen*. He was sentenced to twelve years in prison.

Capucci declares from the dock: "My nationalism is the foundation for my Christianity. Unless I am an Arab down to my blood and bones, then I am not a Christian."

The port of Haifa in the 1940s. A European ship packed with Jewish refugees approaches the shore and drops anchor beside it.

Title card:

"It is in our interest that there be several sectarian states in the region to justify the presence of Israel."

— Ben Gurion

The screen is divided into four sections. In each section shots with a distinct point of view follow one another in succession. Altogether, the shots show Israeli tanks and planes in combat. One of the sections goes back in history, showing Israeli soldiers as they raid homes in a Palestinian village with bayonets. In another section, the streets of Port Said appear after their destruction in 1956. In the third section, Israeli planes jealously guard the ruins of the city of Suez in 1967. The fourth section shows the Israeli attack on the Syrian city of Qunaitra in 1973.

Title card:

"There will be no peace . . . War will continue between us and the Arabs even if they make a peace treaty with us."

— Menachem Begin

A large field. The side of a country road. An Arab family slowly walks by. The family is made up of women and children, with no men among them. They are all carrying bundles and different items. They look out into the distance in fear.

The sound of the announcer of the Palestinian radio program which has been broadcast for thirty years: "People can rest assured that everything is well and they are asked to remain calm. I am fine. Please assure us that you are also fine."

Title card:

> "When a Jew kills a Palestinian or Arab, he rids himself of his fears and becomes worthy of carrying the mark of manhood."
>
> – Menachem Begin

Corpses of an Arab family that had been playing cards. A murdered child is still clutching a card in his hand. Fragments of the bomb that fell on them are mingled with body parts and bloodstains. A pair of child's underpants is hanging on a rope. The refrigerator door is open.

Title card:

> "Israelis, your hearts should not feel pain when you kill your enemy. You should not take pity on them so long as we have not yet done away with what is called Arab civilization, on the rubble of which we will construct our own civilization."
>
> – Menachem Begin

A commemorative photo of the massacre of *Deir Yasin* in 1948. On one side of the photo is a group of European Jews – as is clear from their features and their clothes. They look on in apparent delight at a soldier from the Zionist Irgun paramilitaries. He is carrying on the bayonet of his rifle the head of an Arab, dripping blood. On the other side of the photo, a military truck is carrying a group of naked Arab women tied with ropes.

Title card:

"I believe in our moral and intellectual superiority inasmuch as it serves as an example to reform the Arab race."
                                                    – Ben Gurion

Beirut Arab University. The enormous Gamal Abdel Nasser Hall packed with delegates. In the front row, before the podium, sits Kamal Jumblatt and the leaders of Lebanon's nationalist and progressive parties, and the Palestinian factions. Yasser Arafat walks briskly up to the podium. He turns to the audience with a jubilant look on his face. Everyone stands and applauds for a long time.

Title card:

Yasser Arafat, also known as Abu Ammar, is the leader of Fatah, the largest of the organizations that make up the Palestinian Liberation Organization. He is the general director of the PLO, and commander-in-chief of the forces of the Palestinian revolution, as he is called in official edicts. He is known as "The Choice", or "the old man", by his aides.

Yasser Arafat in a conversation with journalists: "We ask only that our rearguard be secure, and that you don't haggle with us, or over us."

A commemorative photo of Fairuz and Assi Rahbani on their honeymoon in Cairo in 1955.

Title card:

Throughout the civil war, the killing would come completely to a halt at 7 pm every day, so that all the Lebanese could listen to the program of Ziad Rahbani, the son of Fairuz, on Lebanese radio.

The voice of Ziad: "We're still alive!"

Ziad, with his skinny, emaciated face, wears striped pajamas and moves on the stage. Above the theater entrance is a billboard announcing the play that he wrote and acted in: *An American Feature Film*.

A title card fills the screen:

What happened to Lebanon?

The words stay fixed in place while the film credits roll.

Antoinette lifted her hand from the Moviola wheel, and the display stopped. She took off her glasses, and rested her arms on the table, while smiling at me in the weak light. Then she got up in one swift motion, walked over to the light switch, and turned it on.

I looked at my watch and found that it was close to 8 pm. As I looked at the two reels of film that had collected in intertwined piles in the cloth container beside the Moviola, I said: "The introduction took us almost two and a half hours. At this rate, I can finish going through all the scenes in less than a week."

She came back to her seat next to mine, and asked, "And another week to write the voiceover? Does that sound about right?"

"Almost," I replied.

"Is that a problem for you?"

I grimaced. "Not at all," I said.

She lit a cigarette as she busied herself in winding the film reels and returning each of them to its can. When she was done, I helped her carry the film canisters to her office. She left me for a moment while she fetched a wool coat and her purse.

"Where are you headed now?" she asked me as she pulled out a key.

"Home," I replied.

"Me, too," she said, leading me out of the office and locking the door behind us.

"Where do you live?" I asked her.

"In East Beirut."

Perplexed, I stared at her, and she laughed, saying: "Do you find that strange?"

"Do you mean you go back there at night and come here in the morning?"

"Don't forget – it's one city," she said as we went out into the street, which was filled with lights and pedestrians.

"During the fighting, I also used to come here every day. I would leave my family wearing a blouse and skirt or a dress, and the moment I arrived I would put on military overalls and carry a Kalashnikov. At night I would change my clothes before going back to my family."

"Are they . . ."

"Yes. They are Maronite fanatics."

"So you're like Ziad Rahbani?"

"Ziad rebelled against his mother."

"And you?"

"I rebel against the whole situation."

She opened her purse and took out a cigarette. I happened to see inside the purse and noticed the barrel of a small revolver.

I lit her cigarette for her, and then lit one for me. We walked toward an old Volkswagen.

"Have you known Wadia long?" she asked me suddenly.

"We were in school together."

She continued pressing me with questions: "Do you know him well?"

I was at a loss about how to answer. "Ride with me. I'll take you," she said as she opened the car door.

# 9

The gunfire was extremely close and sudden enough that a glass of whiskey nearly fell out of my hand. I was sitting in the living room with Wadia watching a French movie on television.

"The top floor, most likely," Wadia said, without taking his eyes off the television screen.

I put my glass on the table and asked him, "What do you think it was?"

He shrugged. "Could be anything," he replied.

I stood up, walked to the balcony and pulled open the door. I stepped outside and the cold air brushed my face. I stood watching the quiet street plunged in darkness. I glanced at my watch and found that it was midnight.

I could sense Wadia behind me and heard him say in a soft voice: "The best thing to do in these situations is nothing at all."

I turned around and went back inside. He followed me.

"This isn't the first time and it won't be the last," he added. "Only two months ago, three armed men knocked on the door of the apartment directly next to mine. When the person inside opened it, they shot him. He was an Iraqi Communist."

I lit a cigarette. "And who were they?" I asked.

"Iraqi intelligence."

"They killed him and left, just like that?"

"The man who was killed was under Arafat's protection. Lebanese Communists avoided him out of a desire to maintain their relationship with Saddam Hussein. When Arafat learned what happened, he issued his order to Fatah's security apparatus. It arrested dozens of Iraqi Baath agents. After that, things were even among all sides as usual."

The sound of a car speeding in the street rang out. It stopped in front of our building. The sound of a conversation among several people came up to us. The sound of their voices grew distant, then a little later echoed back, muffled, and then broke off. Then a knocking on the doors of the floor below us rang out. Then it was silent.

Wadia had lowered the volume on the television, and I was about to turn it up again when heavy footfalls approached the door of the apartment and the doorbell rang.

Wadia's face grew pale; then he got up and walked toward the door, shouting, "Who is it?"

We heard Abu Shakir's voice: "It's me, Mr Wadia. There are some comrades from Group 17."

"Fatah security," Wadia whispered to me.

Wadia turned the key in the door, and hesitantly opened up, revealing the doorman accompanied by two young men armed with Kalashnikovs. One of them was of medium height, in his twenties. A look of embarrassment appeared on his face – just the opposite of his colleague, who was older than he. His face was clearly lined with experience and authority.

The older one politely asked to see the owner of the apartment, and Wadia presented himself. I pulled out my passport.

"Did the two of you hear the bullets?" he asked, looking back and forth at our faces.

"We heard one bullet while we were sitting here," Wadia replied.

"And you don't know where it came from?"

Wadia shook his head, and the young man asked to take a look around the apartment. Wadia stepped back from the door and we went with the man to my room, where he inspected its contents without touching anything. Then we moved to Wadia's room.

The gun was still in its place on the bedside table. Noticing it, the young man picked it up and raised its barrel to his nose. Then he brought it out to the living room. He pulled a small notebook out of his pocket and wrote down in it the gun's identification numbers, then he left the gun on the table. He tore a white piece of paper out of the notebook and wrote several phone numbers on it.

"Please call one of these numbers if you learn anything," he said, handing the paper to Wadia.

Wadia took it from him. "I know the number," he said. "Will do."

The two men expressed their regret for having disturbed us. They left the apartment and joined Abu Shakir, who walked ahead of them to the next apartment.

Wadia closed the door while I poured myself a glass of whiskey.

"Pour one for me, too," he said, flinging himself into a chair.

I filled his glass and handed it to him. He raised it to his lips, then returned it to the table, saying, "Now I remember. I've met that gunman before. At the time he was in the *Popular Front*."

"Why did he leave it to go to Fatah?" I wondered.

He shrugged. "Who knows?" he replied. "Maybe he got into an argument with his superiors, or he disagreed with them ideologically. Or he made some mistake that they wanted to punish him for. Maybe the salary was the reason. Fatah pays its fighters more."

I reached out for the gun and picked it up. I turned it over carefully.

"Do you know this is the first time in my life I've touched a real handgun? I was well trained with Russian rifles during the Suez War. An old soldier trained us. He was harsh with us because of our political opinions. When we went to prison, he was transferred there. By coincidence, I believe. He enjoyed being in charge of tormenting us. He would have us gather in front of him and order us to squat down and call out 'Long live Gamal Abdel Nasser!' As though cheering for Nasser required all that distress."

I put the gun back. I happened to look at the television set and saw that the film was over; the presenter was reading the latest news bulletin. I turned up the volume.

The situation in Beirut was quiet. The situation in the Gulf was just the opposite. Iraqi and Iranian forces had begun destroying petroleum facilities in the two countries, and the number of war refugees from the two sides totaled over a million.

The final news item came from Egypt, the gist of which was that an American transport plane had been destroyed in the early hours of the morning on its descent into the Cairo West Air Base, during training for the US Rapid Deployment Force. Thirteen American soldiers were killed.

I felt a little elated and poured myself another glass.

"You're drinking a lot," Wadia said, as he slowly sipped his drink.

I turned off the television. "I can't sleep," I said.

"I'll give you a Valium."

"That makes me spacy in the morning. You know I need to be fully alert when recording the shots."

A sly smile played over his lips.

"I see you've become enthusiastic about the film," he said. "Generally speaking, Antoinette is a fantastic girl."

"What do you mean?"

"I mean she's not complicated. She goes to bed with men quickly."

As I lit a cigarette and approached the bookshelf, I told him: "That's completely the opposite of what I want. I go to bed with women slowly."

I flipped through the few books on the shelf and picked an old one by Colin Wilson.

"Read it," said Wadia. "He claims that prolonging orgasms will lead to eternal happiness for humanity."

I put the book back and took another one.

"That's not a problem for me," I said.

"So what is your problem?"

"What do you feel during orgasm?" I asked him.

"Sometimes I haul with pleasure."

"Lucky you."

I picked up my notebook and my pack of cigarettes from the table.

"I'll try to sleep. Goodnight."

I went to my room, took off my clothes and lay down on the bed. My eyes were fixed on the ceiling, and I thought about my ex-wife. Then I thought about the first girl I loved, or to be exact, the first girl we loved. Wadia and I and two other friends of ours were in love with her at the same time. That was at the university, at the beginning of the 1950s, when the wealthy and the aristocratic were the only ones who could break the hidden barriers erected between the sexes. We stood around her all the time and walked with her for hours on end. When it got cold, we would play the hand-warming game, and she would put her right hand in my left pocket and her left hand in Wadia's right pocket.

I also remembered the first time I masturbated, and the time that Wadia and I drank a bottle of wine, and we masturbated in front of each other. I remembered the first girl I slept with. Wadia and I and a third friend from the hand-warming group succeeded in pooling our money, and we picked her up from a shady spot along the banks of the Nile – the same place where Anwar Sadat's mansion and the Sheraton now sit. We brought her back to the house of one of our friends, and when it was my turn, I found her fast asleep. I woke her up, but then I didn't know what to do. So she laid me down on my back and got on top of me. It didn't take more than a few seconds, and while it was happening, the only thing I felt was that I was producing a great deal of semen. When I left the room, she had already gone back to sleep, and resumed her rhythmic snoring.

## 10

The morning papers didn't mention anything about the gunfire incident. While we were having our breakfast, Abu Shakir knocked on the door to let us know that the bullet had been fired accidentally while a gun was being cleaned by one of the top-floor residents.

I was busy cleaning my dark-blue suit with a brush. Then I ironed the shirt I had washed yesterday. I shined my shoes with a piece of cloth I found in the kitchen. And finally, I hung my briefcase over my shoulder and set out behind Wadia.

A taxi took us to the Ain Mreisseh neighborhood, near the checkpoints for East Beirut. Wadia asked the driver to stop in front of a modern building that had scorch marks at its entrance. I got out of the car, which made a U-turn to take Wadia to his office.

The scorch marks extended to a shop selling candy and cigarettes, from which wafted the fresh scent of coffee beans. A group of ball-shaped glass containers of identical size were set out in front of the entrance, containing different kinds of hazelnuts, shelled almonds and peanuts.

Two young men, carrying weapons, accosted me at the entrance to the building. They insisted on searching my shoulder bag, and on using the phone in front of them to call Lamia's office before they would let me go upstairs.

I went up a few steps to the elevator, but it wasn't there, so I opted to continue walking up the stairs, which had blast marks on the walls. When I reached the second floor, I saw "Dar al-Thaqafa Publishing" on a sign above an open door. A metal scaffold was erected in front of it. There was a worker on top of the scaffold busy adding layers of cement mixture to the ceiling.

There was another worker inside painting the walls. A tall man with a gun hanging from his waist was watching him with an unusual level of attention. He only let me pass after I showed him my passport and he had inspected me. Then he handed me over to a plump secretary with a laughing face, who led me to an office at the end of a passageway to the right of the entrance.

She knocked on the door and went in, and Lamia's wide eyes gazed on me. She was sitting behind a metal desk at the end of a large office. She stood up with a smile, and walked around her desk. She extended her hand to me, and I shook it. She held my hand in a tender grip, as she led me to two small couches next to each other in a corner of the room. A small glass table stood between them. We each sat on a couch.

She was wearing a green ensemble, made up of a short-sleeved blouse and a skirt that looked like shorts. My eyes took in her rosy skin and her soft, plump lips.

She addressed me in a refined voice: "How are you?"

"Good," I responded, using the Lebanese word.

"We like the Egyptian dialect, and we have no problem understanding it. Don't wear yourself out imitating ours."

"What if I like the Lebanese dialect?" I asked as I pulled

out of my shoulder bag the envelope containing a copy of my book manuscript.

She took the envelope from me with straight fingers that had long nails painted the color of her skin. As she put it on the table, she asked, "What would you like to drink? Coffee, or something cold?"

"Coffee."

"Bitter, or the way the Egyptians make it?"

"The way you'll drink it," I replied, with my eyes on her lips.

She stood up in an elegant movement, and walked over to her desk. She leaned over it with her back to me. She pressed the button for the intercom, and spoke into it in a half-whisper. I didn't take my eyes off her firm, well-proportioned behind. Our eyes met when she suddenly turned around and walked back to her couch. In her eyes, I noticed the trace of a light smile.

She sat next to me on the adjoining couch and crossed her legs.

"Adnan spoke with me again today," she said. "He sends his sincere apologies for the inconvenience we've caused you. He entrusted me to use my judgment in regards to your book."

"My fate is in your hands."

"I wouldn't go that far," she replied, laughing.

"Did you know that I saw you a few days ago?"

"Where?"

"I've forgotten the name of the place. A café near the American University. You were with a woman who was wearing a black dress."

"Aah . . . that was a friend of mine."

The secretary brought the coffee on a small silver tray and then left. I lifted my cup to my lips and swallowed a sip of bitter coffee, as my eyes ran over Lamia's legs down to her feet and her long, full toenails.

She noticed the direction of my gaze, and looked down at her feet. At that moment the telephone rang and she got up again. She walked to her desk, then walked around it so as to face me. She lifted the phone to her ear and listened for a moment, then pressed a button on the phone.

"Hello," she said, in the same whispering voice.

I saw her eyebrows knit a little, as she listened without saying anything. Then she muttered a word I couldn't make out, and slowly put the receiver back in its place.

I occupied myself by looking at a glass bookcase that held copies of the firm's publications in deluxe editions. She spoke to me from behind her desk as she gestured at the phone: "That was my friend, the one we were talking about. Unfortunately, I have to leave now. Would you like me to drop you off somewhere?"

"I'm on my way to Fakahani."

She leaned over the intercom and pressed the button, then whispered two words into it. She took a small purse from the desk and straightened up.

I placed my cup on the tray, and picked up my shoulder bag as I stood up myself. I followed her outside.

The secretary was waiting for us. Beside her was the tall young man who walked briskly ahead of us out of the building. I walked over toward the elevator, but Lamia put her hand on my arm, saying, "It's better if we take the stairs. Security precautions."

"Why?"

"The elevator might be rigged to explode."

The young man went down the stairs ahead of us. Lamia leaned her head toward me and I breathed in her perfume.

Gesturing at him with her eyes, she whispered, "It's for security precautions, too, that I don't go anywhere without a bodyguard."

Our companion went ahead of us to a late-model Chevrolet; in the driver seat was a chauffeur in a uniform with two rows of shiny brass buttons. The bodyguard held open the back door and waited until Lamia got in. Then he closed it and walked around the car while I followed him. He opened the other door for me, and after closing it behind me, he completed his walk around the car, and took the seat next to the driver.

As the car set off, passing in front of the American Embassy and heading toward Hamra Street, I said, "You can take your time reading the manuscript. I'll be staying in Beirut for at least ten more days."

"Very good," she said, imitating the Egyptian dialect. "I'll call you as soon as I finish it."

The car made its way through narrow streets crowded with pedestrians, then came to a stop in front of the Palestinian Media Bureau. I got out of the car and walked to the building where Antoinette's office was. After the usual security measures, I went up. I found her waiting for me in the editing room, where she had finished loading in place the soundtrack and film reel. I took out my pen and paper, and immediately we set to work.

## THE FIRST PART OF THE FILM

Formations of warplanes carrying the Star of David on their sides. The planes make continual sorties over modest homes and extensive fields. Bombs explode in the middle of the fields. The houses collapse.

Title card:

In the first hours of 1975, Israeli attacks on southern Lebanon stepped up their intensity.

A circle around a paragraph from the Israeli newspaper *Maariv*, dated January 31, 1975. *Mordechai Gur*, the Israeli Army's chief of staff, announces: "We have to create a new geopolitical situation in the region."

The beautiful Lebanese tourist town of Chtaura. Snow covers the streets and the tops of trim-looking houses. A parade for Syrian president Hafez al-Assad makes its way through the streets of the town. The Lebanese president Suleiman Frangieh comes down the steps of his palace and walks forward to welcome the Syrian president.

An official spokesman reads out to journalists an announcement about the meeting between the two presidents. The announcement confirms Syria's readiness to support Lebanon in the face of Israeli hostilities.

Title card:
At the same time . . .

Camille Chamoun stands before a long table surrounded

by people sitting and standing. He raises a glass to his lips to toast the success of the Protein Company.

Title card:

The Protein Company was established with Lebanese and Gulf capital, a loan from the Shah of Iran, and technological support from a number of foreign companies. The founders chose Chamoun as president of the company. From Saeb Salam's government, Chamoun obtained for the company a concession for a monopoly on fishing off Lebanese shores for a 99-year period.

Protest demonstrations by fishermen and nationalist and progressive parties. Signs carrying various slogans, including "The big fish eats the little fish" and "Our sons are soldiers in defense of southern Lebanon".

The city of Sidon. A crowd of demonstration carries the Nasserist parliament member *Maaruf Saad* on their shoulders. The army fires on the demonstration.

Headline from a Lebanese newspaper: "Maaruf Saad hit by gunfire".

Beirut. Several thousand Maronite students in a demonstration in support of the army. Signs demand the removal of weapons from the Palestinians.

Headline from a Lebanese newspaper: "Death of Maaruf Saad".

An enormous demonstration raises up a photograph, draped in black, of Maaruf Saad.

Headquarters of the Ministry of Defense in Beirut. A long, quiet passageway with closed doors on both sides. A senior officer emerges from one of the rooms and loudly slams the door behind him.

Title card:

The army refused to hand over to the court the soldier who killed Maaruf Saad or the intelligence officer who gave him the order to do it.

Leaders of the nationalist and leftist parties around a round table. In the middle of them is Kamal Jumblatt. Journalists record Jumblatt's announcement: ". . . Assassinating Maaruf Saad had several goals: terrorizing the people's movement, manufacturing intercommunal discord, and drawing the Palestinian resistance into Lebanon's internal struggle."

Israeli planes drop bombs on South Lebanon.

Tel Aviv. An American luxury car carries Charbel Qassis, leader of the Lebanese Maronite religious orders, in his black clerical robes. A gold cross dangles from his neck.

Title card:
Father Charbel Qassis arrived in Israel on April 5.

Charbel Qassis waves with a hand adorned with diamond rings and jewels. A close-up of his plump face and full lips. He says: "What do the Muslims themselves think? Are their husbands more virile than our men? On Mount Lebanon we have men who can each have ten or twenty children."

Beirut. The Supreme Islamic Shiite Council building in the Hazmieh neighborhood, the Maronite stronghold in Lebanon's capital. The building's graceful entrance. Twenty thousand Shias are gathered around the building.

Title card:

In the first week of April, the Supreme Islamic Shiite Council elected Imam Musa al-Sadr president for life.

A medium-sized bus, empty of passengers. Bullet marks on its sides and windows.

Title card:

On the afternoon of Sunday, April 13, 1975, this bus was on the way back from an event commemorating the victims of the Deir Yasin massacre. The bus was carrying a number of residents of the Tel Zaatar refugee camp, both Lebanese and Palestinians. When it reached the Ain El Remmaneh neighborhood, the Phalangist militia opened fire on it, killing twenty-six passengers – most of them children – and injuring twenty-nine others.

Bodies covered with Palestinian flags.

Jamil Street. A Volkswagen driven by a young man. The car reaches the Church of Our Lady of Salvation. Bullets are fired on the car from inside the church.

Mar Maroun Street. A speeding Fiat carries a number of armed men wearing the *hatta*, the checkered headscarf usually worn by Palestinians and the inhabitants of southern Lebanon. A number of armed men attempt to stop the car, but it forcibly drives right by them. The car's passengers exchange gunfire with the armed men. One of the armed men falls to the ground. One of the passengers is struck, too.

The roof of a tall building. Three young men behind mounted machineguns. The guns rest on the edge of the roof. Near the young men is a pitcher of water and a tin plate. One of the young men is wearing platform shoes. The second one is wearing a leather jacket. The third has wrapped a military belt around his waist.

A distant shot, seen through the gun-sight of a machinegun. The gun-sight moves, searching for a target. The two crosshairs, in the shape of a cross, follow a moving body. The body gradually approaches the point where the crosshairs meet, and is revealed to be a middle-aged man running quickly. The gun-sight moves away from the man a little, settling on a point behind his feet. A bullet is fired. The gun-sight moves back to the man. It follows him as he runs. Another bullet is fired at a point in front of him. The man falls to the ground, quaking in fear. He gets up suddenly and continues running. The gun-sight focuses on the man's hand. A bullet hits him, injuring him. The man puts his good hand on the injured one and keeps running. The gun-sight shakes in a dance-like movement, searching for a new target. A bullet hits the man in his leg. He falls to the ground. The gun-sight comes to rest on his stomach. A bullet hits the man in his stomach.

Sandbags along the sides of empty streets. A storefront with a sign above it saying "Original Mercedes Parts. Authorized Factory Dealers and Distributors". A wrecked car in front of a closed store.

The asphalt around a demolished gas station. Small signs on the walls with only a single word remaining on them:

"Super". On the ground, a young man with disheveled hair in a shirt and pants, lying on his side. He drags himself forward, blood flowing out of him.

The burned interiors of the domes of the al-Majidiya Mosque near the Wood Merchants' Wharf. A burned corpse showing marks from the rope that tied it up.

A large oil painting of the Virgin Mary holding Jesus in her lap after he had been taken down from the cross, with daggers of grief lodged in her heart. Bullet holes are visible all over the painting.

The main headline of the *al-Nahar* newspaper: "Agreement for ceasefire, withdrawal of forces and removal of barricades."

A circle around a paragraph from an article by Pierre Gemayel in the Phalangist Party newspaper: "Lebanon is the most beautiful land on earth, and the best country in the Orient. Unfortunately, this situation began to deteriorate four or five years ago, when a flood of foreigners of unknown identity and affiliation began to make their way into Lebanon."

A circle around a paragraph from an article in Syria's *al-Thawra* newspaper: "The Palestinian uprising does not stand alone in the face of its enemies. United leadership between Syria and the resistance is the answer."

In front of Lebanon's parliament building. An armored car marked "Lebanese Internal Security". A number of officers. A Mercedes carrying a flag. Inside the parliament building. The members are assembled. The prime minister, Rashid al-Solh, is speaking: "It is clear that the Phalangist Party bears full responsibility for the massacre and the reprisals that followed, as well as the victims and material and moral harm that has descended on the country as a result."

Parliament member Amin Gemayel runs up behind the prime minister and pulls him by the arm, trying to assault him.

Washington. Henry Kissinger is in his office on the seventh floor of the State Department Building, talking to an American journalist: "The situation in Lebanon resembles the one in Jordan in 1970. All you need to fix it is for Syria to send in a brigade."

A wide hall, at the back of which is the Sunni mufti of the Republic of Lebanon, Shaykh Hasan Khaled. He has a white turban on his head. On his right sits the Syrian foreign minister, Abd al-Halim Khaddam. On his left is the Shii imam in his black cloak. Next is the Syrian army's chief of staff. Then there is Kamal Jumblatt, with his arms crossed over his chest and his eyes closed. To the left of the Imam Sadr is the leader of the Sunnis of Tripoli, Rashid Karami, and beside him Saeb Salam, the aged leader of Beirut's Sunnis, with his Havana cigar.

A circle around a news item in a Lebanese newspaper: "Saudi Arabia has placed 40 million lira at the disposal of Saeb Salam to fight heresy and Communism."

The main headline of another newspaper: "A new government headed by Rashid Karami with Camille Chamoun as interior minister."

The main headline of another newspaper: "Israeli attack on the refugee camps in the south. 11 killed and 60 homes destroyed in Rashidiya."

Beirut. The *Maslakh-Karantina* district. Adjoining tin-sheet shacks. Palestinian and Lebanese flags. Another shot of the same location, now turned into ruins. A group of the bombs that were dropped on it. One of the bombs is the same shape and height of a teenager. Another bomb has on it the symbol of Saudi Arabia, consisting of two crossed swords above the slogan "There Is No God But God". The dazed face of an old woman looks out from the ruins. A barefoot little girl in an embroidered dress is carrying an infant in her arms; she sits down beside a smashed wall. A middle-aged woman covers her head with a sheer white headscarf that she has tied around her neck, letting one end of it down over her chest. She weeps, with her hand on her cheek. Beside her is a girl who looks like her, who is crying as well. A family runs in the street. The father has a bundle on his back and clutches a child with each hand. A third child walks ahead of them. Among them are several young men wearing the Palestinian checkered *hatta* headscarf. They smile for the camera as they raise their fingers in the victory sign. Beside them are corpses covered in Palestinian flags.

The main headline for the *al-Safeer* newspaper: "Imam al-Sadr announces the creation of regiments of the Lebanese *'Amal' militia* to defend the south. The imam explains that it is committed to realizing the demands of the dispossessed from all religious communities, ending sectarian distinctions, and defending the Palestinian revolution."

A young man carries a machinegun on the roof of a building. He is wearing a white undershirt with the word "Amal" painted on it in European letters.

A long shot of a street. Two oil barrels on the open street, with several armed men on each side of them. There are not many pedestrians. The armed men stop them and check their ID cards. They detain some and let others go. They blindfold the detainees.

In front of an oven of the Mahallet Abu Shakir neighborhood. A pile of used shoes, modern and traditional, are scattered near the wall. Near the Green Line. A wide pit has come to serve as a cemetery for Muslims. A pile of dead bodies recently thrown onto the pile. Men's genitalia cut off and sticking out of their mouths.

Title card:

> In May, an extremist group of Shia calling itself "The Knights of Ali" killed fifty people, among them a number of leftists.

Young men run, carrying wrapped loaves of bread on their shoulders. A street corner. A woman in a short skirt runs toward a car where an armed man is taking cover.

The front page of a Lebanese newspaper. Main headline: "Phalangist leader confesses". Another headline: "Saeed Naeem al-Asmar admits that he worked as a sniper in the Chiyah neighborhood, and says that it was armed Phalangists under the leadership of Joseph Abu Aasi who caused the massacre of Ain al-Remanneh." A third headline: "al-Asmar accuses officials of the Deuxième Bureau and others from Jordanian intelligence of aiding the Phalangists in their military operations."

A headline in the *al-Nahar* newspaper: "Israeli artillery bombards the south."

A headline in the *al-Safeer* newspaper: "Washington discloses US arms deal recently sent to Lebanon by way of the American Embassy in Beirut."

Another headline in the same paper: "Interpol warns of

the arrival in Beirut of 7 European terrorists acting as Zionist agents."

The village of Bteghrine. Slogans on the walls of houses: "All the idiots support the Palestinian revolution." Another slogan: "Down with Palestine."

An Israeli bombardment of the city of Tyre, by land, sea and air.

A newspaper headline: "Kissinger heads to Egypt on his 11th shuttle diplomacy tour."

Newspaper headlines: "Signing of the Sinai Agreement between Egypt and Israel on September 1." "Agence France Presse says that Washington is the biggest winner in this deal." "Yasser Arafat warns: 'The agreement leaves the Syrians and Palestinians standing alone and will lead to another war. Israel and America are making a delusional mistake if they believe that the Egyptian Army will stand aside and do nothing while the Palestinian revolution risks being wiped out.'" "The Soviet Union officially asks from the United States that the Geneva Conference be invited to convene with the participation of the PLO."

The first page of the magazine *al-Karazah*, published by Egypt's Coptic Church. A photograph of Abba Samuel, in charge of foreign relations for the Egyptian Church, in a meeting with members of the World Council of Churches.

Headline: "Investigations by the US Congress have exposed the connection between the World Council of Churches, which John Foster Dulles helped found, with the CIA."

A paragraph from an article in a West German magazine about the Egyptian Church. A photo of Abba Samuel, with this caption below it: "Abba Samuel, one of the most prominent leaders in the Coptic Church, played a key role in helping members of wealthy Coptic families that were harmed by confiscation orders and Nasserist nationalizations, taking advantage of his wide-ranging international connections, especially in West Germany. For many of them, he obtained significant postings in foreign business and banking institutions, which Sadat's 'Open Door' policy opened up for them."

Beirut. Journalists surround Rashid Karami, the Lebanese prime minister, in a white suit and colorful tie with a grin on his face. He is telling the journalists: "President Frangieh is a great leader and I am confident that the final years of his presidency will go down in history."

Headline of a Lebanese newspaper: "Armed Maronites from Zgharta, the stronghold of President Frangieh, take 25 hostages from Tripoli, stronghold of Prime Minister Rashid Karami, killing 12 of them."

Headline of another newspaper: "Deadly outburst in 3 cities in the north. Phalangists demand deployment of the army. Egyptian 'Voice of the Arabs' radio attacks the Palestinian resistance and calls on the Lebanese Army to be deployed on the streets in order to strike it."

A circle around a paragraph from an editorial in the Egyptian newspaper, Akhbar al-Yawm: ". . . the current clashes are part of a conspiracy of rejection in order to frustrate the peaceful arrangement between Egypt and Israel with the goal of creating a situation that forces Syria to get involved, and if that happens, then Israel will be forced to get involved."

An abandoned street in Beirut. Trash and barrels everywhere. Padlocks smashed and thrown down in front of closed-up bars. An open door to a house. Inside are empty, plundered rooms.

A thief carrying an electric chandelier runs down the street, chased by members of the Palestinian Armed Struggle forces.

Fires blaze at the Rivoli Cinema.

The presidential palace in Damascus. Rashid Karami ascends the stairs.

Part of a meeting in Beirut: Zuheir Mohsen – leader of the Palestinian *al-Sa'iqa* organization that is loyal to Syria – wearing a colorful silk shirt and white pants, holds in his hand a deluxe narghile; Abu al-Hasan, Fatah's security official; Yasser Abed Rabbo, one of the leaders of the Democratic Front for the Liberation of Palestine; Colonel Antoine Dahdah, Lebanon's security chief.

Title card:

Ceasefire agreement, but Phalangists have caused the situation in Zahlé to explode.

Beirut. Martyrs' Square. The rubble of the al-Arabi Hotel with a human leg visible in it. A man lying face-down in the entranceway of a bar; in its glass façade boxes of toilet paper can be seen. Blood stains the man's back.

A blindfolded man is walking between two gunmen.

Headlines of Lebanese newspapers: "307 kidnapped and 200 released. 21 bodies found." "Extremist Palestinian group attacks Beirut Airport. 3 killed. Leadership of the resistance movement disavows the attack and the Palestinian officials hand over one of the attackers."

Trucks carrying armed men leave a village and set off on the back-country road. They pass a village and open fire on its homes.

Beirut. An empty street. An old man with no teeth in a full suit is walking with a bag clutched to his chest. A sniper's bullet hits him in the leg and he falls to the ground. He lifts his head and looks around him, then crawls, calling for help, without letting go of the bag. A man protected by the doorway of a neighboring house ties a rope into a lasso and tosses it to the old man without daring to stick his head out of the doorway. He pulls the old man with the rope far out of the sniper's range. The bag falls from the old man's hand and loaves of bread roll out of it.

Fire blazes in the old Souq Sursock. The destruction extends to the Vegetable Souq, the Opera House Souq and the Goldsmiths' Souq. Women and children in cheap, colorful clothes dig through the piled rubble of souqs and shops. Some armed men join them in the digging. Young men carry piles of clothes and wrapped bundles. Others spread out different items for sale on the sidewalks of Hamra and Raouché.

A house in the Barjawi neighborhood with its walls pierced by shells. The ruins of the Asseily Textile Factory in Chiyah. A Mercedes with its rear end transformed into a deep concavity because of a bomb. Another wrecked car that a gunman climbed onto in order to jump through the window of a grand home. The rubble of a house. The blackened frames of beds, clothes hangers and chairs.

A car speeding over Fu'ad Shihab Bridge, heading toward the Christian district of Achrafieh. A sniper's bullet hits the driver: he smashes into the bridge's barrier and the car juts out over the water.

People surround a dazed woman whose head is covered with a handkerchief. Right beside her is a dead man flat on the ground.

A Mercedes. Its driver is busy tying the suitcases of its passengers to the roof. A family of two women, a man and two children are carrying suitcases and walking on a dust-covered street.

The façade of a demolished building, the ground floor of which is a large, closed store carrying the sign "Installation of All Kinds of Glass and Crystal". A room inside the building with its walls pulverized by rockets. A child's head in the middle of the rubble.

A newspaper headline: "Jumblatt announces that Phalangists alone spend 1 million lira a day for military call-up. Their lowest-paid fighters get 500 to 900 lira, a barricades squadron chief gets 2,000, and a neighborhood commander gets 3,000, in addition to the wages of French mercenaries and their insurance costs."

Yasser Arafat in military clothes puts his hand on Camille Chamoun's arm and smiles with affection. Chamoun is frowning.

Main headline in a Lebanese newspaper: "Agreement to remove barricades and gunmen in battle zones in the capital."

Title card:
Beirut. Martyrs' Square. Four days later . . .

A 21mm mortar gun shoots out flame. Fire and smoke. People hurry to the shelters. Women in nightgowns and barefoot men.

A headline in *al-Safeer*: "Phalangists and Tigers pound the Lazaria district; central Beirut burns."

The Beirut skyline at night. The rockets flying into the air between neighborhoods light it up.

The radio: "Most Beirut streets are unsafe."

A long commercial street in West Beirut. The shops are closed. No trace of a human being. The residential apartments over the shops seem abandoned by their inhabitants. Sandbag barriers on both sides of the street. Shells are launched back and forth between the two sides. A white flag is raised above each barrier and the killing comes to a halt. A gunman walks forward from each side carrying the white flag. The two meet in the middle of the street. They have a brief discussion, then a number of their colleagues join them. They split up into groups of two, one from each side, and proceed to break into the shops on both sides of the street. Gunmen move the contents of the shops outside. Clothes, shoes, electrical appliances and food are gathered into a big pile in the middle of the street. The plundered goods are divvied up between the two sides. Men from each side carry their share to their positions. The fighting resumes.

The aristocratic Christian neighborhood of al-Kantari Street burns. Smoke covers Beirut's sky. Flames consume the Austrian Myrtom House restaurant. An Alfa Romeo burns in the middle of the street. Flames consume an old Ottoman-style building. Men and women push each other in the doorways of houses, coming and going, as they carry suitcases and bundles, tossing them into trucks and cars.

The staircase of a luxury building. Gunmen are carrying out Persian carpets. The entrance of a residence: its expensive furniture appears to be smashed into little pieces.

Title card:

On October 26, the Council of Ministers settled on a
ceasefire agreement.

Range Rovers painted black carry about twenty masked
gunmen from the Tiger militia loyal to Chamoun, the interior minister. The cars stop in front of the St George Hotel.
The gunmen begin unloading boxes of weapons and ammunition. Inside the hotel the employees begin gathering up
the carpets.

Title card:

On October 29, a new ceasefire agreement was reached,
guaranteed by both the president and prime minister.

Black paramilitary cars blast their sirens as they go. Phalangist
gunmen in black hats and outfits jump out of them, carrying
machineguns. One of them runs from one corner to another
with a pair of binoculars swinging on his chest. The gunmen
shout at passersby, then start firing in every direction.

Title card:

On November 1, a new ceasefire agreement was reached.
The Phalangists and Tigers broke it three minutes later.
    Two days later, representatives of the parties and factions
fighting each other met again and agreed to put an end
to displays of arms and to return all hostages.
    The next day . . .

Main newspaper headline: "Shifting barricades kill more than 50 citizens because of their identity. Dozens of bodies discovered. 2 bombs tossed from a car at the headquarters of the Social Nationalist Party."

Main headline of another newspaper: "The nationalist movement and the Palestinian resistance accuse the Deuxième Bureau of working to violate every truce by undertaking terrorist acts against all parties."

Main headline of a third newspaper: "Liaison council made up of civilian and military experts representing NATO acts in the operations room of the Lebanese Ministry of Defense."

Tripoli. A press conference in the city's public hospital convened by Captain Iskender Nicola al-Maalouf. "I have been given a mission," said al-Maalouf, "by Jules Bustani, head of the Deuxième Bureau, along with other officers, to throw bombs in scattered locations in Tripoli for the sake of fomenting discord."

Egypt's *al-Ahram* newspaper. Main headline: "Vice President Hosni Mubarak announces that it was the Communists that precipitated the events in Lebanon, and that there is no national movement, but rather merely a cover for international Communist goals."

Cairo, the People's Council Building. Dr Sufi Abu Talib, president of the Council, confirms that there is a directive from the "believing president", Anwar Sadat, to make Islamic sharia a basis for the nation's laws, so that it applies to non-Muslims. He tells a journalist that there is a bill coming to the Council concerning "apostasy rulings", that will condemn to death by hanging anyone who leaves Islam.

Beirut. Representatives of the warring parties sitting around a table. The attendees exchange lists of the names of those who have been kidnapped. They use the phone to arrange the release of large numbers of them. They all explain to reporters that they have nothing to do with the incidents of kidnapping.

A Lebanese newspaper headline: "Israeli force crosses the borders, erects a barricade and seizes Lebanese citizens."

A circle around a paragraph in the *Washington Post*: "The Lebanese left emerged from the most recent battle in Beirut militarily stronger, but less cohesive. In seven months of fighting, it was able to achieve a clear victory over the Phalangists."

Rashid Karami to reporters: "The ratio of Muslim representation in parliament must be adjusted, and made half."

Lebanese radio: "To our families: We are fine. Please reasure us that you are also fine."

Title card:

The first estimated numbers of victims in the battles: 8,000 killed, and 40,000 wounded.

# II

Antoinette wasn't in her office when I went to see her the next day. The door was closed, so I was forced to wait for her in the editing room. I spent the time reading newspapers and magazines. Then I pulled the telephone over to where I was sitting, and reached into my top jacket pocket where I usually keep my notebook. The pocket was empty, so I searched the rest of my pockets, and in my carry-on. I suddenly remembered that I had put it on the bedside table when I was getting dressed, and left it there.

Antoinette arrived an hour later, accompanied by a handsome young man two or three years younger than she. Her face was flushed with emotion. She apologized for being late, and introduced her companion as a Syrian artist. Then she went to make coffee.

The young man had with him a petition directed at the Syrian government demanding that it release a number of leftist intellectuals who had recently been arrested in Damascus. There were a number of signatures beneath the petition. He asked me to add my signature, so I did.

We drank coffee, then we carried the film canisters to the editing room. The young man left us so he could keep gathering signatures, and we set to work.

## THE SECOND PART OF THE FILM

The front page of Lebanon's *an-Nahar* newspaper. A photo of President Ford. The main headline: "US president says: 'The United States will do all it can to preserve freedom and democracy in Lebanon.'"

The *New York Times*. A circle around a paragraph from an article: ". . . Western arms are inundating Lebanon's right wing, and they are being financed by means of the Maronite Church and Saudi Arabia."

Beirut Airport. Couve de Murville, the French envoy, walks down the stairway from an airplane.

A circle around a paragraph from the French magazine, *L'Express*: "France, sponsor of the pact, is coming today to confirm that it hasn't abandoned the Christians." Another paragraph from the same article: "The French envoy alludes to the Palestinians' responsibility for Lebanon's crisis."

A page from a Swedish magazine with a photo of several young men in beards, in white robes, who are chasing other young men in shirts and pants. One of the bearded men brandishes his "deerhorn"-style knife. In the background, the Cairo University clock tower appears. The camera focuses on a caption below the photo, as its Arabic translation appears on the screen: "A Double-Edged Weapon."

A circle around a paragraph from the same page, with its translation on the screen: "Anwar Sadat listened to the advice of his millionaire friend Osman Ahmed Osman, and delegated him and governor Uthman Isma'il to arm several Muslim extremists, with whom he could intimidate his opponents and curry favor with the Islamic movement in the country. What Sadat forgot is that knives are double-edged swords."

The front page of an Israeli newspaper. A photo of Shimon Peres, Israeli minister of defense, beneath a headline taken from a statement by him, saying: "The Lebanese Civil War is a religious war and proof of the impossibility of establishing a Palestinian state in which all religions have a share."

The Lebanese newspaper, *al-Nahar*. A top front-page headline: "The Kaslik Council urges a declaration of Lebanese neutrality toward the Arabs and Israel."

A squadron of Israeli planes circle at low altitude over fig and olive orchards. Other squadrons pass over the refugee camps flying Palestinian and Lebanese flags.

The main headline of *al-Safeer*: "30 Israeli planes fly over southern Lebanon. 60 killed in the refugee camps and villages and 140 wounded; 70 homes destroyed."

The United Nations building. A meeting of the Security Council. In front of one of the seated people is a PLO banner.

An American broadcaster, speaking quickly: "For the first time, the PLO, despite vehement American opposition, is participating in Security Council discussions concerning Israeli hostilities."

*Al-Safeer*. A photo of Archbishop Hilarion Capucci. The headline says: "Capucci goes on a hunger strike in prison." Another headline: "A smuggled letter from Capucci in prison." A third headline above the text of the letter: "To the people resisting in the south: we are the same as ever, Palestine is in our heart."

Damascus. Pierre Gemayel ascends the staircase of the presidential palace.

Title card:

On the same day . . .

East Beirut. A stream of speeding cars continuously honking their horns, heading toward the Museum where the crossing point to West Beirut is located. Pedestrians are running. Several gunmen in black clothes are chasing them. Pop music blares from radios.

Sahat al-Burj Square. Fruit and crates of Pepsi and 7-Up are scattered in the middle of the street. Men are running. One of them huddles into his clothes for warmth. Another has his head covered with a Russian fur hat. A third has on the common white skullcap worn by Muslim men. In the background, the cinema is showing the Egyptian film, *Keep Those Men Away from Me, Mama.*

Title card:

Black Saturday. On Saturday, December 6, 1975, after a period of relative calm, the Phalangist militia dispatched its fighters to Martyrs' Square and Bab al-Idris. They set about kidnapping dozens of people: they killed most of them, then carried off the rest to their party's centers of operation, and massacred them in front of the doors. They started attacking government offices, especially the electric power company, where they murdered more than 200 Muslims. They also attacked the harbor, opening fire on the dockworkers and then throwing their corpses into the sea.

The office building of the state-owned power company, in East Beirut. The camera focuses on a thirteenth-floor window.

Title card:

> The president of the company, Fu'ad Bizari, a Sunni Muslim, was saved from the slaughter thanks to his solid relationship with the office of the president of the Republic, since he had previously worked as an advisor to two presidents. He telephoned an aide to President Frangieh, who immediately called the Phalangist leadership, and his life was spared.

A Beirut intersection. A handcart with three rubber wheels. Its surface is covered with dishes, cups and home appliances. Its owner pushes it quickly, bending his head to protect his wares. A powerful explosion hits him, hurling him over his cart; blood flows out of him.

Lebanese radio: "Once again, we are with you. Don't leave your homes. All streets are unsafe."

A Volkswagen with its flat tires sunk into the ground. Its frame is riddled with dozens of holes, all of a similar size, except in those places where two holes merge into one.

A hallway in a hospital. Groaning from the wounded. Wastepaper baskets with flies circling around them. The baskets are filled with amputated feet and bloody eyeballs.

*Al-Safeer.* The main headline: "Phalangist leadership confesses. The militia disobeyed orders, kidnapped and killed."

A circle drawn in pen around a paragraph from an article in the French newspaper, *Le Monde*: "Saturday's massacre took place in several Beirut neighborhoods, in an extremely organized fashion. Do they support the division of Lebanon, or are they agents of foreign powers, Israelis and Americans, as the independent Maronite leader Raymond Eddé says? Or are they extremists bringing about a smaller, Christian Lebanon?'

Barricades of mounded dirt. A young man in a military uniform is bent over a Kalashnikov machinegun. Behind him is a young man with the checkered Palestinian *hatta* scarf wound around his face. He is loading a Russian RPG anti-tank rocket into the launcher, getting ready to fire it. The young man is wearing a holder for other rockets on his back.

The waterfront. Fire and smoke rise up from the luxury Phoenicia Hotel.

The main headline in *al-Safeer*: "Lebanese National Movement forces begin clearing out the hotels district."

The al-Mazraa Corniche. The PLO office. An armored car belonging to the Lebanese army fires at the building.

The main headline in *al-Safeer*: "Isolationists occupy the Ghawarna district after burning 300 homes and taking prisoner women, children and old men."

South Beirut Mental Hospital, near the Damascus Road. Within a walled garden. Several patients with their striped clothing are walking about in the sun. The street leading to the hospital. A military car comes up at high speed and stops in front of the hospital entrance. Several gunmen emerge. They storm the hospital by force and take out a young male patient. The patient seems to have some connection to one of the gunmen. A number of patients seize the opportunity and rush outside the hospital. They walk at a rapid clip along the street leading to the city. One of them is a middle-aged man with a red skullcap on his head.

A street in central Beirut. Naked, mutilated corpses strewn at wide intervals in the middle of the road. A naked girl gushes blood from between her thighs. Beside her is a bottle whose neck is stained with blood. A young man with his genitals removed. Next to him is another young man lying on his stomach with the other's cut-off genitals sticking out from his behind.

The street leading to the mental hospital in West Beirut. The middle-aged patient with the red skullcap hurries back to the hospital's steel entrance gate.

A circle around a paragraph from an American newspaper: "The last few days have revealed signs of division within the ranks of the factions of the 'national and progressive' front in Lebanon. Rashid Karami demanded an end to the killing, even as the front announced its determination to keep fighting against the armed presence of Christians. Then a group of factions and organizations linked to Syria, in addition to 'the Dispossessed' – followers of Imam al-Sadr – announced their support for Karami. The Palestinian resistance seems reluctant to get involved in more killing, and thus they are making intensive efforts to make peace between Karami and Jumblatt, and resume dialogue for the sake of a ceasefire."

A newspaper headline: "Tony Frangieh, the leader of what is called 'The Zgharta Liberation Army', announces: We are satisfied with our region and don't need the capital."

The main headline in *al-Safeer*: "The Palestinian resistance is making efforts to stop the killing between the populations of Zgharta and Tripoli."

Damascus. The entrance of the presidential palace. Rashid Karami and Jules Bustani, head of Lebanon's Deuxième Bureau, climb the stairs.

Beirut. Church bells. The headquarters of the Maronite patriarch in Bkerké. A diplomatic car flying the French flag is in front of the door.

Title card:

As usual, the French ambassador presided over the "consular" mass at Christmas.

Damascus Airport. King Khalid of Saudi Arabia walks down the stairway of his plane.

Title card:

Saudi Arabia, with the participation of the Gulf countries, offered 3 billion dollars to Syria as financial assistance in 1975. Syria's estimated budget for 1967 amounted to 16 billion Syrian lira, 9 billion of which came from Saudia Arabia and the Gulf.

Main headline from a Saudi newspaper: "A spokesman for King Khalid says that Saudi Arabia supports Arab efforts to solve the Lebanese crisis by means of Syria alone."

Damascus. The Syrian foreign minister to reporters: "Lebanon was a part of Syria. If fate allows, we will annex it."

Beirut. Camille Chamoun to reporters: "I was hoping they might be able to regain the Golan Heights before they start thinking about annexing Lebanon."

A page from a Lebanese newspaper with a photo of Zuheir Mohsen. Headline: "Head of the al-Sa'iqa organization warns against any major victory over the isolationists because it will invite Israeli interference."

The main headline in *al-Safeer*: "The Phalangists and the Tigers, with the help of the army, storm the Dbayeh Palestinian refugee camp, 20 kilometers from Beirut. 47 inhabitants of the camp dead and wounded."

Headline: "The small Dbayeh camp includes 200 Christian Palestinian families."

The main headline in *al-Safeer*: "Slaughter in Maslakh and Karantina; 500 killed. Phalangists announce their dominance over Karantina and the evacuation of its inhabitants."

General shots of the shacks of tin-sheet and wood that make up the Karantina district, near the three-story "Lebanese Forces" war council building.

Title card:

Karantina had 30,000 inhabitants, most of them Kurds and poor Shiis who had fled from the south.

A posed photograph of several young men dancing over a pile of corpses. One of them is opening a bottle of champagne. In the middle of them is a young woman in a blouse and pants, strumming a guitar.

A posed photograph of men of different ages, standing with their faces against the wall of a building. Behind them are several gunmen with large wooden crosses dangling from their necks.

A posed photograph of a procession of women and children carrying white flags. There isn't a single grown man among them.

The "Sleep Comfort" furniture factory.

Title card:

Inside this factory, several dozen Palestinian gunmen, residents of Karantina, were dug in, and they held out against the Phalangists for three days until they were killed down to the last man.

A Palestinian woman with wide eyes sits at the side of a public street. Her strong, angular features are set in a whitish face framed by an embroidered kerchief tied under her chin. Next to her a crowd of barefoot children look at the camera with a smile as they raise their hands in a victory sign.

Title card:
Two days later . . .

The village of Damur. The estate of Camille Chamoun. A poor person's home, abandoned, on the edge of the village. Two rooms made of stone. A television. Farm tools beside the wall. A color painting of Jesus with sad eyes and long blond hair.

Title card:

In revenge for the Karantina massacre, some Palestinian and extreme leftist Lebanese forces attacked the Christian village of Damur in the south, considered a stronghold of the Tigers and Phalangists. After they encircled the forces of the Maronite militias, they chased the inhabitants from their homes and slaughtered some of them, while others sought shelter in the church. Fatah forces got involved and surrounded the church to protect those inside, and moved them safely to Beirut. They also transported Chamoun and his son in a helicopter to East Beirut.

The Lebanon–Syria border. Truckloads of Syrian soldiers cross the border into Lebanon.

A Kuwaiti newspaper: "2,000 Palestinians, led by Syrian officers, have entered Lebanon from Syria. Chamoun welcomes the step from Syria."

*Al-Nahar* newspaper. A photo of Raymond Eddé above a statement by him: "Kissinger's desire to reach an agreement between Syria and Israel is leading him to try to obtain parts of Lebanon for Syria."

A Kuwaiti newspaper: "Gemayel announces that he is prepared to end the fighting on the basis of 'No winner and no loser'."

*Al-Nahar*. Main headline: "US State Department says it acknowledges the constructive role the Syrian government is playing in Lebanon after reaching a ceasefire agreement."

*Al-Safeer*: "Nayef al-Hawatmeh, leader of the Democratic Front for the Liberation of Palestine, states: 'I don't think that Syria's goal is the absorption of the resistance.'"

A French newspaper: "Elements from the Sa'iqa organization, loyal to Syria, have attacked with heavy rockets two newspapers, *al-Muharrir* and *Beirut*, which are bankrolled by Iraq. Seven were killed in the attack, including the Egyptian journalist Ibrahim Amir."

An American newspaper: "Gemayel tells the Associated Press: 'We are importing new weapons in preparation for the next round.'"

Raymond Eddé to a reporter: "The Phalangist Party, whose slogan was 'God, the Nation and the Family', has violated God's commandments, inflicted its bad actions on the nation, and driven away other people's families, while destroying their homes and exploiting the populace. They are still operating protection rackets, extorting money at roadblocks, and levying taxes that the state should be pocketing."

*Abu Iyad*, Fatah's second-in-command, to an *al-Safeer* reporter: "There are incidents of looting and pillaging done by elements attributed to the Palestinian revolution and the Lebanese National Movement. Some individuals have gotten rich, and some organizations have gotten rich at the expense of the revolution."

The Kuwaiti newspaper, *al-Watan*. A statement by Zuheir Mohsen, head of the PLO's military office, and leader of the Sa'iqa organization which is bankrolled by Syria: "The leadership of the resistance needs new blood."

A headline in another newspaper: "Is Zuheir Mohsen taking Arafat's place?"

Zuheir Mohsen leaving the PLO building in a colorful shirt. He has a cigar in his hand.

Title card:

Zuheir Mohsen was known by the name of Zuheir "Persian Rug", because of his passion for carpets, which he would collect from destroyed and plundered homes. He married the daughter of a rug merchant, then went into the weapons-smuggling business with a Phalangist leader, the brother of Lebanon's ambassador to France, before bullets from an unidentified assassin killed him in front of a casino in Cannes, France.

The French newspaper *Le Monde*: "Gaddafi denies that he offered assistance to any side in the Lebanese struggle."

*Al-Nahar*. A photo of Suleiman Frangieh, and beneath it his public statements, at the top of which is his quote: "Lebanon is a unique human laboratory."

The *Al-Anba'* newspaper. A photo of Kamal Jumblatt below his statement: "I hope the next president of the Republic has more character, virility and culture."

A Kuwaiti newspaper: "*George Habash*, leader of the Palestinian Front for the Liberation of Palestine, accuses Syria of attempting to impose its dictates on the resistance, and invites the nationalist forces to establish the authority of the people over all Lebanese territories."

*Al-Safeer*: "A military rebellion led by Ahmad al-Khatib forming the 'Arab Army of Lebanon'."

*Al-Nahar*: "Soldiers in Sarba mutiny and seize weapons and armored cars on which they have written 'Lebanese Liberation Army'. They have set up barricades which have led to the murders of 15 Muslims."

A street branching off from Hamra Street. Daytime. A group of men and women whose clothes indicate that they are middle class are storming a Spinneys supermarket. They raid the contents of the shop – food, electric appliances and liquor – and bring their loads back to where they left their cars. Some of them are surprised to find that their cars have been stolen. A fight breaks out among them, in the course of which bullets fly.

The Le Relais de Normandie restaurant. During the dinner service. Gunmen rush inside and gather up the diners' money, watches and jewelry. They force two young women to leave with them.

*Al-Safeer*: "Nationalist forces and factions authorize Kamal Jumblatt to act in their name with regards to the government."

*Al-Nahar*: "Imam al-Sadr and the Mufti Hasan Khalid demand an adjustment to the proportion of parliamentary seats divided between Muslims and Christians."

*Al-Anba'*: "Jumblatt says: 'Traditional Muslim leaders who are hostile to secularism are no better than the isolationists.'"

The entrance to al-Mukhtara villa in Jebel Chouf. Below the enormous, ancient doorway stand two rows of gunmen in jackets and checkered Palestinian scarves. They have their machinegun barrels lowered. Jumblatt welcomes the Syrian foreign minister, Abd al-Halim Khaddam.

An Israeli newspaper: "Mordecai Gur, the Israeli army's chief of staff, says: 'The civil war in Lebanon has revealed a new Lebanon, different from the Lebanon as we know it. It will cooperate effectively in any new military confrontation with Israel.'"

A press conference with Kamal Jumblatt. He says: "For 10,000 dead and 20,000 injured, people are asking for a price that is much higher than what was mentioned in the statement given by the president of the Republic . . . The constitution must be amended and the political system completely replaced. The hurdles placed by traditionalists and isolationists – Christian and Muslim alike – must be surmounted, with the aim of secularizing the state and eliminating political

146

sectarianism . . . The Lebanese Nationalist Movement must have a share in a new, expanded government."

*Al-Safeer*: "66 members of parliament from different parts of the political spectrum, including Rashid Karami, Saeb Salam and Kamal Jumblatt, ask for Frangieh's resignation."

Beirut Airport. A destroyed plane belonging to Syrian Airlines.

A Lebanese newspaper: "Jumblatt accuses the Deuxième Bureau of striking the Syrian plane in order to drive Syria into military involvement."

*Al-Amal* newspaper, the mouthpiece of the Phalangist Party: "The Phalangist delegation returns from Damascus with a new plan, one important enough to be kept secret."

Beirut harbor. Phalangists loot the harbor and carry off its contents – cars, electrical equipment, rugs and different tools – to their storehouses.

Title card:

The stolen items were valued at 1 billion dollars. A merchant could then pay 6,000 dollars to a Phalangist in exchange for filling his truck with the looted goods he wanted. Then the Phalangists began to divide up the loot into different types and held a public auction in the Christian Brothers seminary in Gemmayzeh.

Masarif Street in Beriut.

Title card:

This street, lined with banks, changed hands several times before the collapse of the army. But the protection money, which bank owners generously paid, kept them from harm. For the time being. Men from the Phalangists and Tigers began to strip the National Bank of all the cash it had. The Sa'iqa organization looted the Banca di Roma. Gunmen from the Democratic Front for the Liberation of Palestine seized the contents of the vaults belonging to the British Bank of the Middle East, which were valued at more than 130 million dollars. As they left with their spoils, Sa'iqa gunmen blocked their way. Fighting broke out briefly between the two sides and was resolved in favor of the Democratic Front by heavy artillery guns that arrived loaded on top of military cars.

The incomplete frame of the Burj el-Murr skyscraper. Missiles are launched from its thirty-fourth floor and fall on the hotel district where Phalangist gunmen are dug in.

The front of the 27-story Holiday Inn. Hotel workers drape white sheets out of the second-floor windows. The hotel's interior lobby. Expensive chandeliers hang from the ceiling. A crowd of young Palestinian gunmen are gathered in front of the camera in a souvenir photograph. In their left hands are Kalashnikovs. With their right hands, they are making the "V" sign for "Victory".

The main headline of a Lebanese newspaper, in red. The headline takes up most of the top half of the front page: "Holiday Inn falls into the hands of Lebanese National Movement forces."

The façade of the hotel again. On the sidewalk in front of it is a naked, swollen corpse. There are remnants of underwear on his waist. The same shot in a newspaper photo.

Beneath the image are these words: "Phalangist Holiday Inn sniper. He fell like this from the 22nd floor."

A fire blazes in the St George Hotel. In front of the hotel is a tank; the word "Allah" can be seen next to its artillery-gun. Behind it is an armored car carrying a photo of Gamal Abdel Nasser above the words "Arab Socialist Union".

A gunman carries the Phalangist flag and stands behind a Dushka heavy machinegun. He throws down the flag and runs, abandoning the gun.

A newspaper headline: "Lebanese National Movement forces control the Hilton and Normandie Hotel enclosure, and drive the Phalangists back toward Martyrs' Square."

A newspaper headline: "Jumblatt says no ceasefire is forth-coming from the National Movement."

A circle around a paragraph from Syria's *al-Baath* news-paper: "The gravest issue is that the game may extend to some nationalist forces such that they become party to consol-idating the *de facto* division of Lebanon, while the conspiracy reverts to having a group from the nationalist side get into a scheme to divide and isolate the country, while greedily pursuing merely short-term gains."

A headline in a Lebanese newspaper: "Arafat works to close the gap in the viewpoints of Jumblatt and Damascus."

A headline in another newspaper: "Jumblatt meets with Assad for nine hours."

A headline in a third newspaper: "Frangieh flees to Jounieh."

A headline in a fourth newspaper: "Jumblatt announces: 'The other side is in a state of collapse.'"

Mount Lebanon. The latest and heaviest weapons amid piles of snow and ice. The beautiful summer retreat of Aley with its winding roads and one-story modern houses. Fighting takes place from one street to the next.

Tripoli. Fires blaze in the city.

Sidon. A burning car blocks the approach to the city.

The southern border. Massed crowds of Israeli troops.

A newspaper headline: "Nationalist forces are victorious."

The newspaper of the Lebanese Baath Party, loyal to Syria: "Jumblatt is wrecking the Syrian initiative in favor of the American plan."

A headline in another newspaper: "The American envoy, Brown, who was present at the massacre of Palestinians in Jordan in 1970, declares his country's support for the Syrian initiative."

The *Washington Post*. Brown to the newspaper's correspondent in Beirut: "Jumblatt told me that the only solution to the Lebanese problem is to slaughter 12,000 Maronites."

A press conference with Jumblatt following a meeting of the progressive and nationalist parties:

Jumblatt: There is no inclination for a ceasefire, in spite of Syrian pressure.

Journalist: Do you intend to continue fighting if the Palestinians agree to a ceasefire?

Jumblatt: We are a Lebanese movement with independent goals. Because we have aspirations to replace the constitution and change the political system . . . so that a true democratic system can take its place, one that removes the political categorization of citizens on the basis of religion and sect, and that has a separation between church and state . . . But it seems that Arab regimes fear the establishment of a secular democratic state in the Middle East, because there is no

Arab political regime, with the exception of Tunisia, that is founded on the principle of secularism . . . We are not demanding a socialist state or nationalization . . . We are demanding that the political system be changed, a system in which the Lebanese elite can no longer fully dominate . . . We will not end the fighting until the president of the republic resigns."

Kamal Jumblatt suddenly leaves the press conference, right after a phone call, and takes his car to Arafat's headquarters. Jumblatt joins a meeting with Arafat ("Abu Ammar"), Nayef al-Hawatmeh, the Mufti Hasan Khalid, Abu Iyad, Inaam Raad and Bashir Ubayd.

A headline in *al-Safeer*: "After a meeting that went on for two and a half hours, Jumblatt says: 'We went over the situation with Arafat and the extent of the pressure that weighs on the Palestinians. We regret that the Palestinian resistance is subject to any pressure on the level of supplies and weapons from any country.'"

Title card:
The next day . . .

Newspaper headlines: "Arafat welcomes the ceasefire." "The Lebanese National Movement agrees to a 10-day truce during which the members of parliament can meet to elect a new president."

Hamra Street near the Byblos Bank. A crowd of people and cars. Different goods on display on the sidewalks. Two young women and a girl sit on the ground beside the marble wall of a jewelry shop. The two girls hold out their hands to passersby.

Washington. King Hussein climbs the White House steps. He pauses to make a statement to the reporters: "I support any likely Syrian involvement in Lebanon in order to counter attempts by extremists to change the ruling structure for their benefit."

An American newspaper: "Kissinger characterizes Syria's political role as 'a check on the recalcitrance of the most extreme Lebanese elements'."

An American newspaper, dated April 14: "Kissinger announces that the United States and Israel are in agreement that Syria's involvement does not threaten Israel."

The Damascus University amphitheater. President Hafez al-Assad delivers a speech: "We possess complete freedom of movement and we are able to take up positions as we see fit, without anyone being able to prevent us." (Sustained, enthusiastic applause.) "We are opposed to those who insist on continuing the fight . . . I have been told: 'We want to settle it militarily.' I replied, 'If you want an omelet, you're going to have to break a few eggs.'" (Enthusiastic applause.)

A Kuwaiti newspaper: "Frangieh cables Assad to congratulate him on his speech at the Damascus University amphitheater." "Gemayel lauds Assad's speech and his socialism, and attacks the internationalist left."

An Israeli newspaper: "Israeli Foreign Minister Allon: 'With regards to Lebanon, silence is golden.'" "Yitzhak Rabin: 'Israel has drawn a red line for Syrian forces – the Litani River.'"

A Lebanese newspaper: "The Phalangists violate the 35th ceasefire agreement."

Rockets light up Beirut's sky at night.

A Lebanese newspaper: "600 killed and wounded in 2 days."

The Lebanese office of public safety. A crowd of people lining up for passports to emigrate.

A press conference with Elias Sarkis, who announces that he is nominating himself for president and welcomes Syria's support.

A newspaper headline: "The nationalist and progressivist factions call for a general strike and implore members of parliament not to attend the parliamentary session that would elect Sarkis."

The Bristol Hotel in West Beirut. Armored cars pull up together at the hotel entrance and civilians get out, carrying various pieces of hand luggage. Several gunmen accompany them inside the hotel.

Title card:

On the evening of May 7, the Sa'iqa organization started gathering members of parliament into the Bristol Hotel. It became known that millions of lira were paid to members, including 3 million received by Kamil al-As'ad, the speaker of parliament, in exchange for holding the session and ensuring that his parliamentary group attended. Zuheir Mohsen, the leader of the Sa'iqa, emphasized that he only paid those members that Sa'iqa brought to the site of the parliamentary session, and that there were other sources that also paid money.

On the same evening, Shaykh Pierre Gemayel called Camille Chamoun and promised to send him a check for the amount of 2 million Syrian lira in exchange for having him and his group of allies in parliament attend. Chamoun insisted that the payment be in Lebanese lira, because Syrian lira were worth less. He also asked that the payment be in cash. Gemayel called the director of the Lebanon-France Bank, who afterwards became the finance minister in the government of Salim El-Hoss, and asked him to withdraw the amount from an account owned by his brother-in-law, who was on the bank's board of trustees. A Volkswagen was sent to the bank's head office, and it transported the amount in bags, guarded by a group of Phalangists, to Chamoun at his headquarters. He set out with his allies in parliament immediately after receiving it.

Mansour Palace. Armored cars and gunmen surround the ancient building, of Ottoman construction. Sounds of bombardment and bullets. Two foreign photographers seek protection in the hulk of a car. An elderly member of parliament crosses the road to the palace entrance at a run. Behind him are three bodyguards armed with machineguns, running with heads low. In front of the palace entrance stands an enormous man with white hair, brandishing his gun in order to protect the car door out of which a hunched-over member emerges.

Title card:

Moments before the session was held, Kamil al-As'ad surprised the Sa'iqa representative by telling him that the money he took in exchange for holding the meeting and attending it was for him alone. They would have to pay more to his allies in parliament to get them to attend and meet the legal quorum, which meant at least sixty-six members present.

Elias Sarkis leaves Mansour Palace under the protection of several officers and soldiers.

A newspaper headline: "Election of Sarkis as new president of the republic."

Another newspaper headline: "Jumblatt says: 'Arab regimes are all reactionary, even the ones that claim to be progressive. Achieving secularism will break apart all the Arab regimes.'"

A third newspaper headline: "Imam al-Sadr says: there is no difference between those calling for secularism and the Israelis."

A fourth newspaper headline: "300 killed and wounded and clashes between supporters of Iraq and supporters of Syria."

A fifth newspaper headline: "The leadership of the Palestinian revolution condemns the incidents of violence committed by the Palestinian Army of Liberation (subordinate to Syria), Syrian forces and the Sa'iqa organization, and asks the Syrian leadership to remove the barriers they have set up in different districts."

An Israeli newspaper headline, dated May 13: "Syrian forces have killed more Palestinian 'ravagers' in the last week than Israel killed in the last 2 years."

Beirut Airport. A Syrian plane coming from Damascus. The Libyan prime minister, Abdessalam Julud, descends from the plane along with Yasser Arafat.

Washington, DC, the White House. Giscard d'Estaing, the president of France, talks to reporters in a reception room:

"It is likely that France will send an armed force to Lebanon to increase security, and this force may do some fighting in affected areas."

The American University in Beirut hospital. The Maronite leader Raymond Eddé is in a hospital bed and in front of him, in chairs, are Kamal Jumblatt and Nayef Hawatmeh.

Title card:

Following a failed attempt on his life, Raymond Eddé went to Pierre Gemayel in Bkerké and accused him of arranging the hit. On the road back, he encountered gunfire and was pursued, which ended with a bullet wounding him in the leg.

A newspaper headline: "Killing of Linda Jumblatt. Masked gunmen invaded the home of the sister of the leader of the Lebanese National Movement on Sami al-Solh Street, murdering her and gravely injuring her daughter."

Linda Jumblatt's funeral. Thousands come to pay their respects.

*Washington Post*: "There are lingering suspicions that Kissinger is a party to or silent partner in what Lebanon is undergoing."

A Lebanese newspaper: "Forces from the Arab Army of Lebanon, led by al-Ma'mari, attack Christian villages in the north. The Palestinian resistance and Jumblatt accuse al-Ma'mari of a twisted plan with the aim of justifying the entry of Syrian forces into the region."

A Lebanese newspaper: "Al-Ma'mari declares: 'I want to ask them to show me one faction in Lebanon that isn't cooperating with one of the Arab states. So why do they want me to resist Syria and oppose it, when it was and will remain the beating heart of Arabism?'"

Damascus radio. Cables to Hafez Assad from Beirut pleading for help.

Title card:

The next day, June 1, 6,000 Syrian soldiers entered the Zahlé district and began disarming the Palestinian *fedayeen*.

# 12

I dried myself and put on my underwear. Then, after turning out the light, I came out of the bathroom. I passed by Wadia sitting in front of the television, and entered my room. I turned on the light and stood in front of the wardrobe mirror to comb my hair. When I picked up my shirt, I found that it reeked of sweat, so I tossed it to one side. I went out to the living room and asked Wadia to lend me one of his.

He gave me a clean shirt with a nearly worn-away collar. It was the kind of shirt that doesn't need ironing, so I put it on right away. I finished dressing, then opened the wardrobe door. I pulled out my suitcase and took out of it the bag where I kept my dirty clothes. My eye was drawn to the bottom of the bag and I noticed the edge of my notebook underneath some papers.

I thrust the dirty shirt into the bag, picked out the note-book, and flipped through its pages. I looked back and forth at the notebook and the bottom of the bag. Then I put the notebook in my jacket pocket. I carried the bag to the bathroom.

I filled a plastic tub with water and emptied the contents of the bag into it. Then I went out to the living room. I lit a cigarette.

"I finally found the notebook," I said.

Without taking his eyes off the television, Wadia responded, "Didn't I tell you it wasn't lost? Where did you find it?"

"In the suitcase," I said. "But I'm certain I left it on the bedside table this morning."

"'Glory to Him who is not forgetful,'" he said, with a hint of sharpness.

He turned off the television and we left the house. We took a taxi to a side street off the Mazraa Corniche. We got out of the car in front of a demolished building, and entered a modern building next to it, with wide balconies and plants for decoration.

"Would you like to go up Mount Lebanon tomorrow?" he asked me, as we walked up the steps. "I'll be leaving early with a Canadian reporter. Maybe I can ask her to bring along a girlfriend of hers."

I thought for a moment, then replied: "I don't think I can. I have to work."

"Tomorrow's Sunday," he said.

"I know. I'll be working at your place."

Nazar Baalbaki welcomed us with ceremonious dignity. He led us to an elegantly furnished living room, one side of which was occupied by a long table made of heavy wood, groaning with bottles and plates of grilled meat and mezze. Around the table were several men engrossed in a noisy discussion.

I sat down next to an Iraqi fiction writer who worked at a Beirut publishing house. I knew two other people around the table, one of whom was a Syrian film director, whose film about raising rabbits had been banned from screens by the Baathists. The other was a Palestinian scholar who was studying at Cairo University for his PhD.

Nazar put a small empty glass in front of me and another in front of Wadia. He poured them half-full of arak, then added the same amount of water and a piece of ice. I downed the glass in one shot.

It became clear that the discussion concerned the stance of the Lebanese Communists in the civil war. There was a large man with a thick mustache called Marwan, who was accusing them of treachery because they had squandered their chance to seize power.

He was speaking with an unusual amount of vehemence and stridency, and was using phrases like "right-wing opportunism" and "betraying the cause". A Lebanese writer argued against him with the same force, emphasizing that someone wouldn't allow them to act, starting from the factions within the Lebanese leftist front itself, all the way to Israel.

I noticed that Nazar was listening with interest without joining in the discussion. Marwan shifted his attack to a new area, saying: "How do you explain the fact that they aren't lifting a finger to defend leftists who have been arrested in Syria?"

The Lebanese wasn't able to respond, since at that moment we were joined by the artist with the petition who I had met with Antoinette. With him was a young man with long sideburns and rough lips who greeted me warmly. He was on the point of kissing me on the mouth, and would have, if I hadn't turned my face at the last moment. A shudder went through my body as I watched him kiss people around the table on the mouth.

I directed my attention to a large serving-plate of grilled jumbo shrimp. I filled my dish with some as I tried to remember if I had ever eaten shrimp this size in my life.

I drank another glass of arak, and began wholeheartedly stuffing myself with the fresh white meat. Then I lit a cigarette. Wadia noticed I was looking for an ashtray; he put his glass on a small table next to him, picked up an ashtray from it, and handed it to me.

Nazar suddenly stood up in a state of agitation; he produced a napkin and hurried to the small table. He lifted the glass from it and dried its surface very thoroughly.

Wadia was upset and put out his hand to take his glass from Nazar while mumbling apologies. I looked carefully at the table's surface which I supposed was everyday formica.

Suddenly, Marwan addressed me: "Did you hear what Sadat said yesterday to a female reporter from the *Jerusalem Post*?"

I shook my head. Wadia leaned over and said, "I read about it. He mentioned that he was about to make an important political decision."

"He described the decision as being a historical step," Marwan added. "I wonder what he means."

"The only thing left is joining NATO or signing a joint defense agreement with Israel," I said.

One of the people around the table mentioned the name of Ziad al-Rahbani and the conversation turned to his new play called *An American Feature Film*. I asked Nazar what the name meant and he explained that it was taken from television programs, where the late-night feature film is usually described that way.

"Ziad is completely finished," Marwan added, in his cutting, peremptory manner. "He's had nothing new to say ever since the heavy fighting ended."

"He was with the left at the time," Wadia explained to me.

"And now?" I asked.

"No one knows where he stands," he replied.

I filled my glass as I looked at the guests around the table. I asked myself how much of what Wadia just said applied to each one of them.

# 13

The amount I had to drink didn't give me what I considered to be a deep, uninterrupted slumber. I heard Wadia leaving the house early in the morning, but afterwards, I couldn't get back to sleep.

I finally got out of bed, feeling sluggish. I washed my face and had breakfast. I made myself a big cup of coffee. Then I sat down to go over the scenes I had recorded from the film. A little before noon, the phone rang.

I picked up the receiver and heard Lamia's voice.

"How are you? Did I wake you up?"

"Not at all," I replied.

"What are you doing today? Will one of Beirut's ladies be keeping you busy?"

"The only Beirut lady I know is you."

She laughed.

"Did you read the book?" I asked her.

"I read a large part of it. But we can talk about that later. What would you say if I were to invite you to lunch?"

"I'd be honored," I said.

"I'll stop by to see you an hour from now."

"But without an escort," I added.

She laughed. "I'll try," she said. "In any case, today is everyone's day off."

I described for her where the house was, and hung up. I lit a cigarette and looked for the bottle of French cognac that Wadia had bought two days previously. I poured a glass of it and sniffed it with pleasure. I took a sip and held it in my mouth for a moment before swallowing.

I went to the bathroom, looked at my face in the mirror, and felt my chin. I shaved, but the reflection that looked back at me hadn't improved much. After taking a quick shower, I felt invigorated. The sky was thick with clouds and there was a cold bite in the air, so I put on all my clothes and sat down, drinking my glass of cognac in the living room.

My glass was empty so I poured myself another. No sooner had I finished it than the sound of a *zumur* – as the Lebanese call a car horn – came up to me from the street. I heard it again, so I hurried to the balcony. I saw her head sticking out of the driver's window in a white two-seater car. I waved down to her and hurried inside, after locking the door to the balcony. I took a swig straight from the cognac bottle, then went down to the street.

She opened the car door for me, and her perfume wafted lightly over me, surrounding me as I settled in beside her. She was wearing white pants and a silk blouse of the same color. Over her shoulders she had a pink wool vest. Her hair was gathered to the side in a single bunch that rested on her chest. Around her neck was a thick pearl necklace.

The car headed toward Raouché. Cold air came at me through the window, so I felt around for the handle to roll it up, but she stopped me, saying: "Don't trouble yourself with that."

Putting out a red-nailed finger, she pressed a button in front of her, and the door window began to rise on its own.

She pressed another button, and music from *The Godfather* poured out of the speakers. I relaxed in my seat, looking at the empty streets and the locked shops plunged in silence.

"If you stay with us until Christmas," she said, "you'll enjoy the snow."

"I don't like it much," I replied.

"Me, I love it. I'd love to go to Moscow."

She turned toward me and looked at me as if to ask what I thought about that.

"Moscow is a city worth seeing," I said.

"Can you get me an official invitation?"

I stared at her in confusion.

"Who do you think I am? The Comintern's agent in the Middle East?"

"Don't you take money from them?"

"Of course."

We drove through several streets before the sea revealed itself to us, and we stopped under a prominent sign for a restaurant.

I asked her if she had a button to open the door. "Not yet," she replied, laughing.

We got out of the car, and she walked ahead of me to the restaurant's entrance, taking elegant, flirtatious steps. I followed her, observing the movement of her behind in her tight pants.

We walked through the entrance to a wide garden that was divided into separate groves, each of which had several comfortable chairs and a wide rattan table.

We were almost the only patrons, and several servers waited graciously on us with impeccable refinement. We ordered arak and grilled meats. Soon the table was filled with plates of tabbouleh, kibbeh, hummus, tahini, red radish, green mint and yogurt.

I tossed down a glass of arak, while she was content with a single sip.

"The problem with your book," she declared, "is that distributing it is nearly impossible."

"Why?"

"There isn't a single Arab regime you haven't implicated; and then of course, there's a great deal of sex in it."

I lit a cigarette. "I mentioned all that to Adnan in my correspondence with him. But he didn't object to any of it."

"I don't think he imagined you would be going as far as you did."

"So what's the upshot?"

She put out her hand, replete with silver rings, and placed it over mine, saying: "Don't be alarmed. I haven't read it all yet. And Adnan has the final say. I believe he is interested in publishing you."

"So let's drop the subject. Why don't you tell me about yourself?"

She raised her eyebrows. "There's nothing to tell."

"Try."

"I lie a lot."

"No matter."

She turned her glass of arak around in her fingers. "I always wanted to be a writer," she said. "I married for love. Other women were jealous of me over my husband. I have a six-year-old daughter. My work with Adnan is fulfilling: I got the job after a long struggle with his family, who wanted me in the role of a housewife . . . That's everything."

I hadn't taken my eyes off her rosy skin and her tender lips.
"And you?" she asked me. "Are you married?"

"I was," I replied.

"And now, of course, you have a girlfriend?"

"My wife was my only girlfriend."

"Really?"

I lit a cigarette. "I'd like it if you gathered your hair to the back."

She lifted her hands to her hair and gathered it in the back, then fastened it in a ponytail.

She asked my permission to leave the table, and she was gone for several minutes. As soon as she got back, she said: "What do you think about us getting out of here?"

"But the bottle isn't empty yet," I said.

"I have to stop by the house for my daughter."

We left the restaurant and headed downtown. She turned on the radio and light Western music came out at us, but she fiddled with the dial, switching from classical music to a news report and a program for children, before finally settling on a song by Farid al-Atrash.

Farid al-Atrash's lament continued to echo in my ears until we arrived at a place near the television building. She stopped the car in front of a luxury building with a wide entrance, made up of several levels of marble stairs.

There were a number of security guards in civilian clothes, one of whom accompanied us to an elevator. Lamia took out a key from her purse and opened the elevator door. I got in behind her and stood watching the panel, in the middle of which was only one button.

When the elevator stopped, I walked behind her, and my feet sank in layers of lush carpet. I found myself in a luxuriously furnished entrance room, and I followed her to a wide room whose walls were covered with ornate wood paneling.

"One moment," she said.

She left me there.

There was a wide sofa with a plush white exterior that stretched along the length of one wall, with an endless number of small pillows on it, each in varying shades of white and brown. In front of it were chairs of the same design and a low wooden table with a polished surface and a thick edge.

Occupying the second wall were two large sliding glass panels, behind which another large room appeared. Around its walls were high-backed chairs, gilded and decorated with engravings in Arabic, as well as small tables with brass trays on them. Amid them stood a large mirror that almost touched the ceiling.

As for the wall facing the sofa, it was occupied by three oil paintings in a contemporary style, and a wooden bookcase.

I walked up to the bookcase and perused its books. There was a deluxe copy of the Qur'an, and several novels by Ihsan Abd al-Qaddous. Also a mass-market edition of Dr Spock's book on child-rearing, and an English translation of a French novel called *Angelique and the Sultan*, in addition to several American magazines, and another French women's magazine. I noticed what I at first imagined was a row of American mass-market books, but turned out to be videotapes that included the latest Egyptian melodramas. The video-tape player itself was on a separate shelf. A medium-sized photo of Adnan Sabbagh stood by itself in a gold frame on another shelf.

I looked at his smiling face, then I headed for a chair with armrests beside the sofa, and sank into it. I started looking at one of the oil paintings made up of long parallel rows of small white squares surrounded by larger red squares. At a point in the middle of the painting, which wasn't clear at first glance, the situation was reversed: the red squares were smaller and inside the white squares.

A girl with plain features, wearing clean clothes and shoes, brought in a tea tray. The porcelain teapot was in a contemporary style with flowing lines and a wide handle coated in gold leaf. The sugar bowl consisted of a single piece of porcelain with a thin, barely visible line running across it, separating the bowl and its gilded cover.

I poured a cup of tea for myself, and stirred it with a gold spoon. I was about to light a cigarette when Lamia came back, and sat on the sofa. She asked me to give her one.

"Do you like my house?" she asked.

"Very much," I replied. "Even though I've only seen one small part of it."

"You'll see the rest later," she replied with a laugh.

I poured her some tea and asked her about her daughter.

"She went to her aunt's house," she said.

She took a sip from her cup, then put it on the table and stood up, saying: "Come with me."

I followed her to the elevator.

"Would you like to go for a swim?" she asked, as we went down to the ground floor.

"In this cold weather?"

She didn't say anything. We got into the car. With a serious look on her face, she started driving.

"Where to?" I asked her, after a little while.

"I don't know. Where do you want to go?"

"Nowhere in particular."

We passed a billboard with an ad for a film by Roger Vadim, starring Sylvia Kristel. I had seen her in the film *Emmanuelle*, in which she played the role of a woman who enjoyed all kinds of sex.

"I've seen her in person," Lamia said.

"I like her face a lot. Come on, we'll go see her in it."

"If someone saw me in the movie theater with you, it would be a scandal. I'll take you to your apartment."

I stayed silent until we reached the house, and then I asked her, "What do you think about a cup of coffee at my place?"

"You mean at Wadia's place?" she asked.

"Wadia is in the mountains and won't come back before this evening."

"*Okay, bey*," she said, talking the way they do in Egyptian films.

There was a free parking space directly in front of the building, wide enough for the car. But she maneuvered the vehicle several times to park it in a side alley some distance from the main street.

I noticed the filthiness of the apartment and the mess that was spread everywhere as soon as we entered. I sat her down in the living room, then opened the balcony door. I began gathering up books, magazines and clothes scattered on chairs. Then I brought a bottle of cognac and two glasses. I set a glass in front of her, but she put her hand over it. She leaned over to me and said, "Coffee."

I poured myself a glass that I downed in one go, and went to the kitchen to make the coffee. I let it boil for some time, so it could acquire the bitterness that Syrians and Lebanese love. Then I carried it out with two cups on a round tray of colored plastic.

As I was pouring her cup, she asked me, "How is the film coming along?"

"How did you know?"

"Beirut is a small city; there are no secrets here," she explained.

"We'll be done in almost a week."

She smiled wickedly. "Antoinette is a good director," she said.

"She really is," I said, sitting down opposite her.

"I hope the film isn't all about the heroic acts and sacrifices of the Palestinians."

"And what if it is?"

She shrugged her shoulders. "Nothing," she said. "It's just that we've gotten tired of that kind of film. And they're the reason for the ordeal we're living through."

I bit my tongue. A moment later, I asked her: "Were you in Beirut during the heavy fighting at the start of the civil war?"

"No," she replied. "I was in London the whole time."

I began to feel a headache coming on, so I got up to look for an aspirin. I found one in my shoulder bag and swallowed it with a swig of cognac, then returned to my seat.

I looked closely at her lips, and then suddenly told her, "I want to kiss you."

The words came out of my mouth thick with liquor. She fidgeted in her seat with a feigned display of embarrassment. So I moved over next to her on the couch, and took her in my arms.

"The balcony," she said.

I got up and went to the balcony and closed the curtains over the balcony door. I went back to where I was sitting beside her, then turned my entire body toward her.

She lifted her mouth to me, and I savored the touch of her soft lips. She moved her thigh and pressed it against me. Then she brushed against me gently with her knees between my legs. That made it possible for her to notice that I wasn't hard.

She gently extricated herself from me without drawing her knee away. I wanted to say something, so I opened my mouth. My tongue seemed to be moving with considerable difficulty.

The day had been full of mistakes. I had started drinking early. Then I switched between different kinds of alcohol. And now I wanted to tell her something, but I called her by my ex-wife's name.

She drew back from me, her eyes widening and her face going pale. I tried to explain to her how the first letter of her name was the same as my wife's, and that the alcohol had made my tongue heavy. But the attempt wore me out, so I remained silent.

After a moment, she said, "It's getting late. I have to leave."

"Stay for a little longer," I pleaded.

"I can't. Wadia might come. I have to go."

Inside, I was glad she was going, so I stood up. She picked up her purse and asked me where the bathroom was. I pointed her toward it.

I stood waiting for her in the living room until she returned, having straightened her hair and clothes. I started walking her to the door. "You don't have to do that," she told me.

I put my hand on her arm, and she came close to me. I kissed her on the lips, and in a voice that I tried to give the ring of truth to, I told her, "I don't want you to go."

She pressed herself against me, and angled her thighs in such a way that she could touch me. But there was something there that hadn't changed, so she drew back, saying: "I have to go."

She raised her hand to my face and touched my cheek with her fingers, then added, "You had a lot to drink today. Talk to me tomorrow."

"I will."

I opened the door and was about to press for the elevator, but she stopped me, saying that she preferred to take the stairs. She waved goodbye, whispering in English, "*Bye-bye.*"

I waited until she disappeared, then I went inside and locked the door behind me.

# 14

Antoinette returned my "Good morning" without taking her eyes off the scattered papers on her desk. When I sat down in front of her, I discovered that her eyelids were swollen, and that she had put on a good deal of eyeliner to conceal that fact. I sensed that she was extremely nervous.

She headed toward the small kitchen next door, saying: "We'll have some coffee, and then we'll begin."

I picked up the newspapers off her desk, and cast a quick glance at their headlines. Attempts were still ongoing to rescue the Arab summit conference slated to be held next week in Amman. In Muscat, Sultan Qaboos had declared that the Soviet Union was responsible for the instability in the Gulf region, and he demanded that the nations of the West counteract the Soviets' expansionist policy. In Khartoum, a US official was looking into Sudanese defense requirements. And in Washington Menachem Begin declared that his government would not relinquish Syria's occupied Golan Heights. In Paris, *Le Figaro* said that Syria had become another Ethiopia in the heart of the Middle East, after ratifying a treaty of peace and cooperation with the Soviet Union.

Antoinette came back with the coffee, and she noticed I was yawning.

"It looks like you were up late last night," she said.

"Not at all," I replied. "I went to bed early, but I didn't sleep through the night. Perhaps it was because of the climate here, one thing happening after another."

"When the fighting was at its most intense," she said, taking a sip of coffee, "I used to sleep soundly. It's a question of habit. You can easily get used to the sound of bullets. Unlike other things."

"Such as?"

She looked down into her cup. "Sitting down to eat after witnessing a group of rotting corpses," she replied. "Fires blazing and rockets launching while the radio is playing pop music. Several gunmen standing in your way and asking to see your identity, so they can find out your religion, although you don't know what theirs is. Or spending Sunday by yourself inside four walls."

"I've often had that same Sunday experience."

She put the cup back on its saucer and, picking up her purse, led me to the editing room without saying a word. I helped her carry the film canisters from the storage space and then thread into position the film we would be watching. Then I got my pen and paper ready, and took my place in front of the Moviola screen.

## THE THIRD PART OF THE FILM

Title card:

On the same day as Syria's entrance into Lebanon, June 1, 1976, in a move that Western news agencies portrayed as support for the Syrian initiative, the Soviet Premier Kosygin arrived in Damascus at the head of a large official delegation.

Damascus International Airport. Soviet flags everywhere. The large escort for the Soviet official sets out from in front of the airport.

The lead headline of Syria's *al-Baath* newspaper: "Kissinger, after the first round of talks with President Hafez al-Assad: 'We support the resumption of the Geneva Conference as soon as possible, with the participation of all parties directly interested in the Middle East crisis, and we support the Lebanese forces that are fighting for national unity, territorial unity, and a settlement of the crisis via peaceful means.'"

Scattered headlines in Lebanese newspapers: "Islamic Council under the leadership of Shafiq al-Wazzan welcomes Syrian intervention." "Kamal Shatila, head of the Union of Working People's Forces (Nasserist), welcomes Syria's move and attacks reactionaries, isolationists and regionalists under the sway of secularism, sexual license and hostility to Arabism." "Shia, Guardians of the Cedars and Phalangists welcome Syrian intervention and commend Syrian president for his bravery." "Iraq offers 3 million dollars to the Joint Arab Front in the Palestinian uprising."

Beirut. An office of the Sa'iqa organization in Chiyah. Fatah forces surround the building. Other Fatah forces besiege an office belonging to Kamal Shatila's organization in the Caracas neighborhood.

Title card:

In response, Syrian forces moved toward Beirut. So the Palestinian resistance sought the help of the

Libyans and Algerians, asking them to stop the advancing forces in exchange for a return to the *status quo ante*. The attacks on the Sa'iqa and Shatila offices were abandoned.

Headline in a Lebanese newspaper: "Syrian forces occupy all of northern Lebanon."

A paragraph from *Pravda*: "The armed fighting among the parties fighting in Lebanon has virtually ended thanks to Syrian intervention."

Zuheir Mohsen, leader of the Sa'iqa, from Radio Damascus: "Fatah has changed: once it was a tool for the Palestinian uprising, but now it's become a dagger directed against the people of Palestine."

Headline in a Lebanese newspaper: "Syrian forces and al-Sa'iqa rain down rockets on Beirut and the camps. 700 killed and wounded. Nearly 4,000 homes destroyed. Rockets fall at a rate of one explosion every 6 minutes."

Moscow. Headquarters of the Soviet Foreign Ministry. A Soviet authority reads an urgent statement to reporters: "With respect to Syria, which announced that the mission of its forces is to help stop the bloodshed in Lebanon, it is evident that blood is still being shed, and in greater quantities."

Damascus. The entrance to the Republican Palace. The Jordanian prime minister and Zayd bin Shakir, commander-in-chief of the Jordanian Army, accompanied by Mustafa Tlass, Syrian minister of defense.

A circle around a paragraph from an Israeli newspaper: "The largest division of Syrian forces, which had taken up positions in recent months between Damascus and the Israeli lines, was withdrawn and sent to Lebanon and the Syrian–Iraqi border."

A headline in a Lebanese newspaper: "Syrian forces strip citizens of their money, possessions and food." A telegram sent from Maronite leader Raymond Eddé to President Hafez al-Assad: "The Syrian Army robbed my house in Sawfar ... It has not escaped my notice that it did the same to Rashid Karami's house."

Sawfar. A Syrian soldier is talking to a French television crew: "We are waiting impatiently for our turn. Coming to Lebanon was always a dream ... Well-stocked shops, imported goods, movies and women. They selected us from every army division so we won't feel loyal just to our group, and so everyone feels that they all have an equal chance of going to Lebanon."

President Hafez al-Assad addressing a large crowd: "They attacked the Syrian soldiers who entered in order to help them ... We chose these soldiers from different sections of the army, and we made this choice intentionally; we intended for soldiers from every division in the Syrian army to go, for reasons of Arab nationalism, so they could defend the refugee camps, and so that the spirit of defending the Palestinian cause and the camps would be strengthened in all branches of the Syrian military."

Cairo. A television anchorman reads a news bulletin: "Arab foreign ministers decide to replace Syrian forces in Lebanon with Arab security forces."

Beirut. The Achrafieh neighborhood in East Beirut. Abd al-Salam Julud, Libyan prime minister, in the car of Abu al-Hasan, Fatah's security chief. The car stops in front of Pierre Gemayel's home.

Title card:

While a solution for Lebanon was forging ahead into existence under Arab protection, members of a small leftist organization calling itself the Party of Arab Socialist Labor, which was linked to the Popular Front for the Liberation of Palestine (headed by George Habash), kidnapped the American ambassador and the US Embassy advisor, as well as their Lebanese driver. The kidnapping took place in West Beirut before the ambassador's car reached the border separating the two sides, on its way to Sarkis's headquarters. After three hours, the bodies of the three men were discovered in the Janah district.

A headline in a Lebanese newspaper: "The Soviet government offers immediate assistance in the form of food and medical supplies to the Lebanese National Movement and Palestinian resistance via Beirut Airport and other ports."

A headline in Syria's *al-Baath* newspaper: "Syrian minister of media denies that there are battles between Syrian forces and the so-called joint forces (Lebanese and Palestinian), saying, 'What is happening in Lebanon is a battle among Palestinian forces.'"

A circle around a paragraph from the Soviet newspaper, *Sovetskaya Rossiya*: "Despite repeated Syrian declarations about helping Lebanon stop the bloodshed, in reality the bloodshed has increased since Syrian forces entered this country. They are coming down hard in regions that are dominated by nationalist forces and where the Palestinian camps are located."

A headline in a Lebanese newspaper: "President Frangieh – days before leaving the office of presidency – appoints Camille Chamoun as assistant to the prime minister, as minister of the interior, of post, telegraph and telephone, of water and electric resources, and of external affairs and aliens, of national education, of fine arts and of public planning."

A slender young woman in military clothes, with her hair down over her shoulders, inspects several armed men and women, all bearing the insignia "Tigers of the Liberals", Chamoun's militia.

Gunmen bearing the same insignia jump in the air shouting an attack cry.

Narrow alleyways with uncovered drainage ditches running down the middle of them. In front of a tin-sheet shack stands a young man pouring water from a plastic bucket over another young man having a bath on the ground in front of him.

Sunset in the same place. Dozens of men of different ages wearing scruffy clothes appear in the backstreets, shuffling wearily as they return and enter the shacks and low-roofed houses.

Title card:

The Tel Zaatar camp is located in East Beirut, near the industrial zone. Most of its inhabitants are Palestinians and Lebanese, along with poor Kurds, Egyptians and Syrians, Muslims and Christians, in addition to political exiles from several Arab countries.

Maronite monasteries own the largest share of the land occupied by the camp. They were perennially trying to evict the camp in order to reclaim the land, the value of which had increased in recent years. At the same time, the location of the camp kept East Beirut from being entirely under Maronite control.

A general view of the Tel Zaatar camp. Armored cars carrying the "Tigers" emblem surround the camp on all sides. Missiles and rockets fly up over its houses. A mortar on top of an armored car in the fort rains down fire on the camp.

Chamoun, with his carefully-combed silver hair, and with his glasses in his hand, is sitting down, listening to the reports from the leaders of the Tigers, and smiling.

A headline in a Lebanese newspaper: "Jumblatt says: 'The attack on Tel Zaatar is a contest for leadership of the Maronites between Chamoun and Gemayel.'"

Headlines from Lebanese newspapers: "Beirut without water, electricity and gasoline." "Gas at 18 lira." "Blockade of supplies by Syrian forces." "Dollar rises to 330 Lebanese piastres; US and Canadian banks make billions in profits."

A wooden donkey cart, with its back wagon filled with people. One of them carries a wide placard reading: "This is how our ancestors did it. We don't need gasoline."

A street in Beirut. A Palestinian gunman carrying the Fatah insignia distributes flour from a military truck. Hundreds of hands stretch out to him.

The power company building in East Beirut.

Title card:

After the warring factions cut off the thirteen power lines that fed electricity to both halves of the city, Fu'ad Bazri, president of the power company, who came to be known as "Mr Light", succeeded in finalizing an agreement between Yasser Arafat and the Phalangists, on the basis of which the Palestinian leader sent two small seagoing transport vessels carrying heavy fuel to the electric power station in the Christian sector, a few kilometers distant from Beirut, so that it could supply the two parts of the city with current.

A newspaper headline: "Nationalist and Palestinian forces advance in the direction of Ain Remmaneh, with the aim of relieving pressure on Tel Zaatar."

Title card:
On June 27, the Phalangists announced that they had entered the battle of Tel Zaatar.

A press conference with member of parliament Amin Gemayel: "The Phalangists have joined in the assault on Tel Zaatar because those who planned and started the attack were incapable of seizing it."

A poster carrying the insignia of the Tigers with a photo of a beautiful young woman. Below the photo in French: "Saada Khayyat: the first Lebanese woman to fall on the field of honor during the attack on Tel Zaatar."

A press conference with Julud, prime minister of Libya: "The conspiracy is large-scale and international . . . The Syrian Army was drawn into the conspiracy so that it could control all the basic elements in the Lebanese public arena . . . Nationalist forces and people who believe in their Arab character, Christians and Muslims, and those who believe in their nationalist sense of belonging, and the Palestinians . . . My opinion is that they should march in file to Tel Zaatar until the isolationists run out of ammunition. If you start with a half-million Palestinians, and end up with only one hundred thousand, that doesn't matter. This is our view, even toward Israel. If the Arabs weren't afraid of dying, then Israel wouldn't exist."

A newspaper headline: "The resistance takes Bashir Gemayel prisoner after he killed several Palestinians with his own hands. 8 hours later, he was released, following the intervention of President Sarkis and the Deuxième Bureau."

A headline in a newspaper: "Tel Zaatar repels 49th attack."

A headline in the Phalangist newspaper, *al-Amal*: "Leaders of the Phalangists and Tigers follow the progress of the battles directly on the battlefield."

Title card:
On the twentieth day of Tel Zaatar holding out . . .

A headline in a Lebanese newspaper: "PLO leadership to Tel Zaatar combatants: 'The coming hours are fateful, your defiance is key.'"

A headline in a Lebanese newspaper: "Communications between Arafat, Gaddafi and Mahmoud Riyad, and between Jumblatt, King Khalid, Sadat, Boumedienne and al-Bakr, and between Assad and Hussein."

A headline in a Lebanese newspaper: "Tel Zaatar repels 51st attack."

A headline in a Lebanese newspaper: "New 7-hour-long assault against Tel Zaatar repelled."

A headline in a Lebanese newspaper: "10-page Soviet diplomatic note warns Syria against further strikes against the Palestinian resistance and Lebanese National Movement."

A headline in the Lebanese newspaper *al-Anbaa*: "Jumblatt to a conference of Arab foreign ministers: 'You were duped by businessmen of the isolationist faction, who are very close to your kings and presidents.'"

A headline in a French newspaper: "Killing of William Hawi, president of the Phalangist military council, during the battles of Tel Zaatar. Foreign press bureaus in Beirut confirm that his killing was arranged by Bashir Gemayel, who took his place as the head of the Phalangist military council."

In front of the Phalangist military council building. Bashir Gemayel in his military uniform surrounded by his aides.

Title card:

Bashir Gemayel graduated from Jesuit schools and the Jesuit University, where he studied law. But power was more enticing to him than the legal profession he was expected to enter.

Since his youth, he was notable for his hotheadness and his violent tendencies. He resorted quickly to his fists when confronted with a problem. These problems multiplied when he reached adolescence. His face was filled with pimples. He discovered that he was short, and his body not well-proportioned. Soon after, it became clear that the leadership positions within his family were limited to his powerful father and his older brother, Amin, who was distinguished by his slender physique, good looks and intellectual gifts. But he didn't despair. He sought refuge in the street. For fifteen hours a day, during which time he never stopped eating pieces of chocolate, he would attend weddings, baptisms, funerals and masses, currying favor with the petit bourgeois, the semi-employed, minor functionaries, and all the other frustrated people, while waiting for the right opportunity.

The Damascus University amphitheater. Hafez al-Assad is speaking: ". . . Those who are making uninformed opinions must understand that I am not someone who loves power. I am nothing but an individual of this people, and nothing will keep me from feeling the feelings of this people, and taking the decision that I feel expresses the feelings of the citizens of this country and their desires.

"When the events in Lebanon began, some long months ago, we had an explanation for them . . . We said that the conspiracy couldn't achieve its goals except through killing. So in order for us to frustrate the conspiracy, we had to stop the killing. And we set out to act for that reason . . .

". . . But there are some who want the problems to stay the way they are, because they want to work. Some gunmen in Lebanon now are against peace. If peace is achieved, then they will be out of work. And that's a problem.

". . . We welcomed Kamal Jumblatt. I said to him, We want you to let us know what you really want . . . He spoke about secularism. A secular state in Lebanon. I told him that the Phalangists are enthusiastic for secularism. Shaykh Pierre Gemayel told me that he will accept no substitute for secularism. I am insistent on, and hold fast to, a secular state in Lebanon. But the mufti of the Muslims, the Shii imam, and some prime ministers and speakers of parliament have refused secularism.

"Jumblatt said: 'Let us punish them. We have to settle it militarily. They have ruled us for 140 years, and we want to get rid of them.' Here I saw that the mask had slipped. The issue was one of reprisal and revenge.

"A military settlement in a country like Lebanon, between two warring sides in one nation, is impossible. A military settlement for any problem means a decisive elimination of that problem. And in Lebanon that notion is impossible because exercising power should not require having absolute power. Or rather, there should be more than one source of power, although that doesn't exist now. As for the proposed military settlement, if it creates a situation where one side dominates Lebanese public life, then it will result in the emergence of a new problem in Lebanon and in this region. The problem of a certain people, of a certain religion, is the problem of Lebanon or part of Lebanon. The problems of those who are dominated is one that the world will empathize with.

"We can all imagine this solution would not exist at all except through the partitioning of Lebanon. A state filled with hatred would arise. A state more dangerous and more hostile than Israel.

"A third thing: you can all foresee that a military settlement in this way will fling open the doors to every foreign intervention, and especially Israeli intervention.

"On the same day, I summoned Yasser Arafat and this is what I said to him: I told him and I'm telling you now that I cannot conceive of the connection between Palestinians doing battle on top of Mount Lebanon and the liberation of Palestine . . . My friends, do you recall what went on in 1970 in Jordan? At the time, they shouted slogans: Power, all power to the resistance. We are liberating Palestine by way of Amman. The matter is being repeated now in Lebanon. At that meeting, Yasser Arafat promised me that he would withdraw from the fighting.

"Syria is a land of stalwart resistance. Whoever is for stalwart resistance must be for Syria. Syria is a land of liberation, and whoever is for liberation must be for Syria. Syria is a land of Arab nationalism and progress, and whoever is for Arab nationalism must be for Syria. Syria is a land of the Palestinian struggle, and whoever is for the Palestinian struggle must be for Syria. Any talk about liberating Palestine without Syria is ignorance and a deception of the masses."

Title card:

On the same day that the Syrian president gave this speech, Lebanon's mufti sent him the following appeal:

"Today, after the pressure caused by the crisis of hunger, thirst, fear and illness has grown intense, and spreading epidemics have come to threaten the lives of all the inhabitants of Beirut and its environs, not to mention the danger of spreading contagion throughout Lebanon . . . because of the continuation of the squalid 500-day war, and the tightening of the blockade around us from all sides, from land, sea and air.

". . . We turn to you, demanding in the name of Muslim and Arab brotherhood, that you fulfill the call of duty to the human race and to Arab nationalism, namely:

187

"First – that you leave the international Damascus–Beirut road open to all convoys carrying supplies of food, medicine and fuel from brother Arab states through Syria.

"Secondly – that you prevent any threatening move that would block the arrival of ships to the harbors of Sidon and Tripoli . . ."


A separate title card:
Two days later . . .


The headquarters of the Socialist Progressive Party in Beirut. A crowd of journalists and politicians. Kamal Jumblatt, head of the party, holds a press conference. The Lebanese leader announces the establishment of a central political council with him as president that will undertake the functions of political leadership for the nationalist and progressive forces and parties in Lebanon.

In front of the Tel Zaatar camp. Crowds of soldiers. A group of Red Cross ambulances slowly approaches.

A newspaper headline: "Isolationist forces fire on the Red Cross delegation that attempted to evacuate the wounded from the Tel Zaatar camp."

A newspaper headline: "TASS blames Saudi Arabia for what is happening in Lebanon."

A newspaper headline: "The Saudi Industrial Services Company (SISCO) announces that the Middle East will likely settle down once the Palestinian resistance in Lebanon has been weakened."

A newspaper headline: "For 3 days, Syrian forces have been

unable to break through the lines of the Palestinian resistance in Bhamdoun."

Title card:
On July 29 . . .

A newspaper headline: "Agreement in Damascus between the Palestinian resistance and Syria to end the fighting."

A circle around a paragraph from the same newspaper: "The Syrian side confirmed its firm and ongoing position supporting the PLO as representative of the Palestinian people in their struggle against the Israeli enemy and on behalf of liberation; and confirmed that Syria was and will remain a base of the struggle for the people of Palestine . . . Likewise, the Palestinian side praised the position of the Arab nation of Syria with regard to the struggle of the Palestinian Arab people, the Palestinian cause, the assistance of the Syrian nation, and its support for the Palestinian resistance."

Title card:
Two days later . . .

A newspaper headline dated July 31: "Evacuation of the wounded from Tel Zaatar. A Swedish doctor states that the number of killed at the camp has reached 1,400, and the number of injured 4,000."

The Naba'a neighborhood near Beirut. A Phalangist militia fires bullets in every direction. The militia starts expelling residents from their homes.

A crossing-point between the Eastern and Western sectors, near the Museum. Hundreds of residents of the Naba'a district, expelled from East Beirut, arrive together. A narrow street that ends at an overturned bus. Barrels filled with sand. Broken pipes. Women carry everything they own on their heads and drag their children behind them. A girl is carrying a doll, and another carries a gas stove. Everyone advances to the end of the street where the barrier to West Beirut is located.

Title card:

On the fiftieth day of the siege of Tel Zaatar, Yasser Arafat sent letters to Arab leaders, holding them responsible for the fate of the camp. On the same day, the agreement was reached, through the Red Cross and Arab Security Forces, to complete the evacuation of 12,000 civilians from the camp, and to transport them to the Bekaa Valley or West Beirut.

Two days later, on August 12, 1976 . . .

Red Cross automobiles in front of Tel Zaatar. A truck carrying the emblem of the Arab Security Forces. Several women and children – no trace of a man among them – climb onto it. The street is covered with countless numbers of different kinds of shoes: traditional slippers, sandals, women's shoes (high heels and flats). Another truck with sides made of interlaced slats, like trucks used for transporting animals.

In front of the Teachers' College in West Beirut. Crowds. A weeping woman, another woman with torn clothes, and children step out of a small truck. Another weeping woman embraces two children.

The Arab University Hospital. An elderly woman leans over a wounded man with no legs and embraces him.

Title card:

> During the evacuation of non-combatants, the Phalangists and Tigers assaulted the camp in large numbers. Fighting occurred between them and 300 Palestinian and Lebanese young men who refused to submit and continued to resist to the end. At the end of the day, it was announced that Tel Zaatar had fallen.

# 15

The woman really was captivating: she was wrapped in a diaphanous cape that showed off her body's charms. Below the photo I read these words: "The West, enraptured by the Orient and its exoticism. The Orient – like a magic wand, it can turn you into a woman of a thousand faces."

I took my eyes off the advertisement, and went back to reading the news report about the elderly French philosopher Althusser, who had choked his wife. Then I put the newspaper to one side and picked up the phone.

I dialed the number of Dar al-Thaqafa Publishing, and found the line was busy, so I called Wadia in his office.

As soon as I heard his voice, I said, "The maid hasn't come yet and I'd like to leave the house."

"If she hasn't come by now, then she won't be coming today," he explained. "Should I expect you for dinner?"

"I don't think so. Antoinette and I have been invited to the house of a French acquaintance in the evening. We might go directly there from Fakahani."

The sun was shining, making it a warm day, so I went out wearing only a wool sweater over my shirt, and slung my bag over my shoulder. Then I dialed the number for Dar al-Thaqafa again, and since it was still busy, I left the apartment.

I stood waiting for a car to take me to Antoinette's office. An empty one stopped in front of me, so I asked the driver to take me to Ain Mreisseh.

The burly security guard was sitting at the entrance to the building, beside one of the armed guards. Reluctantly, he accompanied me upstairs, and handed me over to the secretary, who called Lamia to let her know, and asked me to wait.

I sat down on a seat facing her. I began looking over into the hallway, at the end of which was Lamia's office. Her door was closed.

After a few moments, the door opened and she emerged. She was wearing a blouse patterned in magnificent colors with long, wide sleeves and gray velour pants. Her hair was plaited in two large braids, and she looked like a teenage girl.

She approached me, taking slow steps, with an absentminded look in her eye, as if she had been taken off-guard. She gave me her hand and forced a smile.

"Nice to see you," she said by way of addressing me.

She turned back toward her office, and I walked behind her. At that moment I saw the hem of her blouse dangling over her pants.

The face of her friend who I had seen in the café looked up at me. She was sitting on a couch, with her legs crossed and sipping coffee.

Lamia headed toward her desk, walked around it, and then sat down, saying: "My friend Jamila. You've seen her before."

I inclined my head toward her, walked to Lamia's desk, and sat on the chair in front of it. I put my shoulder bag on the floor.

I looked over at Jamila and asked her, "Do you work in publishing, too?"

She smiled and shook her head.

"Close to publishing," Lamia said. "She is a bank manager."

I turned toward Lamia.

"I called you yesterday," I said.

She shot a quick look at her friend. "I wasn't at home," she explained.

"I took the manuscript for your book from Lamia, and I'll be reading it today," Jamila said to me.

"Don't worry," Lamia quickly piped in. "I only have the last chapter left to read."

"I'm not worried," I said. "All I want is to finish up this matter before I travel."

"When are you leaving?" Jamila asked me.

"Within a week."

The secretary brought coffee, and I sipped it in silence, while Lamia occupied herself with the papers on her desk. Her friend got out a notebook from her purse, and began flipping through the pages. The vibrant red she had painted on her lips was well-suited to the shape of her broad face, and to the color of her wheat-brown skin. She looked to me at least ten years older than Lamia.

I finished my coffee, picked up my shoulder bag and stood up, while telling Lamia, "I have to be going now. I'll call you later."

She made no attempt to keep me from leaving, and didn't see me to the door. She was content to merely shake my hand while she sat. With a nod of the head to her friend, I left her office.

I fought off an urgent desire for a drink, and took a taxi to Fakahani.

I found Antoinette in the editing room. I noticed that she had arranged her hair carefully, and done her nails in clear nail polish. She was wearing a tight woolen blouse that emphasized her small breasts.

I got my pen and paper ready and turned out the light. Then I took my place next to her in front of the Moviola. She touched the machine's reel, and scenes dealing with the fall of Tel Zaatar passed before us, one after another.

She stopped the machine suddenly, and said, "Do you need to record the next section? It's only the testimonies of a group of women who escaped from the massacre. They don't need any voiceover commentary."

I thought for a moment. "Maybe. But I should familiarize myself with the content of the testimonies, their rhythms, their length, and their connection to the scenes coming before and after. Getting to know them like this will determine the ending for the voiceover that comes before: whether it should be incorporated into them or end before them, with a climax or without one. I will record everything so I can work on it in my own time."

"As you wish," she replied.

### THE FOURTH PART OF THE FILM

Women in the prime of life or in middle age. Their clothes are simple. Their heads are covered in scarves knotted below their chin. Their voices are dry, with no trace of life in them. The camera stays motionless on each woman until she finishes her testimony.

Title card:
Umm Ali Salem, age 50.

"When they expelled us from Palestine, we went to Syria. Then we came to Tel Zaatar. We were always being chased away. The supervisor Abu Aboud from Lebanon's Deuxième Bureau would eavesdrop on us from under the window. Afterwards, they imprisoned my husband because of the leaflets. All my sons joined the resistance when they were young, and they went to training sessions, and then carried weapons. I only have one son left. I used to participate in the illiteracy-eradication units that worked in the camp. The men of the Deuxième Bureau would often take my husband and torture him to make him tell them where the children were. They began coming every day to inspect the house and ask about the children. But all that changed after the resistance took over the supervision of the camp.

"During the siege, five of my sons died as martyrs in the camp. When we left Zaatar, I took with me the shirts that belonged to my martyred sons, so I could smell their precious scent . . . I learned that they dragged my husband: they tied his feet with a rope to separate cars, and then started driving."

Title card:
Zaynab Umm Ali, age 40, mother of ten.

"Abu Aboud met with me individually. One day, at 11 pm, he knocked on the door. I quickly opened it, and there was Abu Aboud, and George Hazini with him. The first one hit me and the second one shouted. 'You coward,' I told him. That's when my children came out, asking, 'What do you want with my mother?' He took me to see

Ahmad al-Azuri. Abu Ahmad beat me five times with a whip. I stayed there for eleven hours. I slept on the floor with my hands over my eyes . . . They kept me in jail with them for three days . . .

"Then the resistance came and killed the agents. I began working in the young men's military camp . . . When the siege of the camp began, a bomb landed, and made a martyr of my sick husband. It also made a martyr of my daughter while she was going to see her father . . . Suddenly Sobhi Iraqi and Hasan Shahrur came to the shelter and said, 'We want some young men to fetch the martyr Namr,' but no one moved. My grown son, who was sixteen, and I went and we removed the martyr Namr. On the way back, my only son was martyred. My son – there was nothing dearer to me than him, except Palestine, because he was my only son among nine daughters."

Title card:
Nuzha Hasan al-Duqi, age 65, mother of five sons and grandmother of ten.

". . . When the events started, my son Ahmad, who was thirty-eight, returned from a trip. He was carrying a gift from a friend of his to his wife and sons in Jdaide, and he didn't return. We found his body after three months in a morgue there.

"During the events, my son Jalal was martyred by a bomb. One day my daughter Fatum went to fill the water buckets and didn't come back, since a bomb struck her and she was martyred instantly.

"When the shelter collapsed, my son Ali was working to remove the rubble. The isolationists aimed a projectile at him and he fell down and died a martyr.

"When the camp fell, my husband and his three sons and my grandsons went out. The isolationists blocked their way at the church, and stood my three sons up against the wall and began beating them with wooden clubs on their backs with all their strength until they fell down. And they killed one of my grandsons. I cried and screamed, but my grandchildren wanted me to be quiet so the gunmen wouldn't take them . . . When we arrived at the hostel, they began having fun with us, and once they told us to run up to the third floor with a hail of bullets behind us. We would run and shove each other, hiding behind each other . . . Finally, they took us out to the street and made us get into trucks. I stood next to my husband, who clung to the truck's metal railing . . . The gunmen brought out young men and killed them in groups in front of us. My husband cried; one of the gunmen noticed him and took him down from the truck. They began torturing the young men in front of him, then they killed him, and he fell to the ground. My grandchildren screamed in terror, so they fired bullets at us and we quickly got down from the truck, without thinking. My grandchildren were all lost, so here I am, living alone. I have no one left."

Title card:
Su'ad Salih, age 42, mother of five sons.

"When the siege began, I had 10 kilograms of flour in my house, so I made dough out of it, baked it, and sent the bread to the fighters. I used to make tea and coffee for them at night. Then the electricity was cut, so we would make candles for the hospital. We got the wax from a nearby warehouse. My son would bring it and we would place it over the fire to melt it, then we would pour it into meat and sardine tins, and put a wick in it. After it hardened, we would cut the can and take the candle out. We got to be very good at it, and started taking X-ray images, rolling them up and tying them in place, and then we would pour the wax in. After pulling it apart, we would get a beautiful, slender candle . . ."

Title card:
Fatima Iwad, age 22, nurse.

"Ever since the siege began, I was working night and day to secure food and water for the wounded. Many of them were dying for lack of medicine. We had nothing to sterilize wounds with except water and salt. Ten days before the camp fell, we were waiting, one day after the next, for the arrival of the Red Cross to evacuate the wounded, but it only came three days later – after the camp had been cut off from the world for forty-two days . . . Around eighty wounded were evacuated, and the next day 150, and on the third day 750, along with several nursing infants suffering from dehydration.

"The night the camp fell, we were told that there were guarantees from the Red Cross and the Arab Security Forces to transport without objection those people living in the camp who surrendered. The next morning, we waited from 9.30 am, at the place where it was agreed that the Red Cross would be at 9 am. But during that time, the bombardment grew insanely intense, and the isolationists entered the camp. We were told that Red Cross trucks were in Dekwane to transport the wounded and civilians, so a group of us – nurses, along with several inhabitants – headed that way. But a barricade manned by Phalangists stood in our way: they searched us, while heaping curses on us. At the next barricade, the isolationists took the male nurses, tortured them, and killed them before our eyes . . ."

Title card:
Fatin Badran, age 23.

"I joined other female volunteers to establish a medical center in the fortified area, under the guidance of the doctors of Tel Zaatar. The night the fortified area fell into the hands of the isolationists, I was with my grandmother in the shelter. All the families in the shelter had Lebanese citizenship except for me and my grandmother. We became more afraid.

"The isolationists entered the district and began firing bullets through the windows and doors into the shelters that were crowded with women, children and old men, since the young men had joined the Tel Zaatar fighters. Then they moved us to the entranceway of another building, without knowing we were Palestinians. A little later, the isolationists brought people who recognized their friends who were among us, so they took them and left. The only people who remained were me, my neighbor and another neighbor woman who was called Wadad Qusur. At this point, my fear grew more intense, so she began reassuring me and telling me that she had friends who would come and take her, and that she would take us with her. But bombs fell on us and we got separated. We walked until we met a Palestinian family carrying Lebanese identity cards, and we went with them in a car. The driver asked us if we were Muslims or Christians, saying, 'If you're Muslims, then you'll have to get out at the Christian neighborhood of Sin el Fil.' But I persuaded him to take us to the edge of the Muslim neighborhood of Furn el Chebbak."

Title card:
Haya Feriha, age 20.

"In our free time, we would prepare the arsenals for the fighters' weapons, and I took part in an assault operation along with the martyred Samira Badran on the front lines in Hazmiye. We returned safely after destroying an armored car, although one of our men was hit. We let them know that we wanted to be with the heavy artillery (the anti-tank guns) on Tella al-Mir, and they agreed, but when I let them know that I wanted to be trained in how to use it, the fighters laughed since they were sure that women couldn't do jobs like that – they could only talk about it. But I was determined to prove to them I could. I really trained, and began by firing fifteen rockets at the opposing position, and I grew more devoted to the revolution. They showed they were prepared to train a squadron of female fighters.

"When the camp fell, we resisted to the last, and finally I destroyed my weapon, according to instructions, and went with my family to Dekwane . . ."

Title card:
Amina Fariha, age 35.

"When the water supply was cut off from the camp, around fifteen women went to the well, and only six of us came back. A cup of water was worth a cup of blood . . ."

Title card:
Shaykha Ahmad Shahrour, age 32, mother of two.

"We were keeping ourselves hidden from one house to the next, until we reached the well. There were Phalangist men there, occupying the heights nearby that overlooked the well. They were shouting at us, 'Two at a time,' and that's when the shooting began. Sometimes we would stay out all night long but come back with no water, and the children would start crying and yelling, because they needed a drop of water instead of milk.

"My little boy, one year old, was sick, so I took him to a doctor with the Red Crescent, but he said, 'We don't have any medicine.' My son's temperature went up to 40 degrees Celsius, and he became paralyzed in one leg. My husband was hit in the stomach and his legs. Before, I would tell him, 'Leave this place, and secure our future for us,' but he would tell me, 'I won't leave Tel Zaatar as long as it has a single stone left.' He kept his promise and stayed there until the last moment, and to this day, I don't know if he is alive or dead."

Title card:
Affar Muhammad, age 32, mother of seven children, three of whom are still alive.

"I went to the Red Crescent hospital on the main street of the camp, to see the wounded. Before I could get there, a bomb fell on the door of the shelter while my children were there, including my oldest daughter Amal, age eleven. She was martyred along with six children her age. After that, my health declined, and I was six months pregnant. The children were hungry and some died from thirst. Mothers nursed their children on the water from boiled lentils, and fever spread among the children. Some of them died of it, and others became dehydrated. By the time I went into labor, the bombing had grown intense, and my daughter was born on the stairs. I couldn't sleep for a single moment."

Title card:
Khazna Muhammad Salih, age 29.

". . . On the day the camp fell, I gave away the weapon I was carrying after they assured us that there were guarantees from the Red Cross and Arab Security Forces. I headed toward Dekwane along with several other women. At a roadblock near Studio Fawzi, a gunman tried to rip my clothes off, but I gave him all the money I owned. At the Hotel School, I saw a woman who was with the isolationists: she was wearing black and beating a boy around fifteen years old on the head and face with a pistol. Then she took him to a trash yard and while cursing the Palestinians, she killed him. I found my mother and brothers in the school. My mother tried to get a car to get us out of there, and my brothers were shaking with fear and terror. She paid a sum of money to the driver and we got in the car. I saw the isolationists tie a rope around the neck of a young man. They hanged him and then drove a car over his dead body. His flesh stuck to the ground. They did all that in front of his injured wife and his small children, who couldn't utter a word.

"The car took us a little way, and then stopped. That's when I saw them bringing out a young man whose name was Muhammad Karum. After they got tired of beating him, they tied his legs to two cars, and his body was torn in half. As for my husband, who left through the mountains, we still haven't heard anything about him."

Title card:
Feryal Shahrur, age 18.

"We ate nothing but lentils and dates. They would brew the tea with dates because there was so little sugar, but the tea ended up having no taste. The men would fight all day on only a little food and drink, and they would smoke rolled-up sage leaves and the leaves that birds eat . . ."

Title card:
Huriya Mustafa, age 20.

"On the day the heavy fighting started, my mother went out to fetch water, and suddenly she came upon a dead body on the ground. She went up to it, in the middle of all the bombs and rockets, and found that it was her son. Yes – it was my brother.

"On the day the camp fell, we came out by way of Dekwane. One of them came up to me and took one of my brothers. He hit him with the weapon in his hand until blood poured over his face. Then he emptied the bullets from his machinegun into his head. My brother turned toward us as if to say goodbye and fell to the ground a lifeless corpse. They took my third brother but my mother intervened to rescue him. She told them that two were enough, and to leave him to me because he was the youngest, but they paid no attention to her and shot him.

"They tried to take me with them but I refused. I didn't budge an inch because I preferred to die. My mother intervened, pleading for help and crying. But they drove her off and opened fire on her, shooting her dead. I seized the opportunity: I picked up my youngest brothers and ran to escape."

Title card:
Fatima al-Musa, age 45, mother of eight.

"I lost three of my sons, bearing in mind that my husband abandoned me, and didn't help me with anything."

Title card:
Fatima Badran, age 36, mother of nine sons.

"I went out while going to get water, and two days later my husband and sixteen-year-old son were martyred. My

205

daughter Samira took care of me. She helped evacuate the wounded under heavy fire. She was hit in the neck and martyred instantly.

"When the camp fell to the enemy, I went out with my mother and father, and the rest of my children. They took my father and killed him. I turned to see him and saw him with blood gushing out of his body and his mouth as he shook on the ground. Just like the eight young men who were with us – they killed them all. I saw a boy with his mother: the gunmen took him and he was standing up against the wall, where the gunmen fired bullets into him from head to toe and he screamed, and his poor mother screamed, too, but they hit her with their rifle butts and they pushed us toward the Hotel School (Ecole Hotelière).

"We looked for a car that would take us to the Museum. The driver wanted 300 lira per passenger. We were shaking with fear: we didn't have that much on us, so we waited for another car. That driver asked for 100 lira per passenger, so we got in and he took us as far as the Museum. They stood us up there against the wall and ordered us to cheer for Pierre Gemayel. They took four girls: they grabbed them by the arms and legs and threw them in the car, then they took my female cousin to a nearby room. She was pregnant and they forced her to take off her clothes and they tried to cut her stomach open . . ."

Title card:
Fawzi Shahrour, age 30.

". . . I saw them rip open the stomach of a woman nine months pregnant, and in front of our eyes, the baby came out of her belly. The woman died instantly. Everyone was terrified, and no one could turn around to look . . ."

Title card:
Zaynab Umm Ali, age 40, mother of ten [continued].

". . . After he threatened me, he took my two daughters from me. He did that in order to rape them. I offered him all the money I had. I ran to his superior officer and kissed his feet, telling him, 'Take anything but our honor' – even after he had completely stripped my daughters before my eyes. I asked him, 'Why are you doing this? You have no conscience if you're going to machinegun the ten of us.' One of them came and told him, 'Let her go.' Then they brought trucks. My children and I got in a truck. As we passed, they threw filthy water on us and slapped us with their shoes. We were driving over the corpses of young men and women. They gunned down eighteen young men at the Museum, sparing only women and children. They would ask women: how do you want your husband to die, by machinegun or a slit to the throat? A woman from al-Duqi was pulling her children along, but they stopped her and told her, 'Bring your son here.' She didn't obey and started crying, so one of them beat her with the butt of his Kalashnikov and killed her son. They pulled out Abu Yasin and killed him right there in front of people. They ran the car over him and crushed him. They brought Suleiman, the military official for the Nationalist Front, and tied his legs to the truck and beat him."

Title card:
A woman who was afraid to have her name used.

"My husband and I and our family were sitting at home when we heard the sound of planes. So we and the neighbors who lived around us hurried to the shelter. A little later I saw my husband with three young men: they were saying, 'Don't be afraid, that's not an Israeli plane circling overhead.' So we weren't afraid, because we knew it was a Syrian plane. We looked up at it and oh, the terror that was in store for us! It began bombing Tella al-Mir, and that's when the slaughter began."

Title card:
Affaf Muhammad, age 32, mother of seven children, three still alive [continued].

". . . I carried my little daughter, who was no more than two weeks old, and my daughters Sonya and Abeer, who was only two. The rest of them held on to the hem of my dress. On the street, my children ended up without shoes. They walked over the rubble and glass, and blood ran from their feet until we reached the Hotel School. We stayed there from 4 am until 2 pm. My children were hungry and I'll never forget the sound of Abeer's voice as she says to me: 'Mama, I want *zaatar* bread in a dish.'"

Title card:
Fatima Mahmud, age 45.

". . . They took the young men and lined them up in a single row with their faces to the wall, and began beating them on the back with wooden mallets until they fell down unconscious. They ordered some of them to kneel, and others to stand with their backs to the wall. They opened fire on the ones who were kneeling. Then they lit fires and heated iron bars in them until they were red-hot. Then they placed them in the shape of a cross on the stomachs of those who were standing. After that, they tied them up with ropes to cars and began dragging them around the streets. The women of that neighborhood were trilling the *zaghareet* at them and singing . . ."

Title card:
Jamila Qa'ur, age 32, mother of four girls.

". . . We got to the modern school and they started searching us. There was a Syrian officer with them. They found 75 lira on me and took it. Then the truck came. My children got in, followed by my mother and father, and finally me. I asked them about my daughters and they said that two of them got lost in the crowds of women and children. I began looking madly for them in the truck as I screamed in terror. After a few moments, I found them under people's feet. The first had died and her body was blue, and the second was nearly dead. I started giving her first aid so I could save her life.

"They made us get out of the truck on the highway. I wanted to get my daughter's body out of the truck, but the gunmen refused and threatened to kill me. They wrapped her in the Lebanese cedar-tree flag and said, 'Come on, take your daughter, give her to Yasser Arafat.' Then they started shooting at us, even though we were standing next to the Syrians and Libyans in the Arab Security Forces, who didn't lift a finger. In fact, we asked these troops for a little water for the children, but they refused, saying: 'Now you're making problems for us. Go get a drink somewhere else.' So we kept clear of them until cars belonging to the resistance arrived. We got in, screaming, crying, and calling out, 'Those poor Tel Zaatar boys!'"

Title card:
Fawzia Mustafa Husayn, age 16.

"A child was screaming and crying from hunger, so they asked his mother to quiet him down, but he didn't quiet down. The Phalangist told her, 'I'll make him be quiet. Give him to me.' He took him from her and threw him far away. He fell to the ground dead. Then he told her: 'Now he's quiet.'"

Title card:
Affaf Muhammad, age 32, mother of seven children, three still alive [continued].

". . . They brought tall, big trucks to transport families, so the women hurried with their children. Because there were so many people running to the cars, the bigger ones were stampeding over the smaller ones. When I had finished lifting my children onto the truck, I tried to get on, too, but the driver started off. I waved at him to stop and let me on, but he refused, and told me to get on another one. In fact, that's what I did. I got to the Museum ahead of the truck that had my children. I waited there until the truck came, and they all got off, except for my children. In the end, my twelve-year-old brother got out and my five-year-old son Feisal, and my four-year-old daughter Norma. I asked about the rest of them and my brother said the people on it were stepping on them, which led to the martyrdom of three-year-old Suham and two-year-old Abeer. As for Sonya, who was nine, she got lost, and to this day, I still don't know where she is, alive or dead. My husband was lost the same way."

Title card:
Maryam Yaqub, age 45.

". . . The day we left the camp, my two children were with me. I told them, 'Walk in front of us.' I saw a girl who had been killed, and then I saw my son, killed, along with several young men. I cried and my husband, who is an old man, told me, 'You're crying now for our son, and soon enough you'll be crying for me.'

"At the Hotel School, they searched us, looking for cash and gold. Then the trucks came to take us and the isolationists got into the back of the truck to see if there were any men among the women and children. They took my husband out of the truck, took the money he had on him, and killed him. At another checkpoint, they took the children out of the truck, including my son Muhammad. When I saw the isolationist boarding the truck from the other side, I hid my son underneath me. I sat on him until the truck started moving . . ."

Title card:
Randa Ibrahim al-Duqi, age 14.

". . . The cats in Tel Zaatar were very fat because they would eat dead bodies. They were dangerous because they would attack people, once they had gotten used to eating them. Our fighters used to shoot at them . . ."

Title card:
Umm Nabil, age 45, mother of ten sons.

". . . I was making dough for bread for the fighters, along with a number of other women from the camp, when I found out that my son Kayid had been martyred. He was twenty-two. So I finished my dough and went to the place where they put his body. I kissed him and left him there, and went back. I didn't tell his brothers so as not to break their spirits.

"A week later, I learned that my son Faris, who was twenty-five, had been martyred, and I was able to endure it. No mother's heart has endured more than that, but I willed myself to be strong because I was a source of strength for mothers whose children were martyrs. My son Nabil left the camp through Mount Lebanon, and to this day I don't know what's become of him. They assaulted the camp while I was there with my fourteen-year-old son Khalid. They lined up the men, took the girls, and performed intrusive, embarrassing searches on the women. My turn came and they asked me where I got a son like that from, since he had blond hair and green eyes, while I have dark skin. They said, 'It's a disgrace for a boy like that to be with the Palestinians.' I answered back at them in a voice filled with defiance: 'This boy is Palestinian – he's *my* son, a son of Palestine.' As soon as I finished speaking, they shot him. I showed no emotion, but stood fixed in place. They ordered me to walk over him, but I refused. I told them, 'I know this is the end, and this is my fate, but we will never kneel, as long as we still have a single nursing baby.'"

Title card:
Maryam Yaqub, age 45 [continued].

". . . We stopped at another roadblock and they took us out of the truck to search us. I had a little sugar and salt in a teapot, and a lot of photos of my children and the deeds to our land in Palestine inside a box . . ."

Title card:
Tharya Qasim, age 48, mother of five.

". . . I had a son – God have mercy on his soul. His name was Muhammad and he was around eighteen. He had fire in his belly. He never let the gun out of his hands. But God made it his fate to die a martyr on July 2, 1976, on the field of honor and heroism. About a week later, my other son Ibrahim was martyred. He wasn't yet fourteen years old. I was very sad. I mourned for them the way any mother would, and also because I no longer had any young men I could offer to fight and defend our honor. My husband is an older man and he's not in good health.

"As for my daughters, may God protect them, wherever they are. I had three daughters: Lamia, who was twenty, Ayida, who was twenty-two, and Dina, who was seventeen. They used to help at the aid stations, and then they went up into the mountains. To this day, I've heard no news, good or bad, about them. I don't know whether they were martyred or if they're still alive . . ."

Title card:
Randa Ibrahim al-Duqi, age 14 [continued].

". . . On the last night, we were able to get through to Yasser Arafat on the two-way radio, and we asked him what we should do. He told us: 'Don't surrender.'"

Title card:
A woman who didn't give her name.

". . . Tel Zaatar was the last holdout in East Beirut. It was obvious that the isolationists won because they had the support of Syria and Israel, and because Tel Zaatar was cut off from our areas. An early surrender could have been negotiated. But instead, more than 2,000 Palestinians and Lebanese were martyred unnecessarily."

Title card:
Watifa Shahada Dahir, age 35, mother of seven.

"It was obvious to everybody the camp would fall, because there were more martyred and wounded than there were fighters. Our brothers in West Beirut didn't send us a single fighter or ammunition for the artillery and other weapons to replace what we lost in over fifty-eight attacks by the isolationists."

Title card:
Nuzha Hasan al-Duqi, age 65, mother of five sons and grandmother of ten [continued].

". . . What did we do wrong, Miss? I don't know. What did we do wrong, that we have to die to return to our land? Is that so wrong? What do they want from us . . . Make us disappear?"

# 16

Jacques LeRot and his wife welcomed us warmly. With a laugh, he began repeatedly welcoming us in Arabic: "*Ahleen . . . ahleen.*"

He was of medium build, like most Frenchmen, around thirty-five, with a sardonic look beaming from his smiling eyes, and always laughing for no apparent reason. His wife had a full head of black hair, and looked older than he was.

They walked us to a spacious room lit by side-table lamps. I shook hands with Marwan, the one with the thick mustache, and his friend the film director, and another young man with a thick beard that covered his entire face.

I sat down in a comfortable chair with polished wooden armrests. Grinning, Jacques addressed me in perfect Arabic that had no trace of a foreign accent: "We're always bumping into each other."

"The last time you were studying the minarets of Cairo," I replied.

He laughed out loud. "Now I'm studying the Lebanese dialect," he said.

He turned to Antoinette.

"How's the film going?" he inquired.

"Good. It's coming along," she replied.

"Are you sure?" he asked, winking in my direction as he leaned over a small table with a row of liquor bottles on it.

He poured each of us a glass of gin, then walked to a big stereo that had a clear plastic cover on it, and asked: "Fairuz or Umm Kulthum?"

"Bach," I said.

He laughed as he flipped through his record collection.

"This is the real reason for the failure of the Arab left. Chasing after European culture and being disconnected from the masses."

"Bach belongs to everyone," I objected.

He picked up a record, and said: "How about something modern, close to Bach and Arab music as well? Have you heard of Charette?"

I shook my head. He put the record on the turntable, and placed the needle on it, then went back to his seat.

Antoinette was engrossed in a conversation in French with Jacques's wife. Jacques directed his speech toward Marwan, while pointing at a piece of paper lying on the table in front of him: "Not a single newspaper in France will publish the petition in its current form."

Marwan's eyes were sharply focused on him.

"Why?" the young man with the beard asked in a challenging tone.

He laughed. "Because it's talking about the detention of several dozen leftists, while there are thousands of others being detained in Syria, from the Muslim Brotherhood and other groups. Plus, it doesn't clearly establish responsibility. We all know that if it weren't for the Soviet Union, the Syrian regime would collapse. The petition doesn't point that out directly."

Marwan bowed his head, saying: "I see your point. The wording of the petition has to be changed."

"That's impossible," the young man with the beard angrily interjected.

Antoinette joined in, saying: "If you change the wording of the petition, I will withdraw my name from it."

Jacques laughed. "You don't have to change it," he said. "You can do a different wording for the French text."

I followed the conversation while listening to the music. It was quite similar to pieces played on the Arab instrument known as the *qanun*. But its structure was complex, and bit by bit it ascended until it was on the verge of reaching a climax, at which point it retreated to the beginning, only to begin a new attempt.

Jacques's wife invited us to a table, laden with platters and gold-trimmed porcelain dishes. We started with soup, followed by the rest of the courses, according to the traditional sequence. We finished with coffee and cognac in the first room.

"Do you know that tomorrow will be the third anniversary of Sadat's visit to Jerusalem?" Jacques asked, as he took a small wrapped package the size of a matchbox out of a cigar box and placed it on the table.

Marwan picked up the package and opened the thin wrapping, then brought it up to his nose and said: "This is an excellent variety."

"I got it yesterday from Baalbek," Jacques explained.

He took a wooden peg out of the cigar box and handed it to the film director. With a practiced motion, the director stuck it into the tip of a cigarette and began moving it in and out. He took a small lump of hashish from the package, rubbed it thoroughly between his fingers, and rolled it between his palms. Then he pushed it into the cigarette, in the empty space made by the wooden peg. He offered the cigarette to Jacques's wife and lit it for her.

The Frenchwoman took a deep drag that made the end of it glow, extending more than a centimeter up the joint. Then she passed it to Antoinette, saying: "I was in Cairo this spring when the Israeli ambassador arrived. The sight of his car making its way across downtown, flying the Israeli flag, was truly jaw-dropping."

"How did people react?" Marwan asked her in French.

She pouted. "There wasn't a large crowd," she said. "And the car was moving fast. There were lots of policemen lined up on the street."

"If he came to Damascus, the crowds would come out to welcome him," said the director as he flicked the wooden peg in a new joint.

"All that because they blocked your film," Jacques added, laughing.

"What could be less important to us now than Assad and his underlings?"

I took my turn with the joint, and passed it to Jacques, who asked me: "Have you found a publisher for your book?"

"Not yet."

"That's how things go with Arab governments," he offered, while giving me a scrutinizing look.

The driving rhythm of the piano was still struggling to reach the climax. It seemed to be towering over it, and was suddenly accompanied by a human moan expressing pain or pleasure or both together.

"Will you be staying long in Beirut?" I asked Jacques.

"Maybe," he replied. "I don't know. I'll be going back to France in two months' time to take part in the election campaign."

I looked at him inquisitively.

"I'm a member of the Socialist Party," he explained. "We have a good chance this time. If we win the elections, then Mitterand will be president."

He laughed. "What . . . you don't like Mitterand?" he added.

"Isn't he the one that declared that Israeli aggression in 1967 was a war that Israel waged to defend itself?"

"You don't ever want to forget? Is that it?"

"Why should we forget?"

He busied himself with accepting the joint from Marwan, taking several drags from it and offering it to me. I took two drags and passed it to Antoinette.

Her nails rested on my fingers for a moment, then wrapped around the joint and pulled it slowly through my fingers, touching me all the while.

The human moaning that accompanied the piano's melody occurred again. A feeling of numbness spread through my legs and my perception of the music grew keener.

Antoinette announced suddenly that she had to leave, in order to get back to her house in East Beirut. Jacques's wife offered to let her spend the night with them, but she refused, insisting that her mother would be worried if she wasn't at home. She flashed her eyes in my direction, so I stood up, too.

"We're headed in the same direction."

She nodded, saying, "I'll take you there."

Jacques and his wife saw us to the door. As soon as we headed out into the street, the cold air hit our faces.

Antoinette was unsteady and clung to my arm, resting her head on my shoulder.

"Can you drive?" she asked.

"No," I answered. "Why?"

"It feels like everything is spinning," she said.

"We'll leave the car and take a taxi."

"We won't find one at this hour. No. I'll drive."

She pulled a keychain out of her purse and we got in the car. She spent a long time looking for the car key before she found it. She turned the key in the ignition and the car started off with a surprising lurch that violently jerked me backwards.

"Easy does it," I said.

"I don't think I can drive all the way to East Beirut."

"So stay with me."

I turned my attention to the road, expecting an accident any second. But the streets were empty. It wasn't long before we crossed Hamra Street, and soon we were heading toward Wadia's apartment.

She stopped the car in front of the building and slumped her head forward on the steering wheel, saying, "I want to sleep."

"Come up with me and sleep at our place," I said.

"Clearly that's what's going to happen."

I stepped out of the car and waited until she got out and locked the door. Then I walked to the door of Wadia's building and called for Abu Shakir. Moments later, he opened up to let us in.

The elevator was on the ground floor so we got in. I held on to her arm just as she was about to stumble on the threshold. Then I closed the door and pressed the button.

She leaned her head on my shoulder, and I held her in my arms. She raised her face toward me and I looked into her eyes.

"Are you sure I'm not putting you or Wadia to any trouble?" she asked.

"I'm sure," I replied. Her eyes were incapable of staying focused, like the eyes of drunks. Her mouth was close to mine. Her lips were open and moist.

"Don't you want to kiss me?" she asked.

At that moment, the elevator stopped. I pulled aside its glass panels, then pushed open the metal door. We left the elevator and I took the apartment key out of my pocket.

I pressed the buzzer first. Then I put the key in the keyhole and turned it. I felt the door pull from the other side, then it opened wide to reveal Wadia.

His face lit up at the sight of Antoinette.

"Welcome," he said, stepping aside for her.

She walked in, saying, "I'm afraid you'll have to put me up for tonight."

Wadia put his arms around her and planted a kiss on her neck, then said, "Only for tonight?"

He directed his words to me while he was still embracing her: "When the heavy fighting was going on at the start of the war, when night fell, you spent the night wherever you were."

She gently freed herself from his embrace and headed to the bathroom without having to ask where it was. I followed Wadia to the living room after locking the door to the apartment. From his movements, I sensed that he was drunk.

He grabbed a bottle of vodka on the table and asked me, "Can I pour you one?"

I shook my head as I threw myself on the couch. He poured himself a glass and added a little orange juice to it.

"The night is wide open," he told me, after taking a swig.

Antoinette came back from the bathroom, having washed her face. He offered her vodka but she declined.

"I've got some pot, if you'd like," he offered.

"A cup of coffee would be better," she said.

I stood up. "I'd like one, too," I said. "I'll make it."

I went to the kitchen and lit the stove. I put the coffee pot on the burner. I waited until it boiled, and then I poured it. I carried two cups of coffee on a tray out to the living room.

I found Wadia engrossed in rolling a joint, while Antoinette rested her head on her palm and was lost in thought. I put a cup in front of her. I sat on the couch sipping my coffee.

Wadia finished rolling the joint, lit it, and offered it to me. I took two drags and gave it to Antoinette, who took a puff and then gave it back to him.

He took several pleasurable drags, then offered it to me, but I declined, saying, "I've smoked enough. I want to go and get some sleep."

"I have to go to bed now, too," added Antoinette, "so I can work in the morning."

Wadia finished the joint and then went off to his room and came back with a wide loose robe that he handed to Antoinette.

"I'll let Antoinette have my room and I'll sleep in the living room," I said.

"I can't take your room from you," she replied.

"I'll sleep in the living room," Wadia offered, "and Antoinette will sleep in my room."

"The problem is that I can't sleep by myself. I won't sleep a wink all night long."

"Then sleep with me in my room: it has two beds," said Wadia, putting his arm around her shoulder.

There were two beds in my room, too, but I didn't say a word. I left them and went to the bathroom to wash my face. Then I went to my room, took off my clothes, and put on my pajamas.

I stretched out on the bed. A little later I felt thirsty and went out to the living room and then the kitchen. The door to Wadia's room was open and the light was on. I noticed Antoinette in her underwear in the middle of the room. When I passed by again on my way back with a glass of water, I saw the door to his room was shut.

## 17

## THE FIFTH PART OF THE FILM

Jenin. Nablus. Jerusalem. Jericho. Bethlehem. Hebron. Black flags fly over the cities of the occupied West Bank. Posters lament the martyrs of Tel Zaatar. Israeli Army jeeps cruise the streets and city squares. Jeeps with two-way radio in the plazas and at intersections. (Note to self: Israeli military jeeps, with lowered carriages, are noticeably distinct, in the same way that Gestapo motorcycles with side-seats were.)

The road leading to Mount Lebanon. Syrian armored cars advance, firing their artillery guns.

A circle around a paragraph from a public statement by Kamal Jumblatt in the *al-Anbaa* newspaper: "The battle for Mount Lebanon approaches, so take up arms and hold firm; holding firm means we won't despair too much when one place or another falls."

Beside the previous paragraph are two headlines: "Jumblatt in a hurry to hold the Arab summit conference." "Abu Iyad criticizes Arab silence in the face of Syrian military acting alongside the Phalangists."

Washington. Dean Brown speaks to journalists: "We are trying to keep Lebanon from turning to the left." "Israel is a key player in the situation, since it is supplying the Maronites with weapons."

A circle around a paragraph from *Time* magazine, published September 13, 1976: "In the darkness of night, Israeli commandos dashed ashore in the Christian-controlled port of Jounieh, some 9 miles north of Beirut. As soon as they established contact with the Lebanese garrison, both forces spread out and secured a landing area. A helicopter slowly whirred up from an Israeli cargo ship standing offshore, guarded by a small armada of missile ships. The helicopter, *Time* has learned, brought to Jounieh a top Israeli official who spent the night in a series of secret conferences with various Lebanese leaders, then climbed back aboard his helicopter and flew out to sea again, just before dawn.

"The official was Israeli Defense Minister Shimon Peres. His brief 'invasion' of Lebanon – a nation with which Israel has no diplomatic ties – was the first of four trips between late May and late August. As if that were not extraordinary enough, he was accompanied on his third trip into Lebanon by none other than Israeli Premier Yitzhak Rabin, who held talks with as yet unnamed Lebanese leaders. Out of these negotiations has come a secret but potentially decisive Israeli intervention in the seventeen-month-old Lebanese Civil War. Acting with the agreement of Lebanon's Christian leadership and a moderate group of Muslims, Israel is moving to wipe out forever the Palestinian guerilla bases in southern Lebanon. As Foreign Minister Yigal Allon said last week, 'A situation will be created in which we will not permit any faction to allow the Palestine Liberation Organization to act against Israel from Lebanese regions close to the border.'

"Beyond that, the Israeli–Lebanese agreement has opened the way to an important readjustment in the Middle East lineup, one that could prove to be a genuine turning point in Israel's relations with its Arab neighbors."

Beirut. Jumblatt to reporters: "We've put our neck on the line."

Headline in a Lebanese newspaper: "The first Soviet official statement calling on Syrian troops to withdraw from Lebanon."

A statement by Yigal Allon in the Israeli newspaper, *Davar*: "The flame of civil war in Lebanon has consumed the PLO's utopian idea of eliminating Israel by establishing a binational Arab–Jewish secular democratic state to take Israel's place."

A circle around a paragraph from an American magazine: "The women of Cairo who are covered from head to toe are still a minority, as are those groups that call for dealing with the Copts by considering them '*dhimmis*', as was the case in the Islamic empire ten centuries ago. *Dhimmis* were excluded from full citizenship – that is, they were second-class citizens – and they either had to pay the non-Muslim *jizya* tax or become Muslim."

A headline in the newspaper, *Voice of the Tigers*, the mouthpiece of Chamoun: "The theory of coexistence in Palestine came to an end in Lebanon."

The headquarters of the Tigers forces. Chamoun reviews 3,000 Phalangist fighters in black uniforms on the drill field at their graduation from basic training. He addresses them, saying, "The war is a long one, and we are still at the beginning of the road."

A Lebanese gunman carries an artillery piece, wearing an armband with the cedar emblem. He speaks in French in a filmed interview carried out by British actress Vanessa Redgrave: "Every Lebanese should kill a Palestinian."

Pierre Gemayel and Camille Chamoun and Suleiman Frangieh walk through the gateway of an old palace. They are joined by Charbel Qassis in a sumptuously furnished reception hall.

A headline in a Phalangist newspaper: "Formation of a united military leadership headed by Bashir Gamayel."

A headline in *al-Safeer*: "Jumblatt calls on the Palestinians to organize and form a provisional government."

A newspaper headline: "George Habash, leader of the Popular Front for the Liberation of Palestine, criticizes the hesitation of the Lebanese National Movement to establish popular sovereignty."

A newspaper headline: "Moscow criticizes the extreme right and extreme left in Lebanon."

A newspaper headline: "Nayef al-Hawatmeh, the leader of the Democratic Front for the Liberation of Palestine, says: 'A military settlement is impossible.'"

A newspaper headline: "Habash says: 'No compromise. We will establish an Arab Hanoi.'"

A newspaper headline: "The fifth newspaper closure in Kuwait after parliament was dissolved and the constitution annulled due to fear of Lebanonization."

Lebanon's presidential palace in Baabda: the new president Elias Sarkis ascends the stairs.

Title card:

On September 21, 1976, Sarkis assumed the presidency from Frangieh, and immediately called on the Palestinian resistance to withdraw from Mount Lebanon.

Yasser Arafat to reporters: "All we ask is that he not stab us in the back and doesn't bargain with us or over us."

A newspaper headline: "Chamoun's Tigers fire at Jumblatt's car after his meeting with Sarkis."

A newspaper headline: "Attack on the ship carrying Jumblatt to Cyprus."

Damascus. Hafez al-Assad delivers an address to soldiers of the "Defense Squadrons": "Your efforts in Lebanon and your opposition to the conspirators have prevented the division of Lebanon."

West Beirut. Tripoli. Tyre. Sidon. Public events commemorating the sixth anniversary of the death of Gamal Abdel Nasser.

A newspaper headline: "The Soviet news agency Novosti on the anniversary of the death of Gamal Abdel Nasser: 'His absence is strongly felt.'"

Newspaper headlines: "Syrian forces enter most villages on Mount Lebanon. Joint nationalist forces fight and retreat." "Israeli sea blockade of Tyre and Sidon prevents the arrival of provisions and weapons for national forces." "The political council for the Lebanese National Movement criticizes Arab silence and the neglect of international progressive movements." "Bashir Gemayel declares: 'We will liberate Lebanon even if the Syrians halt.'"

A newspaper headline: "Yasser Arafat to fighters: 'To arms, for victory is at hand.'"

Damascus. President al-Assad makes a speech on television on the anniversary of the Yom Kippur War: "We are determined to continue to help Lebanon in order to rescue it from its sufferings and to preserve its independence and unity, and to save the Palestinian resistance."

A circle around lines from a Soviet newspaper: "Events in Lebanon have cast doubt on the nationalism of Arab regimes with regards to Palestine."

Riyadh Airport. King Khaled welcomes Sadat, Assad, Sarkis, Yasser Arafat and the Emir of Kuwait.

Beirut. Jumblatt to reporters: "The situation is in the hands of the oil states now."

Large headlines in a Lebanese newspaper: "Riyadh conference resolves on a ceasefire in Lebanon beginning from October 21, 1976. The conference resolves to change the Arab security forces into a Deterrent Force under the command of Sarkis. The new force will be made up of 30,000 troops, the bulk of which will be Syrian forces (21,000 troops) in addition to two Saudi and Sudanese battalions."

A photograph in a newspaper of the meeting between Jumblatt and Abu Jihad, the leader of the joint forces in Mount Lebanon and one of the most prominent Fatah leaders. Below the photo are two captions: "Abu Jihad: 'All is lost in the civil war'" and "Jumblatt: 'I demand a united position from the Palestinians.'"

Title card:
Finally the war halted.


Crowds of Beirut's civilians welcome the armored cars of the Deterrent Forces. A welcome and a slaughtering of sheep in Chouf, Keserwan and Jbeil. The Deterrent Forces occupy military barracks next to official military organizations. Their tanks cruise through bombed-out streets.

Newspaper headlines: "Return of telephone service between the two parts of Beirut. Electricity back for 8 hours a day."

A Beirut street. A bulldozer clears away rubble. In the middle of the street, a barricade made of two burned-out passenger cars.

A hospital room. In the center of it is a bed, with the independent Maronite leader Raymond Eddé lying on it. Jumblatt enters to visit. As he leaves he announces to a reporter: "I expect further assassination attempts."

A newspaper headline: "Al-Sa'iqa organization attacks the Democratic Front to reclaim its headquarters in the Studio Building."

Title card:

- The Swedish Red Cross announced that 700,000 Lebanese had been harmed in the war. And that 10,000 people are missing or unaccounted for in Lebanon.
- Losses to the telegraph and telephone systems were estimated at 110 million lira.
- Losses in capital in the years 1975 and 1976 were estimated at 700 million lira.
- Indirect losses to the national income in the manufacturing sector were 2.274 billion lira.
- Losses in imports were 5.35 billion lira.
- Losses in exports were 2.225 billion lira.
- The war made it necessary to restrict the number of Australia's visas for Lebanese citizens to 9,000.
- It was estimated that the war left behind a quarter-million orphans.

Kamal Jumblatt to reporters: "America has paid out 250 million lira during the course of the war."

The headquarters of the United Nations in New York. Votes are cast on a resolution for Israel's withdrawal from occupied Arab regions, and for the founding of a Palestinian state. The resolution is approved, with ninety votes in favor and sixteen against.

Damascus. Abd al-Halim Khaddam, Syria's foreign minister, to reporters: "Disarmament includes the Palestinian resistance movement. The criterion for its Arab nationalism is its relationship with Syria."

Amin Gemayel to reporters: "The Syrian position has saved us some very difficult steps."

The Beirut street where Kamal Jumblatt's home is located. The remnants of a detonated car-bomb near his home. Pieces of flesh on tree branches. Blood stains a nearby white car. An ambulance carries the victims of the explosion. A doctor makes a public statement to a reporter: "So far, two killed and twenty-four wounded."

A newspaper headline: "Elements from the al-Sa'iqa organization attack the offices of the *al-Muharrir*, *Beirut* and *al-Dustur* newspapers. Syrian spy agency attacks the offices of *al-Safeer*, arrests several of its editors, and transports them to a Damascus prison."

A newspaper headline: "Jumblatt demands the resignation of Colonel Ahmad al-Hajj, head of the Deuxième Bureau, whom Sarkis appointed as chief of the Arab Deterrent Forces."

A newspaper headline: "Phalangists refuse to shut down their radio broadcasts."

Zgharta. Frangieh's palace. The former president to reporters: "We won't throw down our rifles until calm returns."

A newspaper headline: "The Lebanese National Movement informs the Deterrent Forces' leadership of the two places for collecting their weapons."

Abu Mazen to reporters: "The resistance will not hand over its weapons but it will move them from the cities to the south."

The French magazine *Nouvel Observateur*. A circle around a paragraph from a conversation with Jumblatt: "The Palestinians had carried on a kind of mandate over us: military administration and the means of subsistence and communication were in their hands."

A newspaper headline: "Censorship of Lebanese newspapers has begun."

A newspaper headline: "United political leadership between Egypt and Syria. Agreement to hold the Geneva conference before April, provided that the Palestinians are represented by an independent delegation."

Alexandria. Saint Mark's Cathedral.

Title card:

On January 17, 1977, Egyptian Copts in Alexandria held the first conference of its kind in modern Egyptian history. In attendance was Pope Shenouda III, who, since his election to the papal chair in 1971, had won great popularity among the Copts. Abba Samuel, the official in charge of foreign relations for the Coptic Church, had played a prominent role in organizing this conference. The conference examined "freedom of belief" and "the freedom to practice religious ceremonies", "protection of the family and Christian marriage", "equality and equal opportunity and the representation of Christians in parliamentary bodies", and "the danger of extremist religious movements".

The conference presented several demands to the authorities: "cancelling the proposed law on apostasy from Islam", "abandoning plans to apply laws derived from Islamic sharia to non-Muslims", "revoking Ottoman-era laws that restrict the right to build churches", "rejecting sectarianism in filling government employment positions at all levels".

On the same day . . .

Egyptian newspapers carry giant headlines: "Cancellation of subsidies for some commodities in compliance with demands of International Monetary Fund. List of 25 commodities whose prices have 'moved'."

Title card:

Early morning the next day, January 18, 1977, demonstrations set out to protest the new price increases in Alexandria. Then, hours later, they broke out in Cairo. Before noon, the demonstrations had struck the length and width of Egypt.

On the next day, the demonstrations were joined by some elements that rashly gave in to looting and destruction. Angry masses in Aswan marched by the presidential retreat there that Sadat loved – it was his favorite winter headquarters – and he was forced to flee and return to Cairo under the protection of Central Security troops.

Dozens were killed, fallen victim to the bullets of Central Security.

Chouf in Lebanon. Mourners flock to the funeral of a local resident. Kamal Jumblatt joins the mourners. Some form a circle around him. He talks to them about his philosophy of death, saying: "A person smells the odor of his impending death three days beforehand."

Title card:

Two days later, on March 16, 1977, Kamal Jumblatt (age sixty) gets into his black Mercedes on his way from al-Mukhtara palace to his country house in Chawiya, where he was accustomed to secluding himself every Friday, immersed in books and nature, 1,500 meters above sea level.

But this time he wore khaki clothes, and helped several laborers move rocks in order to level a piece of land he had chosen for his private bodyguard. Afterwards he brought for his companions food consisting of eggs, local cheese and apples, to a table made of two large stones. When he finished lunch, Jumblatt stood up and said, "Let's go, we should be on our way." He put on his clothes, then got into the car with his companions – his driver and his private bodyguard – on the road to Beirut.

At the crossroads for Deir Durit monastery . . .

Blood fills the ground. Jumblatt's car pierced by bullets from every direction.

In front of the ancient al-Mukhtara palace. Beneath a cloth awning: Jumblatt laid out on a wide bier made of white silk, between his companions in life and death. Weeping women in black clothes, and white sashes, surround the bier. Long lines of people in black clothes pass in front of the bier in the rain. Machinegun volleys in the air mingle with sounds of thunder and flashes of lightning.

Beirut. A solemn procession of tens of thousands of people paying their respects at Jumblatt's funeral.

The site of the crime once again. A car with this license plate number: Baghdad 72719.

Title card:

> The car used by the perpetrators. But suspicions are directed toward another Arab capital.

A still photograph of another two-person meeting between Kamal Jumblatt and the Syrian President Hafez al-Assad in Damascus.

# 18

"There's only the last part of the film left, and it's about Operation Litani," Antoinette said as she took the reel out of the machine. "Do you think we'll be able to finish it tomorrow?"

"Why don't we try today?" I wondered.

She looked at her watch.

"It's three o'clock now. We have to have something to eat. And then I want to take you somewhere," she said.

I gave her a quizzical look.

"I want you to meet someone I know," she explained.

"Who?"

"I won't tell you now."

I stared at her in surprise.

"Do you trust me?" she asked.

"Of course."

"Then don't ask."

We left the office and went out into the crowded street. We entered a small, hole-in-the-wall restaurant. We had zucchini with tomatoes, meat and rice, along with lentil soup. Antoinette insisted on paying the bill, which came to 20 lira.

We went back to where she had left her Volkswagen, and we got in. A little later, we were setting out on the road leading to the airport.

We reached the Sabra refugee camp, and she turned the car off the road toward it. Several gunmen accosted us at a barrier made of barrels. They were wearing the insignia of the Palestinian Armed Struggle. One of them recognized Antoinette and greeted her affectionately, so they let us pass.

Antoinette stopped the car a few meters further on, beside a falafel vendor who had several chairs and wooden tables set out – an open–air restaurant. She got her purse and rolled up her window, so I did the same thing with my window. Then I got out of the car and stood there looking at the jars of colorful pickled turnips distributed among the tables of the small restaurant.

She pulled me by the arm and we set out on a street crowded with boutiques and shops, including one for used clothes, which hung from hangers attached to the ceiling. The walls were covered with slogans, political posters and pictures of martyrs.

We headed toward a network of back alleys, with humble homes – most of them no more than two stories tall – set on the sides. The smell of fried onions and coriander with garlic slipped its way into my nose. I nearly bumped into several children who were playing football. We were forced to stop and stand against the walls to make room so that three women in black frocks, with their heads wrapped in white kerchiefs, could walk three abreast.

The sound of a heated argument reached us through a window overhead. I heard a woman yell in a real Egyptian accent, asking for her passport so she could go back to Egypt. We passed the three women again and then kept walking for several minutes. Then we went inside a house and knocked on a door belonging to one of the two first-floor apartments.

A tall young man in pants and a sweater opened the door. A beaming smile lit up his face at the sight of us. We walked inside to a clean living room with a metal table and several chairs. At the far end was a desk with bookshelves above it.

He gestured for us to sit, then slowly took a step, moving one of his legs with difficulty. He took a chair facing us. He observed me silently without letting the smile disappear from his face. It was a handsome face, with sharp features, and filled with lines belied by the luxuriant black hair. A lock of it hung down over his brow, and there was a strange expression in his eyes, the significance of which I couldn't make out.

Silence settled over us and I lit a cigarette. Antoinette did the same. Finally, I forced a smile and asked her, "Aren't you going to introduce me to your friend?"

"Walid is Palestinian, originally from Jaffa. He is an art teacher at the camp school. He also does translating for the media institute."

After a moment, she added: "I talked to him about you. He is happy to meet you."

I looked at both of them in confusion. I noticed that he didn't take his eyes off her lips.

"He can't hear or speak," she said in a trembling voice.

I looked at him, and he exchanged looks with me. I got the feeling he understood what she had said.

"What do you want to drink?" she asked me. "I don't think we'll find alcohol here."

"I don't want anything to drink," I said quickly.

"I want some coffee," she said. "Should I make one for you, too?"

"Sure."

She walked to a door at the side of the room. I could see a gas cylinder through it. I looked up at the walls, and began scrutinizing the posters all over them. Among them was a newspaper aimed at children, of the kind printed to be displayed on a wall. I happened to glance at Walid, and I found him watching me with a friendly smile. I realized that the strange expression reflected in his eyes was the same one we always see on people with disabilities connected to hearing and sight. It makes them seem as if they are seeing you, but thinking about something else at the same time.

Antoinette walked in on us with a tray of coffee. I reached out for a cup, and she said:

"No. That's for Walid. He takes it with a lot of sugar."

"Why the surprise?" I asked her, helping myself to another cup. "Why didn't you tell me from the beginning?"

She hesitated. "I don't know," she replied.

Walid took two sips from his cup, then put it back on the tray. He turned toward the office, and picked up a piece of paper and a pen. He wrote several lines, then handed the paper to Antoinette.

"He welcomes you," she said, after reading the first line.

She silently finished reading what was on the paper, then folded it and put it in her pocket. She turned to look at him.

I finished my coffee, and fidgeted in my chair. I told Antoinette that I had an appointment back at the apartment in half an hour. She stood up. "We can leave," she said.

Walid's expression changed. A hint of worry appeared in his eyes. Antoinette gave him an inquisitive look, so he got out of his seat. He walked, limping, to his desk and sat there. He picked up a thick Flo-master pen and a piece of white paper.

Antoinette went over and stood behind him, telling me, "One minute."

Walid busied himself with the paper for several seconds, and then put it to one side and pulled out another one. Antoinette picked up the piece of paper, and then handed it to me.

I was looking at a drawing, the meaning of which I couldn't make out. It was made up of several lines and black marks. I turned the paper over in my hand. Eventually I recognized the map of Palestine as it had appeared in 1948, when Zionists cut out a small part of it where they declared their state.

Walid finished the second piece of paper, and was busy with a third. Antoinette handed me the paper, and I found that it was the same map, but the black mark that looked like Israel had grown bigger and expanded, and contained the West Bank up to the River Jordan, and the Sinai Peninsula, and Syria's Golan Heights, and the cities of Gaza and Rafah.

On the third piece of paper, arrows extended from the black mark to southern Lebanon. On the fourth, the arrows reached Beirut, Amman and Damascus. On the fifth, they extended to Baghdad, Kuwait, Dhahran in Saudi Arabia, and Benghazi.

I felt annoyed. I felt as if he was treating me like a student in his school. What he wanted to make me understand was something all Arabs "from the Atlantic to the Gulf" knew about. Soon my annoyance dissipated, and I saw that, on the face of things, circumstances proved just the opposite.

I folded the five pieces of paper and put them in my pocket, then I shook his hand. I left the apartment and stood waiting for Antoinette at the entrance of the building. On the wall opposite I saw a poster of a martyr. It had a bad photograph of a smiling face overflowing with youthful virility. Beneath the image was his name, and a notice that he had received academic military training, and that he was killed while dismantling an explosive charge.

Some time later, Antoinette joined me and we retraced our steps in silence to where we had left the car. As soon as we passed the barrier with the gunmen, we headed out on the road to the center of West Beirut.

"Walid's leg was hit during the massacre that King Hussein orchestrated for the Palestinians in Jordan in 1970," she explained. "I got to know him at the end of '75. He was completely normal. He talked and sang and everything. After Tel Zaatar, he went silent."

"Didn't he go to a doctor or a hospital?" I asked her.

"Everyone who examined him agreed that his hearing and vocal apparatus aren't damaged."

She slowed down to avoid hitting a car that had Syrian plates and was driving in the middle of the street. She pressed the horn several times, but to no avail. In the end, she was forced to stay behind the other car.

"He leaves me the freedom to do what I want. I can leave him if I want," she went on.

I gave her a puzzled look. Flushing red, she hastily added: "He doesn't touch me. But I won't leave him. I love him."

We traveled the rest of the way in silence. I wanted to get out of the car on Hamra Street, but she insisted on bringing me to the door of the building. I stood out on the street until she left, then I crossed to a grocery on the sidewalk opposite. I bought a kilo of grapes, several pieces of cheese, some canned goods, and a few cans of beer.

The elevator was on the top floor, so I opted to take the stairs. Wadia was out, so I set my purchases on the kitchen table. I took out a can of beer from the refrigerator. I put my finger in the pop-top ring but yanked it too quickly and it twisted. A spray of beer shot out of the can and landed on my face and clothes.

I poured the contents of the can into a glass, and dried myself. Then I carried the glass to the living room, and sat down next to the telephone. I gulped down half the glass in one swig, picked up the phone and dialed.

The phone rang for a long time before her voice came to me, cold and reserved.

"It's been two days since I've seen you," I said.

"You saw me yesterday."

"But you weren't alone."

She didn't reply, so I went on: "I want to see you."

"When?"

"Now."

"Impossible."

"Why?"

"Adnan's family came from their country home, and I can't leave them."

"What about your office?"

She laughed. "Wait until tomorrow."

"But I want you so badly now."

"Are you drunk?"

"All I've had to drink today is half a can of beer. I decided to abstain from alcohol."

She let out a sardonic laugh.

"I want to kiss you," I said. "All of you. Even your feet."

"Really?" she asked coyly.

"Really."

"I have to go now. Call me in the morning."

"It's better if you call me."

I hung up the phone. I poured the rest of the beer into the glass and drank it in one swallow. I lit a cigarette and turned on the television.

I watched the last scenes from an American TV series, where police cars converged as usual from all directions, their sirens wailing. After that came the news. It carried a report about an Arab summit meeting in Amman to be held within days. And statements by Egyptian officials on the occasion of the third anniversary of the historical peace initiative. The Egyptian foreign minister appeared on the screen, announcing that the peace treaty made the 1973 war Egypt's last. He was followed by the Egyptian chief of staff, Abu Ghazaleh, declaring the readiness of the Egyptian armed forces to defend the Gulf states.

I heard the sound of the outer door opening. Wadia walked in, carrying a bag of apples. I took the bag from him and put it on the table. He took off his jacket and threw it on the couch.

He gestured to the television, and asked, "Did you watch the news from the beginning?"

I nodded. "The states participating in the summit haven't been determined yet."

"I'll be going to Amman in the morning," he said. "I see you finished early today. Have you finished the work of going through the film?"

"We will be done in two days' time. After that, two or three days to write the voiceover, then I travel immediately after that."

"And the book?"

"The owner of Modern Publishing called me to apologize. As for Lamia, she hasn't finished reading the manuscript yet."

"Didn't you say you had an agreement with Adnan? I don't understand what she's up to. I'm afraid there's something funny going on."

"You mean they are trying to get out of the contract?"

"Something like that."

I shrugged. "In that case, my only option is Safwan."

"But Safwan won't pay you anything. For now, at least."

"So, all I have left is my payment for the film."

"How much will they pay you?"

"I don't know . . . We haven't talked about that yet."

"You should bring it up with Antoinette. There's nothing to be ashamed of. Everyone is paid. Do you want me to talk to her for you?"

"No need for that. I'll talk to her."

He put his hand in his jacket pocket and pulled out his notebook, then headed toward the telephone.

"Don't you need cash?" he asked as he dialed a number.

"Not yet," I replied.

"Why don't you write an article or a short story for a newspaper?" he asked, dialing again. "You can make some real money if you want."

"I know."

He put the phone up to his ear. "Write anything. Everyone does that. You know the current terminology – it's all straight from the revolutionary lexicon."

"I'm very stressed. And I haven't been sleeping well. I have a hard time holding the pen. I wouldn't even know how to write an opinion piece."

He put down the receiver and flipped through the pages of his notebook, adding: "How about an interview with a fascinating personality?"

"How much would an interview with Carlos be worth?"

"The international terrorist? There's a rumor going around that he's in Beirut."

I nodded. "If I meet him, I'll sit down and have a talk with him. I believe that's something I could do."

He looked at me in astonishment.

"You mean you know where he is?"

"No, but I might come across him."

He walked toward me in a state of excitement. "An exclusive interview like that would be priceless. All the newspapers and wire agencies in the world would compete to buy it. Are you being serious about this?"

"Of course."

"You would be the first person in the world to interview him."

"That's why I asked you about how much I could get for it."

"You would be the one to set the price. Listen. Let me come with you. We'll put together an unprecedented face-to-face interview."

"I'm not certain yet that I'll succeed in meeting him."

He looked at his watch, and then walked over to the phone. He stopped suddenly and started pacing back and forth in the living room while thinking. Then he picked up his jacket, put the notebook back in its pocket and put it on, saying, "I'd advise you to make this matter a priority. It would be the opportunity of a lifetime for any journalist. If you get cold feet or change your mind for any reason, I'm ready to go in your place. I'm going to the agency now. Call me there if you need anything."

I nodded, and my eyes followed him out the door.

# 19

I ate my breakfast quickly, then swept the apartment and tidied up the living room. I scrubbed the bathroom sink, the tub, the toilet seat and its cover. With some difficulty, I was able to remove the bits of soap stuck to the sink. I washed the dishes piled up in the kitchen, and brought a little order to its chaos. Then I shaved and showered. I changed my underwear. Then I hung the wet towel out to dry on the balcony, and put a clean one in its place.

Around 10 am, I called Lamia.

"Are you going to Fakahani today?" she asked me.

"Yes. Why?" I replied.

"I can drive you there. I won't be going to the office."

"Excellent. I'll be waiting for you. What would you say to coming up first for coffee?"

She hesitated for a moment, then asked me, "Is Wadia with you?"

"Wadia's in Amman. He won't be coming back before tomorrow."

"Okay."

"And what about your bodyguard? Will he be coming with you?"

"I'll get rid of him before I come," she said with a laugh. "Bye bye," she added, in English.

I poured myself a glass of cognac and sat down to drink it in the living room, as I observed the cloud-covered sky through the balcony door. Fifteen minutes later, the buzzer rang.

I hugged her with one arm while locking the door with the other arm. She gently extricated herself, saying:

"I escaped Abu Khalil, but I'll have to go back soon, otherwise he'll think I've been kidnapped."

She undid the buttons on her raincoat as she walked toward the sofa. Then she took it off and tossed it on a chair, followed by her purse. Only then did she sit down.

She was wearing tight brown chamois pants and a yellow blouse. There were thick woolen yellow stockings on her feet, in open-back platform shoes.

"Where's that coffee you claimed to have?" she asked.

"Coming right up," I said.

I hurried to the kitchen, made the coffee, and brought it out to the living room. I put it on the table. I sat next to Lamia and put my arms around her. Then I kissed her on the lips.

"What's that?" she asked suddenly, pulling away from me.

She was referring to a small black box mounted over the apartment door.

"The buzzer," I said, with an air of bafflement.

"Are you sure?"

"What else could it be?" I replied.

"A recording device or a hidden camera."

I laughed. She took a sip of coffee and put the cup back down on the tray, saying: "I'd like to use the bathroom."

I stood up to let her pass.

"You have to leave the apartment," she said.

"But why?" I asked, perplexed.

"I won't be able to if you stay here. I'm embarrassed."

"But where should I go?"

"Buy me something. Do you have mineral water?"

"I think so. There's a bottle or two of Sihha."

"I don't drink Lebanese water. Buy me a bottle of Perrier."

I put on my jacket and she accompanied me to the door. I locked it behind me. I had just gone out onto the street when it started raining heavily. I found that the grocery across the street was closed, so I ran to the corner and went into another store.

I bought a bottle of Perrier and hung around inside the shop in the hope that it would stop raining. When I saw it was starting to come down harder, I bought a newspaper, put it over my head, and ran back to the apartment.

She opened the door for me.

"Is everything all right?" I asked.

She laughed. "Everything's fine, *ya bey*," she replied.

I poured her a glass of mineral water, and offered her a glass of cognac, but she declined. I poured one for myself. I went to the bathroom and closed the door behind me. I stood and surveyed the room. Nothing gave away that she had been there. Then I discovered that the towel was not in the place I had put it. My eyes fell on a spray bottle on the edge of the sink that wasn't there before. I picked up the bottle and found that it was French. It said on the label that it was the best product for "cleansing intimate parts of the body and giving them a fresh scent and taste".

I put the bottle back where it had been, and stood there thinking: Did she forget it by accident? Or did she intend to leave it there so I could see it? Either way, it led to the same conclusion.

I went back to the living room and found that she had closed the door to the balcony, and lit the electric heater. She had taken off her shoes and socks, and had her legs stretched out in front of her on the table.

I sat down next to her, looking at her white, symmetrical feet and her slender toes, with the shiny coat of deep-red nail polish on her long nails. I saw her give her feet a meaningful look.

I got down on my knees and clasped her feet, running my hands over them.

"No corns or calluses," I said.

"Why would I have them?" she asked.

"Everyone has them," I explained.

"It's because of their shoes. I pay good money to get comfortable shoes."

"From Beirut?" I asked.

"No, from Xavier."

I hadn't heard the name before, so I stayed silent. I leaned my head over her feet. I brought my mouth to her toes, took one of them between my lips, and slowly sucked it.

I looked up at her and found that she was watching me in concentration. Her face had drained of any expression. I licked between her toes, then passed my lips over the back and sides of her feet up to her ankles.

After a moment, I bumped up against the hem of her pants. I adjusted my position on my knees and put out my hand to her middle. She refused for a little, but then helped me. Soon her pants were in a pile at her feet.

Her white thighs were revealed before my eyes. I felt her

soft skin with the palm of my hand. Then I leaned my head over them.

Her hidden scent made its way into my senses, light and captivating. I kissed her under her knees and between her thighs. The taste of her was cool and fresh, like the taste of a body directly after a bath.

A diaphanous fabric embroidered with lace presented itself to me, and I licked its rough texture that mingled with her softness. I pulled it down, and her hair – light, carefully trimmed – was exposed.

She leaned her body back until she was lying flat on the couch with her face toward me. I brought my face close, and her silky skin surrounded my cheeks. My lips attached themselves to her damp flesh. The taste of the salty sea made its way to my tongue, and I lapped it up with pleasure.

My jaw began to hurt, so I looked up at her. I saw she had her eyes closed. A moment later, I couldn't move my jaw any longer, so I backed away. I flung myself on a chair, dazed and exhausted.

After a moment, she opened her eyes. She sat up feebly and began putting her clothes back on. Then she asked me for a cigarette.

I lit one and gave it to her, then she lit one for me. I noticed that her eyes were brimming with tears.

"Today is the anniversary of my mother's death," she said in a whisper.

I moved over next to her and took her in my arms. She rested her head on my shoulder. Then she looked at my lap. Hesitantly, she put her hand on my crotch, then looked in my eyes and asked, "Did you . . . ?"

"Nothing happened. That's not what usually happens with me."

"And I wasn't doing anything to turn you on."

I looked at my watch over her head. "It's twelve o'clock now," I said. "I have to go. You should, too, otherwise they'll be asking about you."

"*Ouf* – this city gets on my nerves. It's so small! You can't move around freely in it without someone seeing you. I wish we were together in Paris. By ourselves. We could have fights and yell at each other. And sleep together."

"There are Arabs there everywhere you look."

"True. Alright then, Geneva."

"Do you know it well?"

"Of course. I've visited it several times."

"And did you stay at the Noga Hilton?"

"How did you know?" she asked in astonishment.

"Because all Arabs like you stay there."

"And what's wrong with that?"

"Nothing. Except that the owner of the hotel is an Israeli who gives Israel two million dollars a year. He accompanied Begin when he visited Cairo for the first time. He was with him to welcome Sadat at Beersheba last year."

She raised her eyebrows in disapproval: "And what do I have to do with all that?"

"True. What do you have to do with all that?"

After a moment, I added, "Also, I don't have the money to travel."

"I'd pay for you," she said eagerly.

I shook my head. "What makes you think I even want to travel with you?"

"What's gotten into you?" she asked, putting her hand on my chest to push me away.

Smoothing her hair, she stood up, picked up her bag and hurried to the door.

I hurried after her, and grabbed hold of her. Then I put my arms around her and kissed her. Her legs buckled and I clung to her body. She began to move slowly, then pulled away, saying:

"I have to go."

"Did you forget that you promised to drive me?" I asked.

"It's better if I don't, so that no one sees us together."

I let her go. I straightened out the couch and adjusted my clothes and hair. Then I put on my jacket and headed outside.

# 20

**THE SIXTH AND FINAL PART OF THE FILM**
Title card:

In May 1977, Menachem Begin became prime minister of Israel. Two months later, he visited Washington, carrying with him a plan to restart negotiations to settle the Middle East crisis. Before he traveled, he declared that Israel was prepared to participate in the Geneva summit, provided that the PLO was excluded.

But the visit resulted in his agreement with President Carter to get around the Geneva conference and remove the Soviet Union and the PLO from the negotiations.

There were clear indications about Sadat's aims, and about the keys to his personality. Begin found the opportunity was a suitable one for conclusively removing Egypt from the Arab bloc.

Begin began by making hints to Sadat via the royal palace in Morocco that he had information about a Libyan conspiracy against Sadat. He made it clear that he was prepared to give the details directly to a designated Egyptian deputy.

Sadat hastened to send the director of Egypt's military intelligence services to Rabat, where he met the head of the Mossad, who gave him the details of the conspiracy. Sadat immediately ordered a punitive attack on Libya. For a full week, Egyptian planes bombed Libyan positions at the borders, and beyond. With these raids, Sadat hoped to prove that he was capable of opposing a regime hostile to the United States.

Over the course of the following months, there was a flurry of secret communications, capped by a secret meeting between Moshe Dayan, Israel's minister of defense, and King Hussein of Jordan on August 24, and between Dayan and King Hasan of Morocco the next month.

Two months later, on November 19, 1977 . . .

Jerusalem Airport. President Sadat comes down the stairway from his private plane (which cost 12 million dollars, paid for by the Saudis) with Ephraim Katzir, president of Israel, beside him.

Title card:

On the first visit of its kind by an Arab president, and under the slogan of "Permanent peace at any price", and under the auspices of American hegemony, Sadat acknowledged the historical right of the Jews in Palestine, and in the Holy City, not to mention the right to the presence of Zionist settlers.

This admission was the turning point. Begin started talking about acknowledging the right to the presence of the Palestinians who remained until Zionist occupation, in the form of a plan of self-administration for the inhabitants of the West Bank and the Gaza Strip. As for those who were not under Zionist occupation, they had no right to Palestine, and had to be dissolved into the state they were living in.

The Israeli Knesset. Sadat makes a speech, declaring: "There will be no other wars . . . between Egypt and Israel . . ."

Title card:
A few days before . . .

Israel began testing Kfir planes, which were produced in their factories, in a surprise attack on the village of al-Izziya in southern Lebanon.

Headline in the Israeli newspaper *Yedioth Ahronoth*: "The leader of the Kfir squadron states that the execution was flawless, and the advanced systems worked outstandingly."

Jerusalem Airport. Sadat prepares to board his plane to head back to his country. He shakes hands with the leader of the Israeli Kfir squadron which attacked the village of al-Izziya; he himself is entrusted with accompanying Sadat's plane in the sky over Jerusalem.

A circle around a paragraph from an article with the byline of the journalist Jim Hoagland, in the *Washington Post*: "Investigations carried out by Congress, by way of the committee headed by Senator Frank Church, with some of the CIA leadership, have confirmed that King Hussein received sums of money from the CIA. While Gamal Abdel Nasser tried to bring down the conservative Saudi regime in the 1960s, Kamal Adham, the director of Saudi intelligence and its liaison officer with the CIA, was able to mobilize the greed of Sadat, who was vice president of Egypt at that time. At one point, Adham provided Sadat with a fixed personal income, according to a well-informed source who refused to provide detailed evidence."

Ismailia. The Egyptian president's luxury retreat. Sadat and his wife welcome Menachem Begin and his wife on Christmas Day, 1977. An open-air press conference. Sadat reads from a piece of paper: "We have agreed that the war of October, 1973 will be the last war between Egypt and Israel." Directly behind Sadat in the photograph, Moshe Dayan's black eyepatch can be seen.

Title card:
Two and a half months later . . .


South Lebanon, near the Israeli border. Small green tobacco shrubs spread out on the hills and lowlands. Entire families bent over doing farmwork. Camels and beasts of burden. Farmers lie down on the ground, in front of baskets of figs, grapes and prickly pears that they sell with the skin on. Palm fronds and orange tree branches. The Mays al-Jabal pond. Lebanese women wash clothes and household dishes in the muddy waters. Pack-animals drink from the same water. On the surface of the road Palestinian nationalist slogans have been drawn.

A young Lebanese woman wears a blouse with rolled-up sleeves. Her head is wrapped in a large kerchief tied behind her hair. In front of her is a long low board. On it is a layer of flour. To her right is the oven, consisting of two pieces of stone supporting a brass tray. The woman flattens a piece of dough on the low board, then spreads it out on the tray so it covers its entire surface.

The same place after sunset. The farmers return to their homes. The roads gradually empty out. From one house comes the sound of a girl singing:

> *"Oh Mama, from Tel Zaatar*
> *I'll send you a letter*
> *From a green tent*
> *To tell you what it's like here.*
> *Oh Mama, from Tel Zaatar*
> *Rockets burns the houses.*
> *Oh Mama, the wounded are dying*
> *Beirut wails and weeps*
> *There's no more houses there . . ."*

Darkness wraps itself fully around the roads. The howling of a wolf echoes in the distance.

Title card:
And suddenly . . .

Illumination bombs rain down one after the other on the fields. Massive explosions. Tongues of flame dart out in every direction.

Title card:

At 1 am on March 15, 1978, the concentrated Israeli attack began for the operation which computers had electronically assigned the name "Father of Wisdom", but which afterwards was known as Operation Litani. Thirty thousand soldiers participated in it, reinforced by planes, tanks and squadrons. The stated goal of the operation was "creating a security zone 10 kilometers deep".

Some hours later, Begin issued a statement in which he said, "There are days in which all citizens of Israel, as well as those of goodwill in different countries, say: 'Full respect to the Israeli Army.' And this day is one of those days. Over the last twenty-four hours, in poor geographical and air conditions, the Israeli Army has accomplished the task which the government placed on its shoulders, along a 100-kilometer-wide front."

A circle in pen around a paragraph from a book by Ezer Weizman, *The Battle for Peace*: "A few minutes after the first Israeli tank crossed the border into southern Lebanon, the telephone rang in the office of Eliazer Raymond, the head of our delegation in Cairo. In spite of the late hour, the leadership in Tel Aviv issued instructions to Raymond to call the head of the Egyptian spy services – General Shawkat – to deliver to him an important message. Raymond notified Shawkat: 'A short time ago, our forces began a limited operation on the Lebanese border to remove terrorist bases from the region. I hope that this limited operation will not hinder the talks between our two countries.' "

Dust-yellow Israeli Army tanks advance along a country road. On both sides are Palestinian children, handcuffed and blindfolded. Fires consume entire villages. People run in fear. Houses collapse. Blood on faces. Corpses in the road. A three-year-old girl with blood gushing from her severed leg.

A gunman wearing Palestinian insignia fires from the top of a hill. A mortar strikes the hill and it explodes.

A circle in pen around a paragraph from the memoirs of Muhammad Ibrahim Kamil, Egyptian foreign minister: "The morning after the Israeli invasion . . . I called President Sadat in his presidential retreat in El-Qanater El-Khairia to show him the statement I'd prepared . . . concerning the attack . . . but I wasn't able to talk to him because he was still sleeping. After that, I continued to try to reach him several more times, at regular intervals, but without success . . . So I went ahead and published the statement without waiting for Sadat's opinion about it, since the situation was embarrassing to Egypt, especially in the eyes of the Arab world . . .

"At 1.30 in the afternoon, Sadat called me at the ministry and asked me in a yawning voice why I had been trying to reach him by phone several times that morning, and I replied that it concerned the Israeli attack on Lebanon.

"With a laugh, Sadat said: 'Have they given them their thrashing yet?' I didn't know what he meant by that, so I asked him, 'Sir?' And he replied, 'I mean, have they taught them a lesson yet or not?' And I finally understood that he meant, 'Have the Israelis taught the Palestinians a lesson?'"

The town of Marjayoun. Two beautiful young women in the uniform of the Phalangist militia have guns slung over their shoulders and are directing Israeli tanks through the narrow village street. They exchange words in Hebrew with Israeli soldiers.

A van carrying several European journalists makes its way along a dusty road surrounded by trees and rocks. Along the side of the road are wrecked Soviet-made armored cars. From a distance the sound of bombs from Israeli planes reverberates. A Lebanese gunman is in charge of steering the van. Through a loudspeaker, he says: "We Christians have made an alliance with the Jewish people." Young men in the military uniform of the Phalangist militia and Saad Haddad's forces wave to the passengers in the van. The van approaches the village of Klayaa. People come out onto the roads. Some of them call out: "*Shalom*! Welcome!" Several girls run behind the van and throw rice on it.

The village of Tibnin. White flags on the roofs and balconies of some homes whose appearance suggests that their owners are wealthy. A Lebanese vendor leans contentedly against a Mercedes, having spread out on the ground packets of cigarettes, bottles of whiskey, playing cards and condoms.

The town of Khiam. Wind whistles through shattered windows. An empty tin can rolls around, making an eerie clatter. The town is completely destroyed, with no trace of human life.

Title card:

The town of Khiam had a population of 140 thousand Shia before the Israeli attack.

The town mosque.

Title card:

Under the supervision of Israeli forces, the troops of breakaway Lebanese leader Saad Haddad gathered over one hundred Shia – men, women and children – in this mosque, and set them on fire.

The town of Marjayoun. Ezer Weizman, Israeli minister of defense, inspects the village. Saad Haddad walks up to Weizman and his companions. He stands at attention silently in front of them, then gives the military salute. He puts his arms around Weizman's neck and hugs him for a long time, with tears pouring from his eyes.

Haddad: "All our respect to the Israeli Army. In the name of all Lebanese, I offer a greeting to the Israeli Army."

A circle around a paragraph from Israel's *Davar* newspaper: "The leader Haddad and the scholar Francis Rizq, teacher of literature in Klayaa and Haddad's political advisor, are two cheerful and goodhearted individuals, especially when they are under the protection of the Israeli Army. Their happiness shows because they are basking in the light of Israeli and world opinion. They are prepared to answer questions from the press in Hebrew, Arabic, English and French."

A convoy of green Land Rovers. The first car carries the leader Saad Haddad who wears the uniform of the Lebanese Army. He is surrounded by his men, armed with American machineguns. The cars pass through an abandoned village. Some of them stop in the village square.

One of Saad Haddad's gunmen emerges from a house in the village balancing a wooden table on his head. He heads toward the Land Rover, puts the table in it, and goes back the way he came. Another gunman helps a colleague carry a big gas oven. A third gunman, annoyed, examines the contents of an abandoned house. He only finds a long steel rod, and in exasperation, he picks it up.

Title card:

> On the fifth day after the start of the operation, the UN Security Council issued Resolution 425, calling for the withdrawal of the Israeli Army from southern Lebanon.
>
> Two days later, at 6 pm on March 21, 1977, the Israeli Army held its fire after reaching the Litani River, following consultations by telephone between Begin and Washington. The day before, in Damascus, the foreign ministers from the Arab states who refused any acknowledgment of or negotiation with Israel (Syria, Libya, Iraq, Algeria and South Yemen) adjourned their meeting without deciding on any action against Israel.

Beaufort Castle, which has looked out over southern Lebanon since the days of the Crusaders. Israeli armored cars surround the castle. The main gate to the castle is blocked from inside by the piled bodies of the dead and wounded wearing Palestinian insignia.

A circle around a paragraph from an Arabic newspaper in East Jerusalem: "This war has restored respect to Palestinian dignity. It can be boasted that the Palestinians by themselves plunged into a war against Israel in full view of a feeble Arab world. The anger from the Arab world has created a feeling of shared involvement and unity, the likes of which the Palestinians have not witnessed for a long time."

Washington. The US State Department building. An official spokesman to reporters: "The State Department is still studying whether Israel violated its purchase agreements for American weapons, which it used in South Lebanon. The agreements prohibit the use of advanced weaponry (such as

F-15 planes) for attack purposes, although they are allowed to be used for defense."

A circle around a paragraph from the Israeli newspaper *Yedioth Ahronoth*: "The commander of the Israeli Air Force, David Ivri, commented on the statement from the US State Department regarding weapons, saying, 'I can state clearly and decisively that we did not violate any clause in the agreement. We used the planes to defend our forces from the air. This weapon is a kind of powerful shield for our forces, which didn't result in any violation, because we are only talking about defense.'"

The Israeli minister of defense, Ezer Weizman, speaks with a correspondent from the Israeli newspaper *Maariv*:

Journalist: "In the course of the advance planning, did you take into consideration the complicated aspects of an operation of this size: 150,000 refugees fleeing in fear of the Israeli Army, and hundreds of civilians – or perhaps more – killed and wounded?"

Weizman: ". . . the Lebanese Civil War has produced lots of refugees, with no end in sight and in numbers that surpass those produced by the Israeli Army's operation and the operation by the Jordanians in 1970, and by the Syrians when they entered Lebanon, when they slaughtered a lot more 'ravagers' than the Israeli Army has in the last ten days."

Journalist: "You are an experienced soldier: didn't you feel a pang of conscience when you saw the Israeli Army using its most advanced planes and artillery, and with a force such as this, against opponents supplied with – at best – Kalashnikovs, and in many cases opponents who have nothing to defend themselves with?"

Weizman: "In every war you have a heart, a conscience, and all kinds of remorse. Military men who have known the terrors of war and its atrocities up close love peace more than others do. But what should we have done? Should we supply our soldiers with Galil rifles because they have Kalashnikovs? Like anyone else, I have what we can call things that keep me up at night. But I have visited the Lebanese wounded in Israeli hospitals, and I was struck by a feeling that was not entirely pleasant."

Title card:

- The cost of Operation Litani, according to Israeli sources:
- 30 million dollars.
- 1,300 Lebanese and Palestinian dead.
- Several thousand wounded.
- 150,000 inhabitants of South Lebanon who lost their homes and have taken refuge in the north.

A circle around a paragraph from the Israeli magazine *Bamahaneh*, under the byline of Haim Raviv: "The 'ravagers' and their organizations had two surprises in store for them last week: the first was the large scale of the Israeli Army's operation in South Lebanon, and the second was the hope-crushing response from the Arab states.

"Egypt and Syria, the two leading states of the opposition, have made it known, each in its own way, that they are unprepared to enter into a confrontation with Israel. Egypt announced that it would continue to adhere to the peace initiative, and Syria acknowledged that it would not be dragged into a war with Israel prematurely.

"But there had to be some pretense of action: in Damascus, an unscheduled conference of rejectionist states was held. And King Hussein rode the Palestinian horse, calling for an Arab summit meeting. Statements were issued condemning the Israeli attack. The Egyptians sent a medical team to aid non-militant casualties. Everyone is pleased with the opportunity to weaken the PLO."

A circle around a paragraph from the Israeli newspaper *Haaretz*: "No doubt the Americans were informed of the operation before it began. We would not be mistaken if we were to say that they knew, in a general way, the primary points that Israel would occupy in the sector along the border."

A circle around a paragraph from an American newspaper: "The information provided to various Arab parties, and which reached them by way of the United States, informed them that the operation would be limited in duration and in geographical extent. That is why Syria's rulers took a very low profile at first. On the first day, Syrian media devoted only a few sentences to it. Thus, the expansion of the operation from 10 kilometers to 40 was a surprise. America was either in collusion with Israel in a campaign of deception, or it had itself fallen prey to Israel's deception."

The town of Taybeh in South Lebanon. It looks like a ghost town.

The town of Qantara. Most houses are still standing, but the windows have no glass, and the entrances have no doors. Water pipes and faucets have been pulled out. Enormous holes in the walls. Shop doors torn away. Their contents plundered or destroyed. An Israeli jeep weighed down with televisions, refrigerators and furniture.

A circle around a paragraph from the Israeli newspaper *Haaretz*: "A soldier told us: 'Looting has been a part of all of Israel's wars. We had good luck here. I was in Egypt in '73, and because of the bad living conditions in Egyptian villages on the west bank of the Suez Canal, we hardly found anything of value. We only confiscated blankets and sheets, and clothes that were sent to the country via the American air resupply route. They were excellent quality and worth millions of lira. They were distributed to tens of thousands of soldiers. During the long months leading up to February 28, 1974, the date of our withdrawal from the west bank of the Suez Canal, the Egged buses that carried soldiers to spend their leave in Israel were packed to the gills with those goods."

A circle around a paragraph from the Israeli newspaper *Davar*: "Material and human assistance continues to be offered by the Israeli Army to Lebanese villages that have been damaged during the course of the recent battles. Yesterday, around fifteen prefabricated freestanding homes were brought from Israel to the Muslim village of al-Abbasa. The homes were set up on public land in the village. The first group of Lebanese families whose homes in the village were destroyed during the battles took up residence in them. Around 600 individuals remain in the village out of 6,000 who lived there before the outbreak of the war. Most of the inhabitants fled to Beirut."

The US Secretary of Defense Harold Brown on American television: "The Israelis have admitted that they violated their agreement with the United States with respect to the use of cluster bombs in certain cases. The United States have examined with Israel Israel's promises not to repeat this violation.

But I don't want to place any more emphasis than necessary on this matter. Because the important thing with regard to Lebanon is that there is withdrawal from this area."

Title card:

> Fragmentation bombs are considered the most dangerous and lethal weapons in the US arsenal. They are extremely effective when used against tanks and armored cars. If they are used in civilian areas, the result is a bloodbath.
>
> These bombs were dropped from planes in cylinders, each of which carried a large number of slivers. At a certain height, these cylinders open up and each one releases 650 burning slivers, at 5.6cm diameter each. They fly outwards in different directions. One kind contains a timing device that makes the shards explode some time after the target is hit. Israeli planes used this kind in their bombardment of hospitals and children's shelters in southern Lebanon.

A spacious dining hall. Several American and Israeli military officers and civilians surround a table piled high with different kinds of food. Enormous electric chandeliers hang from the ceiling. At the head of the table sits Mordecai Gur, chief of staff of the Israeli Army. He is making a speech to those in attendance, saying, "When I ordered the use of fragmentation bombs in Lebanon . . . I never had any doubt that it would be in keeping with the spirit of the agreement made between our two countries, and the spirit of the American people."

Gur in an interview with a reporter from the Israeli magazine *Al HaMishmar*:

"Journalist: When bombing targets, did you make any distinction between the 'ravagers' and civilians?"

"Gur: I don't have a selective memory. I've served in the army for all of thirty years. Don't you realize what we did all those years? What we did along the Suez Canal? We created one and a half million refugees. We bombed Ismailia, Suez, Port Said and Port Fu'ad. One and a half million refugees."

A circle around a paragraph from *Haaretz*: "Israel's success lies in the fact that the United Nations – which in reality is the forces of NATO in blue helmets – is currently standing on the Litani River, not on Israel's borders or within the Occupied Territories. Then there are the Christian pockets, and Israel is asked to pull back, but it hasn't done so, and the Syrians haven't gotten involved. Also, prominent Shia in Lebanon's parliament have laid the blame on the Palestinians for the disasters that have befallen Lebanon. And the Druze cohort has issued a similar statement. Hostility to the PLO has become noticeably prominent among the Lebanese public."

A circle around a paragraph from the Israeli newspaper *Davar*: "We must secure a peace treaty to be signed in the future with Lebanon's government, which will make possible the joint exploitation of the waters of the Litani River."

Title card:

"It is inconceivable that Palestine will remain confined by its present borders. For the Jews have the ability to spread out and expand into all the lands that surround it, from the Mediterranean to the Euphrates, and from Lebanon to the Nile. These are the lands that have been given to the Chosen People."

– Norman Bentwich

"We will never abandon Israel."

– Henry Kissinger

# 21

The final scenes of the film depicted the Israeli forces' withdrawal operation from South Lebanon, and the arrival of United Nations forces to take their place. I suggested to Antoinette that these scenes should be removed, and the movie should end with the Israeli occupation at the Litani River. I said that that solution would elevate the film from being merely a record of events to the level of a vision of the future. Because Israel has a history of growing, expanding and swallowing up territory. If it left Lebanon in 1978 after a three-month invasion, then it left behind in its place "NATO forces with blue helmets," as Israeli leaders themselves put it. Likewise, nothing could prevent them from coming back at any moment.

Antoinette concurred with me about this, and we agreed that I would buckle down in the apartment for two or three days, during which time I would finish writing the required voiceover.

I left her as she was winding the last reel of the film, and went back to the apartment. Wadia hadn't yet returned from Amman, so I took a bath. I made a cup of coffee. I sat down and flipped through the pages where I had recorded the film's scenes. I wrote down some observations, then I put the papers to one side. I made myself a light dinner and ate it, accompanied by two cans of beer. Then I headed to bed.

My sleep was light and restless. I was aware of Wadia's return, and his departure in the morning. Finally I got myself out of bed, feeling sluggish. I had breakfast and stood out on the balcony to smoke. I noticed that the streets were completely quiet. The shops were closed. Then I remembered that today was Lebanon's independence day.

I sat at Wadia's desk. But I didn't have the energy to work. I pulled the telephone over and dialed Lamia's number. I listened to the phone ring for a long time. Then I put the receiver back and walked to my room.

I put on my jacket. I made sure I had my passport in its inner pocket. I counted the cash I had on me and found that it came to no more than 200 lira. Then I left the apartment.

I headed toward Hamra Street, crossing streets that were almost empty of pedestrians. When I reached that familiar thoroughfare, I walked by Wimpy's and the Mövenpick, then the Hamra Cinema and the Red Shoe. I stood on the corner by the Red Shoe and observed the Modka café on the sidewalk opposite.

I crossed the street and walked by the Modka. I kept walking as far as the Café de la Paix.

I pushed open the glass door and went inside. I sat down at a seat covered with artificial leather. A girl caked in makeup brought me a cup of Arabic coffee.

I sipped the coffee while smoking a cigarette as I watched the few other patrons. Then I paid my bill and left the café. I turned left and took a leisurely walk. I passed by the al-Nahar newspaper offices, and the Banque du Liban. I reached Burj El-Murr Square, then I looked out from the vantage point of the Fu'ad al-Shihab Bridge.

I passed through an abandoned checkpoint made of barrels into the neighborhood of Zuqaq al-Blat. The whole area seemed completely abandoned. Soon the street descended toward the left. A checkpoint blocked my path, with some gunmen standing there whose identity I couldn't make out. But they paid no attention to me, and I walked through. A little later, I found myself in Riad al-Solh Square. I headed right and entered Martyrs' Square.

Old Beirut's main square appeared, surrounded by ruins on all sides. The old houses, most of which dated to the Ottoman era, were still standing. But their windows and the doors to their shops had been turned into dark holes pierced by twisted iron rods. On the roofs lingered the remaining frames of neon signs, which transformed the square at night into a blaze of light – prominent among them were the traces of an advertisement for Laziza Beer and Gandour Chocolate beside a Coca-Cola bottle.

In spite of that, the square teemed with activity. In front of the demolished buildings, wooden carts were lined up, carrying all kinds of goods, such as clothes, shoes, dishes and electrical appliances. In the entranceways of some demolished shops sat money-changers. Looking over all this were several armored cars bearing the emblem of the Deterrent Forces.

I walked around the square, looking for an alley that had a shop selling used foreign books, which I had dealt with on my previous visit. I entered an alley with a shop for cigarettes, newspapers and magazines at its entrance. A large poster on the wall next to the shop caught my eye: it consisted of a photograph duplicated several times of the top half of a naked woman, with her right arm wrapped around a naked man's head. He was leaning with his mouth against her ear. His hair was draped around her head; she had her lips open and her eyes closed. The multiplication of the image suggested that this moment was drawn out and repeated.

I looked at the photo for a long time. Beneath it I could see a line of text in small print, so I got up close. I could make out the words printed in English: "The orgasm is a response that humans alone possess. No other mammals experience moments of intense climax like that during sexual intercourse."

Looking at the poster wholly engrossed me, so I only noticed the sounds emerging from a dark door at the end of the alley when a group of shabby-looking men came out of it all at once. Soon I could make out the sound of women moaning: that's when I realized it was coming from a theater. From the men coming out, and the fact that there was no billboard out front, I gathered it was a cheap movie hall showing the worst kind of X-rated movies.

I walked down the alley all the way to the end, and then found myself at an intersection where three streets met. A locked storefront carrying the name Gemayel Pharmacy looked out over it. I didn't grasp the significance of the name until the stern face of the Phalangist leader, with mad-looking eyes, stared out at me from small-size posters on the walls. I realized that I had unwittingly entered the other section of Beirut.

I was about to retrace my steps when a black car pulled up beside me, and its two rear doors opened at the same instant. The next moment, two men surrounded me, grabbed my arms and then pushed me into the back seat. Instantly, the car shot forward and took off at high speed, its tires letting out a high-pitched squeal.

Before I could make out the face of anyone else in the car, a thick blindfold came down over my eyes, and practiced hands tied it forcefully behind my head. The hands reached into my pockets, under my arms, behind my back, between my legs and above my socks.

My body tensed up in anticipation of being hit. It occurred to me that I was in a better situation than I was the time I was arrested, when I was put into a similar car, next to the driver, and then punches rained down from behind on my neck and head.

The car slowed down and then came to a stop. I heard the sound of someone opening the doors. The person sitting to my right moved, while roughly pulling me out of the car.

I stumbled and would have fallen if one of them hadn't propped me up from behind while cursing me out. Then he grabbed my left arm and pulled me across a narrow stretch of sidewalk that ended after several steps. After that, we walked for a little. Then we went up two other steps and continued walking. A little later, we went down a long staircase and through a damp place where our footfalls echoed loudly.

My escorts halted, and I heard the sound of a key turning in a lock. Then cold air brushed my cheek. The hands that had been clutching my arm let go of me. One of them gave me a rough push forward, and I nearly fell on my face. Then I heard the sound of a nearby door slam, and the sound of footsteps getting fainter.

I stayed frozen in place, and sharpened my senses to make out whether there was someone nearby. My hands were free, so I hesitantly lifted them to my face. When no one tried to stop me, I tore the blindfold from my eyes.

A few seconds passed before I was able to see anything. I found myself all alone in a long, semi-darkened room with a high ceiling. Light made its way in through a skylight obstructed by iron bars. The room was bare of any furniture, and there was nothing in it that gave any suggestion of the character of the place or its owners. At the far end of the room, I saw several cardboard boxes. I walked toward them, and found they were empty. One of them bore the name of an American cleaning powder.

I searched for my pack of cigarettes but didn't find it. I noticed that all my pockets were empty. And my wristwatch had been taken from me. I estimated the time to be close to two or three o'clock.

I walked up to the door and found that it was made of solid steel. I leaned down to the keyhole, and put my eye up to it, but I couldn't distinguish anything outside, because of the lack of light. I moved my eye away and stuck my ear to the hole, but I didn't hear a sound.

I backed away from the door and walked to the end of the room, then I turned and walked to the other end. I began walking back and forth across the room until I felt tired. So I sat down on the bare ground, leaning my back against the wall. Soon dampness began spreading into my body, so I stood up. I went to the door, and put my ear to the keyhole and listened.

My ears picked up the sounds of doors slamming, footsteps and muffled shouts. Footsteps approached and I heard some-one say angrily: "The bastard was shooting at us." Another one answered him, saying: "Come on. What do you want her for? There must be a thousand girls who wish they could get their hands on your salary." A third voice reached me, this one in a tone of command: "Do you have authorization from the party?" The voices clashed with each other and I couldn't make out a single word. It wasn't long before they gradually grew faint and distant.

I stood up straight and noticed a light switch beside the door. There was an electric lamp hanging from the ceiling. I flicked the switch several times, but without result. I could feel the cold more strongly, so I jumped up and down repeatedly, then started some warm-up exercises until I felt tired.

There was one corner in the room protected from the draft coming through the skylight – the one taken up by the cardboard boxes. I walked over to it, and started moving the boxes, taking them to another corner. Then I flattened one of them between my hands, put it on the floor, and sat on it. I did the same thing with another box and put it behind my back.

I enjoyed a little warmth until darkness fell, and the two boxes became saturated with the dampness of the walls and floor. The cold was soon penetrating into my bones. Coiling myself up did me no good. A little later, I had a strong urge to urinate.

I knew by experience that as long as I was by myself and didn't have a way to resist or put pressure on them, then no matter how much I yelled or banged on the door, I wouldn't change anything about what had been decided for me. Most probably I would run the risk of getting myself hurt. So I decided to wait until my kidnappers revealed their intentions.

But urine pressed on my bladder, and made me abandon my wisdom or fear, so I walked up to the door and started pounding on it with all my strength while shouting and calling out.

After a while my hands hurt, so I stopped the pounding and listened. I heard footsteps approach. A key turned in the lock and then the door opened up onto a dim electric light, and a young man carrying a machinegun slung over his shoulder, with a cigarette dangling from his mouth that gave off the smell of hashish.

"What are you knocking for?" he said to me sharply.

"I want to go to the bathroom," I said.

He shut the door without saying a word. I stood there, confused and contemplating whether I should start pounding on the door some more. Soon the door opened again. The young gunman appeared, holding a plastic bucket that he tossed at my feet. Then he closed the door in order to lock it, but I objected, saying: "I want to speak to the person in charge here."

"Not my concern," he replied.

He pushed me away, then pulled the door closed, and turned the key in the lock.

I carried the bucket over to the corner that was occupied by the cardboard boxes, and urinated. I felt relief. I resumed pacing the room back and forth, groping about for a little warmth. Then I sat down on the floor in the corner I had prepared for myself. I lay down with my knees bent and my arms beneath my head. I fixed my eyes on the thin strip of light underneath the door.

I must have nodded off for some time, because I suddenly became aware of a sound at the door. I found that it was open, and a broad-bodied man had planted himself in the doorframe. He had a machinegun in his left hand. Dim light fell from behind him onto part of the floor in the room, concealing his face from me. But I perceived the movement of the machinegun in his hand, gesturing me to come out.

I stepped outside, and he forcefully grabbed me by the arm. I saw that he was a man noticeably advanced in age, with a head of white hair, although obviously endowed with bodily strength. We walked along a long passageway lit by a single electric lamp, and with two other doors opening onto it. The smell of the air, the heavy dampness coming from the walls, and the tiled floor made me feel that we were below ground.

We went up a steep staircase to another passageway, this one flooded with the warmth of strong light from fluorescent lamps. The floor was covered with colorful linoleum. The passageway was long, and at the end of it hung a flag next to a photograph I couldn't clearly make out.

My escort came to a stop in front of a door and knocked on it. Then he turned the handle and pushed me in front of him. He entered behind me and closed the door.

I was struck by the heat coming from the radiator on one side of the room. I saw that I was facing a desk, behind which sat a heavy-set, rough-lipped, clean-shaven young man. He was talking on the phone with his eyes on a color television screen that rested on top of a wooden table beside the desk. He was wearing a short-sleeved shirt with the top buttons undone, revealing thick hair on his chest and arms. The hair on his head was fine and black, carefully trimmed and parted on the left.

I couldn't understand anything he was saying on the phone because he was speaking French in a low voice. I directed my attention to a piece of cloth hanging on the wall above his head with a colorful cedar tree embroidered on it. On another wall there was a piece of paper with a line of Arabic written on it in a substance like liquid gold: "Of the repositories of knowledge in the world, their treasures are from Lebanon. Of the languages of nations, their most beautiful letters come from Lebanon. Of the Seven Wonders of the World, their greatest legend comes from Lebanon. The tree of eternal life selected for its everlasting abode a mountaintop from Lebanon. The Son of God was baptized in water from Lebanon. I wonder: did Adam leave Paradise for your sake, O Lebanon?"

The young man finished his phone conversation, put down the receiver, and continued watching the television screen for a moment. Then he reached out and turned it off. He directed his attention to several pieces of paper in front of him, among which I recognized the contents of my pockets. He flipped through them with short, plump fingers that had long, manicured nails.

He addressed me without taking his eyes off the papers in his hand.

"I can't find any indication here of your sect."

"I don't understand what you mean," I said.

"Your religion," he asked. "What is it?"

For the first time, he lifted his eyes up at me, and two cold, yellowish circles looked out from a bloated face with oily skin.

"Aren't you going to introduce yourself to me first?" I asked. "And tell me why I'm here?"

A ghost of a sardonic smile appeared on his lips.

"You don't know yet?" he asked.

"I could guess where I am. But I don't know why I've been abducted."

He slowly lit a French cigarette, then explained: "You'll find that out after you tell me first what you're doing in Beirut, and where you're staying. You're living in West Beirut. Isn't that right?"

I nodded.

"So you won't tell me what your religion is?"

"What does my religion have to do with it?" I asked.

He stared at me for a moment, and then spoke in the tone of someone using self-control: "Religion is the mark of a man. His identity. It's what determines his relationship to his Creator."

"Then defining it is of no importance," I replied. "Every individual determines his relationship to his Creator according to his religion. And as far as I'm concerned, religions are all the same to me."

"That's not how we see it. For all of its existence, Lebanon has been threatened with annihilation by Islam."

"I have another idea of the danger that has threatened Lebanon, and which is threatening it now."

"You're in luck that I want to talk logically with you. It gives me a chance to explain my point of view."

I paid no attention to him and went on: "It's based on you being a majority in Lebanon. That's a subject for debate. Because there are those who say that Muslims are the majority now. In any case, whether you are the majority or minority, this doesn't change the nature of the danger that is threatening Lebanon. It's the same danger that threatens the Arab and Muslim countries and all the states of the third world."

He shook the ash from his cigarette into a silver dish on which the white bayonets of three rifles embraced each other, and said, "You're talking about an imaginary danger. I'm referring to Arab expansion, and that's a real danger."

I laughed. "Where is this Arab expansion? There's only an Arab nationalist awakening that is uprooting all religions. In fact, some activists in this awakening are Christians, as you know."

"They are Arabs. As for us, we are Phoenicians."

I looked at him in disbelief.

"Are you being serious? I'll say it again: whether you're Phoenicians or Arabs, it won't change the reality of the shared danger that confronts all Lebanese, Syrians, Iraqis, Egyptians, Iranians and so on."

He put out his cigarette in the gun-ashtray and lit a new one.

"So what do you think about the oppression that Christians are confronted with in Egypt?"

I took my time in answering as I thought of a suitable response. He put on a victorious smile and said, "Have you thought about it? Have you considered it?"

"I won't claim that there isn't discrimination," I hastened to say. "But it doesn't rise to the level of oppression. Also, part of it is artificial. The other part is a legacy of the past. When we imposed secularism on the state, we put an end to all trace of it."

"What I've seen in Egypt is just the opposite of that. It's a profound and historical oppression. And it's also growing."

"This is what I meant when I said that a part of the existing discrimination is artificial. It's what Islamist groups are practicing and calling for. I myself have heard one of these fanatics say that Pope Shenouda is more dangerous to Egypt than Begin is. In that regard, he is entirely in agreement with you. You are allied with Israel against your fellow countrymen."

He shrugged. "You can't blame a drowning man for asking the Devil for help."

"How do you know he will really help you? That he won't seize the opportunity to devour you?"

He laughed derisively. "Will he devour a corpse that foreigners have squeezed the life out of?"

"You mean the Palestinians? Their presence in Lebanon is what protects you from the Israelis."

"No one protects Lebanon from anything. Our weakness and our neutrality is our weapon. So long as we don't attack anyone else or threaten them, no one will put us in harm's way."

"Do you really think that?"

His cheeks flushed red. But he continued to hold fast to his outward calm.

"What matters to me is your admission of the actual oppression of Christians in Egypt. It makes me happy that we are in agreement on that point."

"On the contrary," I replied. "We are not in agreement at all. There really is discrimination. But you oppose it with reverse discrimination, while I oppose it with the complete elimination of religious division. During the fighting in 1975–76, there appeared among you a movement to remove religion as a category from identity cards. That's what we need. Secular states, not religious ones, where the place of the individual is determined on the basis of his ability, not on the basis of religion, family or tribe."

"You mean, abolishing sectarianism?" he said disparagingly. "That's impossible. The end of sectarianism means the end of religion."

"I don't think I can persuade you to come around to my point of view," I said, with a note of weariness. "What I'm asking of you now is to give me my papers and my passport and to let me go."

He raised his eyebrows. "Just like that?"

"Yes, just like that."

He let out a short laugh. "I didn't expect that you would get bored of our hospitality so quickly," he said.

I followed his lead, saying: "What hospitality? I haven't eaten a thing all day. The room is cold, with no bed, blankets, or light. There isn't even any water to drink."

He feigned interest and turned to the old man who had escorted me, saying, "Is this possible? No water?"

The old man muttered something about how he would get me some.

"Unfortunately, today is a holiday," the young man said to me with a malicious smile. "Shops are closed. Our warehouses are, too. But we'll make everything available to you tomorrow."

"Tomorrow is Sunday," I said. "Everything is closed as well."

"That's your bad luck," he said coldly.

He nodded to the guard, who came up to me, grabbed me by the arm, and led me out.

# 22

My bad luck was confirmed when the following day arrived without sunlight. I kept my eyes on the skylight, waiting for light and the warmth it would bring. But the sky stayed dark. Soon rain was pouring down in torrents. Drops of it scattered across the skylight, and then collected beneath it on the floor, in a small puddle.

I resisted the cold by continually moving. I avoided thinking about what could happen to me at the hands of the Phoenician and his men. From time to time, I put my ear to the keyhole. But I couldn't pick out a single sound that revealed that anyone except myself was there in the building.

After some time, there came to my ears the sound of footsteps approaching and stopping at the door. The door opened to reveal the young man who had brought me the urine bucket the day before. On the floor, he put a tray that had on it a loaf of white round bread, a paper carton of milk, and a cup of tea with steam rising from it. He had hardly turned away before I hurried over to the tray. I held the cup of tea in my hands and savored the warmth of its contents. Then I turned to the loaf of bread and milk.

The paltry meal only compounded my desire for coffee and cigarettes. But I distracted myself by walking and jumping, and by a series of waking dreams. From there I quickly moved on to making big plans – a stage known to every prisoner after a period of confinement. I worked out plans to quit smoking and drinking, develop an exercise regimen, live near the ocean, and double the number of hours I spent writing.

Darkness was about to fall when I set about propping up my corner with more cardboard boxes, and then I coiled myself into a ball and my eyes succumbed to sleep.

I entered a deep, uninterrupted slumber that I didn't emerge from until dawn. I watched the light spread out without leaving my place. But soon enough I moved when the sun's rays fell on the wall next to the skylight and spread out over it in the shape of a rhomboid heading toward one of the corners below. I stood under the sunny rectangle, looking for a little warmth. Its area gradually expanded, and I was able to put my hair in it, then my forehead, my ear, and my eye.

I enjoyed the warmth spreading on my face, and then my chest. I spent the following hours between the patch of sunlight and the door. Muffled sounds, coming from different directions, were penetrating through it. Several feet passed by it without stopping. But I didn't lose hope that the person who carried the tray would be here at any moment.

The sun's heat reached its high point, and then began to recede. I amused myself for a time by hunting a fly that had settled on yesterday's tray. Finally, I heard the sound of the key turning in the lock. The door opened to reveal the old guard.

He gestured to me to come out, and I obeyed. I had hardly stepped outside the room when I sensed the presence of someone else. Before I could make out his face, a cloth blindfold was put over my eyes and tied around my head. Then a hand on my back pushed me and I walked forward, stumbling. One of them grabbed my arm and pulled me through a long passage. We went up a set of stairs and continued walking. Then we went down a long staircase. It seemed to me as though we were taking the same route as the first time. My idea was confirmed when I sensed that we had gone out into the street.

There was a car motor running nearby. A hand pushed me forward toward the source of the sound. Then it pushed down on my shoulder, and forced me to lean over. My leg bumped against a metal edge. The next moment, I was settling into a car seat between two guards.

The car set out at a normal speed. A little later it doubled its speed. Then I smelled the ocean. I heard one of the people sitting with me say, "Here."

The car stopped; no one moved. The one sitting to my right lit a cigarette. The sound of the lighter being flicked was repeated a few times. Then the car filled with cigarette smoke. No one said a word.

The silence was total. We seemed to be in an out-of-the-way place. I thought I detected the sound of a car at a distance. I listened closely. Some time passed before I could make out the sound. Gradually, it began to grow louder, until it came to a stop near us. The one sitting on my left moved to open the door next to him and got out of the car. His footsteps receded, then disappeared. A little later, he came back and ordered me to get out.

He grabbed me by the arm as I stepped outside. He walked several steps with me, then stopped. Then he let go of me.

I heard the sound of his feet moving away in the direction we had come from.

My heart pounded violently. I thought about putting my hand up and pulling off the blindfold, but I didn't dare. Then I heard the car I had come in start its motor. I thought about running, or throwing myself on the ground. Then I heard the car take off in the distance.

Several heavy, unhurried feet approached me. A hand reached up to my blindfold and removed it. I blinked several times before I could make out the man who was standing in front of me. He was heavy-set and elegantly dressed, and wore sunglasses.

He touched my arm with his hand, pointed me to a black American car standing at a distance, and said: "This way, please."

I walked beside him in a daze. We reached the car and he opened the back door, stepping aside so I could get in. Then he closed the door, walked around the car, and proceeded to get in on the other side.

There was a young man wearing similar glasses sitting beside the driver. As for the latter, I only saw one side of a bald head covered by a cloth cap.

"Where are we going?"

No one bothered to answer me. I understood what they wanted and kept silent.

The car passed through semi-deserted streets surrounded by demolished houses. Then the view changed, as we traveled through a high-class neighborhood that hadn't suffered much destruction. Then after fifteen minutes, the scenery of ruins returned.

The sun had set by the time we headed to a sloping street leading up to a large building on a hill. Electric light radiated from its windows. We rode alongside a high fence made of iron bars. We slowed down in front of a gate guarded by soldiers, on top of which was a brass plaque declaring it to be the Ministry of Defense for the Republic of Lebanon.

The soldiers raised the barrier to let our car through. It crossed the entranceway and turned toward the right. Then it stopped in front of a flight of ascending marble stairs.

My escort left the car, then gestured to me to follow him. We went up the marble stairs, followed by the other man who had been sitting beside the driver. We passed through a wide door to a large hallway crowded with soldiers and civilians. We went up another flight of stairs, and walked along a long corridor between two rows of closed doors. Finally, we slowed down and stopped in front of an office. My escort knocked on the door and went inside, while I remained outside with his colleague.

A few moments later, the man came out and gestured to me to come in. Then he closed the door behind me.

The office extended to the left of the entrance to where an enormous wooden desk stood. Behind it sat a short, elegantly dressed man. The man stood up and put out his hand for me to shake, saying: "Welcome, sir. A pleasure to meet you."

He pointed to one of the two facing chairs that sat near his desk.

He went back to his seat. As I sat down, I looked closely at him. I read his name on a small wooden nameplate on his desk: "Colonel Muhsin al-Attar".

He was also looking closely at me, and when he saw that I was reading his name, he said: "There – now we have gotten to know each other."

I nodded.

"Wouldn't you agree with me that you are quite fortunate?" he went on.

I arched my eyebrows, and didn't say anything.

Shuffling several dossiers on his desk, he said, "Apparently you have many friends in Lebanon."

He picked up a small notebook from one of the dossiers – I knew it had my passport in it – and flipped through its pages. When he realized that I was refraining from saying anything, he pointed out, "Your visa expires in three days' time."

"Yes," I said.

"Do you intend to travel before then?" he asked.

I looked up at him in confusion. "Would it be possible for you to let me know where I am?" I asked.

He smiled. "You haven't noticed yet?" he said. "You are here in the military intelligence bureau. The Deuxième Bureau, as they call it."

"Why?"

He arched his eyebrows dismissively. "Why? Because we saved your life. We searched for your kidnappers and persuaded them to release you."

I looked at the soft skin of his cheeks that hung loosely outside of his tight shirt collar.

"Thank you," I said.

"I think we deserve more than a word of thanks."

"How do you mean?" I asked.

"By having you stick to being candid and honest with me."

"But I haven't lied to you. I haven't said anything to you."

He smiled meaningfully.

"Exactly," he said.

"Are you saying I'm a free man?"

"Of course."

"Can I go?"

He tossed my passport to one side and picked up my notebook.

"Of course. But don't you want to take your papers and your passport? And then there are a few small questions. You are free to answer them or to refuse. But if you want a proper way to express your appreciation for us . . ."

"What do you want to know?"

"First we'll have some coffee. How do you take it?"

"*Mazboota* – medium-sweet."

"Just like I do."

He talked into a small intercom on his desk, requesting Egyptian-style coffee. He offered me a pack of Marlboros. I couldn't stand the taste of them, but I took one, and let him light it for me. Then I took a deep pull on it that made me feel dizzy.

"Beirut is an important city as far as writers are concerned," he said, "because it has a lot of publishers. Unfortunately, some writers and publishers don't stay within the confines of their work, and they get themselves involved in matters that can cause them serious harm."

A young man brought two cups of coffee. I took my cup, while he busied himself in changing the filter of his cigarette holder. Then he fixed his cigarette in it and lit it with slow deliberation as he cast a glance at a piece of paper in front of him. With no warning, he leaned over the desk and stared sharply at me.

"Where is Carlos?" he demanded.

Perplexed, I looked up at him.

"Carlos who?"

And suddenly I remembered, and smiled in spite of myself.

He jabbed a finger at me in a state of agitation.

"There – so you know!"

"You mean the international terrorist," I said.

He grew even more agitated.

"That's him exactly."

"But what do I have to do with him?" I asked.

He pounded the dossiers with his fist.

"Sir," he said in exasperation. "You should be talking candidly with me the way I am with you. We have information that you know him well."

"Not true."

"Our information has been corroborated."

"Your information is wrong. I have nothing to do with terrorism or politics. I came to Beirut to publish a book, that's all."

He smiled wickedly.

"And what about the film?"

"What about the film?" I riposted sharply. "They asked me to write a voiceover for it. And why wouldn't I do that? That's my job."

"So what's the story with Carlos?"

"There isn't any story. What I've told you is everything."

He began examining me closely. He seemed to be uncertain about which of two options to take. Then he came to a decision, and slumped into his seat. He took the cigarette out of the holder and put it out in the ashtray, telling me, "Sir. Listen to what I'm going to tell you. We aren't able to rescue a person in your circumstances every day. If we succeed today, then perhaps we won't be able to the next time. My advice to you is to stay away from troublesome matters. If you find yourself in a fix, maybe you can turn to us. We hold some strings, and we can pull on some others."

He picked up a card from the brass tray and handed it to me, saying, "Here's my name and number. There's no need for you to come here or for us to meet. You only have to pick up the phone and talk to me. Afterwards, you will find that we can show our gratitude. On the right occasion. This book you were talking about. Have you found a publisher for it?"

"Not yet," I said.

"Give me a copy of the manuscript, and maybe we'll find you one," he offered.

"Unfortunately, I don't have any more copies."

He stood up and reached for my passport, my notebook and the rest of the papers that had been in my pockets. I stood up too, and took them from him.

"I had around two hundred lira with me," I said.

"That's all we got from your kidnappers," he explained as he pressed a buzzer on his desk. "If you need cash, perhaps I could loan you some."

He put his hand in his pocket, but I stopped him, saying, "There's no need. I don't need anything. I will manage."

I insisted on refusing, and he took his hand out of his pocket. The escort from the car entered the room, and the colonel addressed him, saying, "Accompany this gentleman to the gate and call him a taxi."

I shook hands with him to say goodbye, and left the office. I walked ahead of my escort to the floor below, the marble staircase, and then the outer gate.

# 23

The taxi made its way in the dark of night through deserted streets and dusty fence-walls, and groups of gunmen affiliated with different groups. Some of them stopped us and then let us pass. We finally reached Hamra, and then pulled up to the house.

I looked for Abu Shakir, but couldn't find him. I went up the stairs at a run, hoping Wadia would be there. I knocked on the door, and he opened it for me. As soon as he saw it was me, his jaw dropped in astonishment, and he gave me an affectionate hug.

I asked him to pay the taxi fare, and hurried to the kitchen. I took a can of beer out of the fridge, and drank it in one gulp. I brought another one out with me to the living room.

I lit one of Wadia's English cigarettes, and walked up to the telephone. I dialed Lamia's number, and a child's voice answered. Then her voice came on the line: "You?"

"Is someone with you?" I asked.

"Yes," she said, whispering. "Where have you been?"

"I'll tell you everything when we meet. Maybe in half an hour?"

"That's impossible," she said. "I can't go out."

"Then I'll come to you," I suggested.

"That's more impossible."

"At your office?"

"I'll be waiting for you at the office in the morning," she said in a normal-sounding voice.

"I'll come on one condition."

"What's that?"

"That you wear your hair in a ponytail."

She laughed. "No problem," she said.

"And another thing. Don't wear a bra."

"What?"

"Your breasts don't need a bra."

"In the past, I didn't wear one, but now I'm older."

"Not at all. Promise me?"

She laughed again. "I'll see," she said. "*Bye-bye.*"

I heard Wadia's voice behind me as I put the receiver down, and I turned to him. He was looking at me nervously as he lit a cigarette.

"A real miracle. A kidnap victim comes back – and so quickly. Everyone will be eager to buy the interview I'll be doing with you."

I scrutinized his face carefully, as though I were seeing him for the first time.

"How did you know I was kidnapped?" I asked as I opened the second can of beer.

"When I noticed you weren't sleeping at the house, I called Antoinette, Lamia and Safwan, and everyone who knows you. But none of them had seen you. There was no other explanation. Antoinette promised me she would prod the apparatus of the Palestinian resistance into action. Listen: you must be hungry."

"Like a dog," I said. "I want meat and whiskey. And first of all, a bath."

"Go take a bath. I'll get everything ready for you."

"Did Safwan mention anything about the book?" I asked as I headed to my room.

"He said he can't publish it in the current circumstances," he answered.

I brought clean clothes from my room, and carried the can of beer to the bathroom. I took off my clothes and put them in a pile in a far corner. I brushed my teeth, then ran hot water in the bathtub. I shaved as I drank the beer. And finally, I sat down in the tub and leaned my head against the wall. I raised the beer to my lips.

But it wasn't long before my happiness disappeared. My bowels moved for the first time in two days. The reason wasn't that they would imminently be returning to normal regularity. Rather it was the idea that began to nag at me.

I finished my bath, put on my clean clothes, and went out to the living room. I found that Wadia had brought from outside two chickens grilled over charcoal, with familiar plates of salad. I recounted to him, while we ate, how I was kidnapped, and the conversation that took place between me and the fanatical Phoenician, and then the conversation between me and the man from the Deuxième Bureau.

Puzzlement came over him when he heard about the question that the man from the Deuxième Bureau had asked me about Carlos, and he muttered: "Strange. What did you tell them?"

"The truth."

He looked bewildered. So I added, "I mean that I don't know anything about him."

His face went pale. "Is that true?" he asked.

"Of course."

"But you told me . . ."

I laughed. "You're the one who misunderstood."

"Strange," he repeated, astonished.

I dipped a mouthful of food into a plate of yogurt and crushed garlic. "Really strange," I said. "I only mentioned Carlos's name once. In this living room, during a conversation with you. So that means only one thing."

He stopped eating and looked at me expectantly.

"What's that?"

"Either you had a chat with someone about the conversation we had . . ."

"Absolutely not," he burst out.

He went quiet, and then added, "I don't think so. Maybe."

I continued: "Or your apartment has been bugged by the Deuxième Bureau."

He turned to look around everywhere in the living room, and then looked down, saying, "Maybe."

I sipped from a glass of beer. "I don't think so," I said.

His eyes widened.

"If you're saying –"

I held up my hand to stop him.

"Let's not talk about that now. What I want to understand is: why did they kidnap me, and why did they let me go?"

He cut a slice of chicken and said, "Your kidnapping may have been by chance. A strange face that appeared in their area. And especially if the stranger seemed to be curious."

He put a morsel in his mouth and continued: "There's no basis for it as far as kidnapping operations are concerned. Sometimes the kidnap victims are executed immediately. That's often done in revenge for a similar operation done by the other side. And sometimes it happens for no apparent

298

reason, like what happened recently when the Phalangists killed around forty Egyptian workers. A lot of times, the kidnappers keep their victims so they can be traded for others, or for fixed sums of money. That's why the Phoenician was being patient with you – it was so he could assess your situation, and whether he could profit from you in some kind of exchange. If it became apparent to him, for example, that you were a Christian, he would try to persuade you to come around to his view, and gain from your support. I think you've heard that there are links between them and some Egyptian Copts."

"What about the Deuxième Bureau?"

He focused on wiping up what remained in the bowl of hummus with a morsel of food and explained: "The Deuxième Bureau is a strange institution. It is subject to the influence of the ruling families, Maronite and Muslim. But those who are in charge of it are also subject to other loyalties, foreign and mutually opposed to each other. And on top of all that, sometimes they operate independently in the game of the struggle for power between the different blocs, domestic and foreign."

He lit a cigarette and continued talking: "And now we come to the Palestinian resistance. Circumstances have forced them to maintain lines of communication with the different blocs. They are channels that are not affected by events. For example, while there may be bloody fighting between Fatah and the Phalangists, the line of communication between them works normally."

He looked at his watch, then went up to the television set and turned it on, putting it on mute while waiting for the news report. He continued what he was saying, as he returned to his seat: "So your kidnapping was by chance. Antoinette succeeded in prodding PLO officials into action. Naturally, they took an interest in the matter for two reasons: the first is that they are keen to support their relationship with all the progressive Lebanese groups, such as Antoinette's, to safeguard their presence in Lebanon. The second reason is connected to the first: Antoinette's use of the facilities at the media institute affiliated with them makes her a client of theirs in some way. In that light, your kidnapping infringes on their standing, even if indirectly. First, they began with the different organizations in West Beirut until they were sure you weren't with them. At that point they opened up their line of communication with the Deuxième Bureau, and then with the Phalangists, the Tigers and the Guardians of the Cedars, and the rest of the Maronite factions. They all denied they had anything to do with the matter. But the Deuxième Bureau – either to pay off a debt to the PLO, or to do them a favor that they can call on later, or to win a point in the struggle for power with the Maronite parties, or to follow up on an entirely side issue like Carlos – the important thing is that the Deuxième Bureau didn't stop there, and it took an interest in your story. Within a few hours, it learned where you were being held via its agents spread out among the various factions. The matter was settled with a phone conversation. The kidnappers found that by letting you go they would have a point in their favor with the Deuxième Bureau, or they could pay back a favor to them. Apologies were exchanged and future favors made note of, and you get your freedom back. And you become indebted to the Deuxième Bureau in some way."

I nodded, adding, "Very likely. Even if it's a frightening scenario. And laughable, too. But it explains the rest."

He gave me an inquisitive look.

"Your role in it," I explained.

A look of astonishment appeared on his face, and he forced out a laugh.

"My role was that I set this chain of events in motion when I looked for you and called Antoinette."

"Of course, of course. No argument about that. But I mean something else."

"What?"

"Carlos."

His face grew pale. "What about him?" he asked.

"Maybe we are being bugged here. But I am confident that the Deuxième Bureau heard about Carlos from you personally."

"Meaning that I'm a Deuxième Bureau agent?"

"Not necessarily. I don't think so. There is a modern, civilized way for these things. You pick up the phone and call a friend of yours, someone you know has some connection to the Deuxième Bureau. Someone like the owner of the café where we saw Lamia. You chat with him. And during the course of the conversation you throw out some information that you know very well the Deuxième Bureau will be interested in. Practically speaking, you didn't do anything that professional agents do. All you did was have a chat in the form of a response to the traditional question: 'Any news?'"

"And what would I gain from this chatter?"

"A little security, perhaps," I replied. "Some support in a moment of crisis. Life is hard here. Beirut is a den of tangled and contradictory loyalties. And then, isn't it likely that you are obligated to them for what happened with me today?"

"I never imagined that you thought so poorly of me."

"I wish it was like that: that it was just about thinking poorly of you."

His fingers were shaking. Without looking at them, I knew that my fingers were shaking too.

"Would you like me to give you another example of thinking poorly?" I asked. "There's the subject of the notebook. I am confident that I left it on the bedside table. So how did it end up in my bag?"

"If I took it, then logically, I would put it back in the same place."

"On the contrary. You know I looked all over for it on the bedside table, around it and under it. If it turned up in the same place, then it would be obvious. The smarter thing to do is to have it turn up somewhere else to convince me I had forgotten where I put it."

"So I took your notebook and gave it to the Deuxième Bureau?"

"Maybe you only flipped through it. You were afraid I had contacts that could expose you to danger."

"And what else?"

I laughed. "Isn't that enough?"

"I want to hear this."

"As you wish. Maybe we'll begin from prison, which you left after one week. Or from 1968, when they appointed you to Beirut, while all your friends were either in prison or just coming out."

"And how do you explain that?"

"Weren't you one of those responsible for organizing the Socialist Union? You used to write reports about trends in public opinion; that is, the opinions of your colleagues in the newspaper?"

"You're amusing me quite a bit with your detective-novel revelations. I always considered you my closest friend. And here you are, proving me wrong in my estimation of you."

"Life is a series of letdowns. The strange thing about it is that I – in my heart – don't blame you for anything."

I happened to glance at the television screen, and found that the news had started. I turned up the volume and listened to the anchorman talk about 3 billion dollars that Iraq had received from Saudi Arabia to make up for its losses in the war with Iran. Then a photo of Sadat appeared on the screen in relation to an interview he gave with the German magazine *Der Spiegel*, in which he stated that Egypt and the US had a strategic relationship, and that "his country" was ready to offer facilities to the United States and Western nations so those states could defend their interests in the Gulf.

Sadat seemed to have monopolized the evening news, since he soon appeared at a convention for his political party in Cairo. This time his distinctive voice came out to us as well: "On May 27, 1979 . . . that is, after I raised the Egyptian flag over Arish . . . On the 27th I was in Arish and Begin came up to me . . . We went 'n' visited Bir Saba . . . Y'know, the topic of Sinai is totally over . . . uhh, by raising the flag over Arish . . . I told him, c'mon, let's sit down . . . That happened yesterday when I raised the flag over Arish . . . That means a lot . . . Why? It means that you really respect your agreements . . . I know that . . . You really carry out your obligations . . . OK, what's still to come is we have a year left for Palestinian self-rule . . . Starting from now, we get rid of the agreement . . . What's still to come, Begin . . . Begin said, That's OK . . . What do you think? He didn't need – he didn't ask me for anything more than security measures . . . All the security measures they asked for, I told them, I'll give 'em to you and more. He told me something really great . . . I told him what would you say to a million square meters a day of Nile water . . . He told me something really great . . ."

I suddenly felt overtired and wanted to sleep. As I stood up, I said, "I'm going to bed."

He didn't say a word and kept looking at the television screen in an anxious silence. I leaned over him and put my hand on his head.

"Believe me, Wadia," I said, "I don't blame you at all."

# 24

The macho bodyguard had a serious look on his face. He occupied a seat next to the secretary's desk, stretching his long legs out in front of it. He nearly blocked the way. As usual with him, his gun hung from his waist.

"Madame is waiting for you," the secretary said, gesturing to the inner office.

I walked down the corridor leading to her office. I saw her standing at the door, with her hands out to me. She took my hand between her palms and drew me inside. Then she pulled back from me and headed to her chair behind the desk, saying, "Have a seat and tell me what happened."

I sat down in the chair by the front of her desk. I noticed she had combed her hair back and gathered it into a knot. She was wearing a pink silk sleeveless blouse, and a full skirt of the same color. I immediately noticed she wasn't wearing a bra.

She saw where my eyes were looking and her face went red.

"The sun is strong today," she said. "Happy, *ya bey?*"

I told her all about what had happened to me; we laughed together at the Carlos story.

"What's the news with my book?" I asked her.

"I really liked it, and we'll take it. When are you leaving Beirut?"

"I have a reservation for the plane on Friday."

"I'll draw up your contract today."

"What about the money?"

"As soon as you sign it, you'll get it."

She pulled out some paper and said, "Can you wait for me a little bit? You can drink some coffee and read the papers until I'm done."

The secretary brought coffee. I picked up one of the newspapers. The front page was shared by news about the Arab summit conference in Amman, a new sweep of arrests against the Palestinians there, and Sadat's two interviews, which I'd listened to yesterday. There was a reference to a third interview with Danish television, in which he was quoted as saying: "It has been confirmed that God is preparing me for a special mission."

I flipped through the newspaper and on the last page, I saw a photo of a boy around seven years old, with a handsome face and wide eyes. He sat between two friends behind a desk in a schoolroom. The photo was taken from the front, and at a low angle, so the legs of the three schoolboys showed, as well as a bookbag belonging to one of them on the floor. They all had their legs crossed, revealing their socks and shoes, except for the handsome-looking boy, who put the tip of his pen in his mouth, quietly thinking. His left leg, thrown over his right one, consisted of an empty pants leg.

The accompanying article talked about artificial limbs, on the occasion of the International Year of the Disabled. I read that the market for artificial limbs in Lebanon had been flourishing recently, despite the difficulties it faced. The progress that had been made in their manufacture meant that only the rich were able to benefit from them, while the overwhelming majority of injured people in Lebanon were among the poor.

Below the photo of the boy, I read this caption: "An artificial limb is not like a natural limb, as many believe, but is a device to help people make some of the essential movements they need to get around."

There was another photograph of the same boy on the street: he supported himself on crutches next to his two friends, and had his bookbag slung over his back. His neck was turned to follow a soccer game among boys his age.

In a third photograph, another boy, around four years old, appeared. He was wearing a vest over his shirt, and he was standing between two metal barricades that revealed his lower half, while the doctor was bent down over his amputated leg, fitting him for an artificial limb. Beneath the photo I read: "Walking is a series of movements made by several joints in the leg, hip, knee, anklebone and toes. Amputation usually takes place above or below the knee."

Lamia got out of her chair and walked to the bookshelf. She pulled out a folder and brought it back with her. She stopped next to me, laid the folder flat on her desk, and bent over it.

The office door was open, and I could see one side of the hallway leading to the outer reception room. Without taking my eyes off the door, I leaned over a little, and placed the palm of my hand on her calf. Slowly, I traced my fingers up to the back of her knee, then I wrapped my hand wrapped around her knee from the front, and continued moving it up her thigh.

Her skin was firm, smooth and warm. After a moment, my hand bumped against a piece of cloth. I stopped and looked up at her. She was still bent over the folder, but her eyes were closed.

Slowly, she opened her eyes, and they met mine.

"I'm not embarrassed in front of you," she said.

The noise of the explosion was powerful; the building shook down to its foundations. I quickly pulled my hand away, while she stood up straight and smoothed out her skirt.

"It's the sonic boom," she said, hurrying to the window.

The noise was repeated again. Then several weak, sporadic explosions echoed back, similar to anti-aircraft gun rounds. The secretary walked in on us in an agitated state, saying, "Israeli planes."

She joined us at the window. We stood there, looking at the sky without seeing anything. The noise didn't occur again, so the secretary left, closing the door behind her.

I brought my mouth up close to Lamia's bare arm, and imprinted a kiss just outside her armpit. I noticed that her face was pale.

"Are you afraid?" she asked me.

"Of course," I replied.

I put my arms around her and plucked at her ear with my lips. She rested her breasts against my chest, then pulled away from me, whispering: "Someone's coming in."

She picked up the folder and brought it back to the cabinet. Then she sat down behind her desk and became engrossed in her work. I went back to my chair, lit a cigarette, and began observing her.

Suddenly she tossed the pen aside and pushed back her chair.

"*Oof*. I can't concentrate."

"Let's go – we'll get out of here."

She thought a moment and then said, "I have to go home."

I put my hand out on the desk and clutched her hand. I felt her nails with my fingertips.

This time the noise was extremely close to us. I could distinguish the sound of two gunshots, one after the other. The door swung open violently and the secretary appeared, looking pale and trying to speak. Right behind her came two of the young men who worked in the office, and behind them one of the two armed men who guarded the entrance to the building.

From the flood of rushed and contradictory words, we were able to piece together that Abu Khalil had gone out to buy cigarettes, and when he came back in the elevator, he noticed an armed man he didn't know on the stairs. The man raised his machinegun to shoot Abu Khalil. But Abu Khalil was faster: he shot two bullets at him but missed, and the gunman was able to escape toward the roof.

We all rushed out together. We stood in front of the elevator; the glass on its wooden doors looked shattered.

We heard the sound of heavy feet and heavy breathing. Abu Khalil appeared at the top of stairs, his gun in his hand.

"I chased him up to the roof, but he managed to escape."

The outer door guard shook his head.

"No one came into the building that I didn't recognize."

"So where did that guy come from?" shouted Abu Khalil. "Out of thin air? He must have come through the door, while you were asleep on the job!"

The guard was furious. "You're the one who's sleeping all the time!"

Lamia intervened to break up the fight, and asked both of them to check the building thoroughly.

We made our way back to the office. She closed the door and leaned her back against it.

"It's a good thing Abu Khalil saw him," she said, tapping her fingertip against her lower lip.

Still thinking, she walked over to her desk.

"What time is it?" she asked me.

"Two thirty," I replied.

She walked toward me and stood in front of me, then she put her hand out to my chest and pressed against it. I leaned my head against her chest and took the tip of her breast between my lips. She drew her legs close and held them against my body.

"*I'm very turned on*," she said in English.

"I can't take much more of this," she added in Arabic. "Do you know what I mean?"

I nodded. "Let's go to my place."

"What about Wadia?" she asked.

"I can call him now at his office and make an arrangement with him."

"I don't want that. I won't feel relaxed that way."

She looked at the two sofas leaning against each other in a corner of the office, and said, "Not here, either. Not after what happened today."

Suddenly she made up her mind and picked up her purse.

"Come with me," she said.

"Where to?"

"To my place."

Abu Khalil was waiting for us in the outer reception area, and he walked ahead of us to the stairs. We followed him down to the front door, where we were met by the two guards, brandishing their guns.

Abu Khalil asked us to wait inside; he gestured to Ibrahim, one of the guards, and left the building. After a few moments, he reappeared in the front seat of the Chevrolet, next to its driver wearing an official uniform.

At a nod from Abu Khalil, Ibrahim raised his gun to his chest, as his eyes swept across the rooftops, windows, and entrances of nearby buildings. He walked up confidently to the car; pulling open the back door, he nodded at Lamia. He remained standing there until she got in, then he closed the door behind her. Then he walked around the car and opened the other door. Stepping aside, he addressed me: "This way, sir."

Ibrahim closed the door, then wheeled around the car and opened the door next to Lamia. She moved over in my direction to make room for him, so that she was pressed up against me. He sat down with his gun in his hand.

"*I was planning to get rid of His Excellency here at the end of the month,*" Lamia said to me in English. "*But it seems as though I still need him.*"

The driver set off through a network of intersecting streets, carrying out the instructions from Ibrahim, who kept his eye on the cars, watching them come up behind us until we reached her house.

Before the car came to a complete stop, Abu Khalil had opened the door and jumped onto the sidewalk with his gun in his hand. The armed man did likewise, and he stood next to the car with his machinegun up to his chest and his finger on the trigger.

We got out of the car and walked up to the building under the protection of the gun and the Kalashnikov. We were joined by two of the armed men standing in the entranceway. We went up the wide marble stairs, then we crossed the inner reception room. Ibrahim took the key to the elevator from Lamia, and rode up to the top floor to make sure there were no explosives.

The elevator came down after a few minutes, and Lamia and I took it to her apartment. She led me to the room I had sat in the last time, and she left me there.

I headed to the library and stood looking at its contents. I saw that the shelf with the photograph of Adnan was empty, and I discovered the photo placed on the floor, next to the library, with Adnan's face to the wall.

I pulled out a fat, strangely-shaped volume, and found that it was an Arabic–Hebrew dictionary. I flipped through its pages until Lamia walked in on me. I noticed that she had added a new layer of eyeliner to her eyes, making them appear wider.

"The food is ready, *ya bey*," she said.

I put the dictionary back in its place, and followed her to the living room. Sections of carpet hung on its walls, as well as giant trays made of silver engraved with Islamic decorative motifs. In the middle of the room sat a large wooden table, with a large number of chairs lined up around it.

The table was set for only two people, so I asked her, "Won't your daughter be eating with us?"

"Salma ate with her nanny and they went out for a walk," she explained, sitting down.

I sat down in front of her and looked around me.

"Isn't there anything to drink?" I asked.

She pointed to a bottle of orange juice and smiled.

"We don't keep any liquor in the house. You forget that we're Muslims."

Two waiters in white jackets and black pants took charge of serving us. We moved from various kinds of salads to *kishk* with chicken breasts and stuffed grape leaves. Then pieces of cooked meat with the light-green zucchini known as *kusa*, and boiled carrots.

Dessert was a concoction of chocolate. I contented myself with an apple I took from a wide bowl filled with apples, plums and grapes.

I lit a cigarette and we moved to the library, where they brought the coffee to us. Lamia left the room for some time, and when she came back, she sat down next to me and took my hand. My hands were cold, so she let go of them.

"Come with me. I'll show you my room," she said.

We walked down a long corridor with a marble floor. She stopped in front of a room.

"Is the bathroom near here?" I asked.

She pointed to the opposite door, so I opened it and went in. I found myself in a wide cave made of black marble streaked with pink veins. Mirrors covered a large part of its walls.

I urinated and washed my hands and mouth in a wide sink with gleaming yellow faucets that looked as though they were made of gold. Then I dried my hands while contemplating my face, which had several reflections in the mirrors. Finally, I left the bathroom and quietly closed the door behind me.

The room where she was waiting for me was medium-sized. In the center was a low, round bed without pillows, but covered by a thick pink bedspread.

She pulled me by the hand and led me to a plush couch, then she sat down in front of me on the edge of the bed, watching me with interest, and observing my mood.

My eyes wandered from the thick carpet topped with wavy tufts of wool to the enormous curtains that revealed a glass panel looking out over a wide balcony. I relaxed into the couch, burying my body among the soft cushions.

I felt at peace as I cast my eye over the clean, carefully arranged furniture, and the dark sky visible through the glass. The peaceful feeling was total. I felt the desire to succumb to the couch and its cushions. And the desire not to move or speak, in order to prolong this moment a little.

She leaned over to me and put her hand on my knee. I took her arm and gently pulled her toward me. She moved over to sit next to me and buried her head in my neck.

Her body was warm, and I felt her tremble. But my nerves were relaxed, and I was enveloped in a kind of numbness.

I put my hand on her leg, and felt her soft skin. Then I ran my hand along the curves of her thighs. I looked up at her and saw that she was breathing heavily, with her eyes closed. Soon she began trembling with every touch of my fingers.

My fingers grew tired after a little while and my wrist started to hurt. But I continued touching her without taking my eyes off her face until her shudders subsided, and I took my hand away.

She collapsed on my chest, with her eyes still closed. After a while, she opened them, then sat up straight and readjusted her clothes, saying, "We'd better go back."

I followed her to the library and sat facing her. I lit a cigarette as I watched her. She had a serious look in her eyes, lost in a flow of inner thoughts.

"I have to go now," I said, glancing at my watch.

"Hmm?"

I repeated what I'd said.

"Stay for a little," she said without enthusiasm. "I have an Egyptian movie starring Nadia El Guindy."

"And I have a movie that needs a voiceover commentary."

"As you wish," she said.

She walked me to the elevator door.

"Will you be here tonight?" I asked as I walked into the elevator.

She nodded.

"Should I call you or will you call me?" I asked.

"No. I'll call you," she replied.

"I'll be waiting."

## 25

It seemed to me that the commentary should be reporto-
rial and terse, without a trace of stirring emotions or
sorrow in the tone. What would be the value of an impas-
sioned, eloquent speech in the face of indelible scenes of
bloodletting, conflagration and destruction? I was troubled
by doubt for a moment about the need for a voiceover at
all. Then I remembered that film required many things to
give it vitality, and it could be that one of them was a
human voice.

I had to get rid of most of the original title cards, or to
be more precise, I had to incorporate them into my voiceover.
Likewise, the length of this commentary had to progress in
tandem with the amount of material in the film. In many
places, the voiceover had to be synchronized with the scenes
running through it.

I resorted to Antoinette's abbreviated list recording the
time of each shot. I knew that twenty seconds on the screen
takes up, on average, thirty words. So I calculated the required
number of words for each scene, which was composed of
various shots. That made it possible for me to determine the
amount of material I was being asked to write.

I decided to treat the voiceover as an integral text, with a
beginning and an end, not as a collection of captions suited

to each scene. I also had to take into account some scenes that needed explanation, and others that didn't need a single word.

I threw myself completely into the work, and it was midday Thursday by the time I finished a draft of the voiceover. I reviewed it carefully from different angles – the logical sequence of events; good writing and a smooth style; the political viewpoint; getting the facts right; and from first to last, being in sync with the film's scenes and shots.

The tight schedule gave me a sense of urgency, and I set myself to writing a final, clean copy, until the phone rang and pulled me out of my deep concentration.

I picked up the receiver, and a female voice that I didn't recognize came to me down the line: "Sir . . ."

"Hello," I said.

"I'm Jamila."

I said hello again.

"I'm sorry to bother you," she went on. "But I really need to talk to you."

"By all means."

"Maybe we can meet somewhere a half-hour from now?"

"Where?"

"It's up to you."

"Would it be a problem for you to come to my place?"

"A café on Hamra Street would be better. Like the Modka, for example."

"All right," I said. "The Modka it is."

I pushed my papers aside. I put on my jacket and left the apartment. I walked slowly toward Hamra Street. Then I strolled over to the Modka, and chose a table in a prominent spot. Not long after, I saw her looking for me, so I stood up. She came over, walking quickly. She squeezed my hand forcefully and sat down.

She was wearing a tweed jacket and skirt. She seemed a little thinner than I remembered. She had no makeup on, and there were faint wrinkles around her eyes.

I asked the waiter for two cups of coffee and two glasses of cognac. I lit her cigarette for her. She took a deep drag, and said, "I apologize for intruding on you like this. Are you flying out tomorrow?"

"Yes. In the evening."

"I want you to break off your relationship with Lamia as soon as you leave."

I had raised the glass of cognac to my lips, but I put it back down and looked at her in astonishment.

She nodded and repeated what she had said.

"Strange," I said. "First of all, you are assuming that there is a relationship between me and Lamia. Then, you are asking – "

She cut me off. "I know everything, so you don't have to deny it."

"Even if we assume that that's true," I went on, "don't you see that what you're asking for is a little unusual?"

"I have my reasons, and you'll be persuaded by them once I explain them to you."

"There's nothing between me and Lamia," I said. "The relationship between us is only a professional one."

She stubbed her cigarette out in the ashtray, and held the glass of cognac between her hands.

"Listen. I've known Lamia for many years now. She tells me everything."

"If she was the one who told you about this so-called relationship we have, then she was lying."

"I have two eyes, you know."

I looked at her two powerful, masculine hands, with their trimmed nails carefully painted a seashell color. I feigned the nonchalance and confidence of someone with nothing to hide.

"I'm sure you'll understand," she went on.

She looked intently at her glass, hesitating; then she looked up at me and said: "There is a special relationship – a very special relationship – between me and Lamia."

"Why does that concern me?"

"Sir, you have your life in Cairo. I don't have anyone except Lamia. She is a delicate creature who needs to be completely protected and given a high level of affection. No one understands her, values her and loves her like I do. But sometimes something happens that I don't understand. Let's say an attempt to prove her femininity or her ability to attract men. Or maybe boredom."

She laughed bitterly, adding, "Or a midlife crisis."

"Maybe she belongs to both sides," I added.

"Probably. But I haven't lost hope that I can win her over completely to my side."

"If she is using me to thwart the relationship the two of you have, then what makes you think she won't do it again with someone else?"

"Leave that to me to worry about," she said. "What I want from you is for you to end your relationship with her as soon as you leave. No promises of any kind."

"I haven't conceded that there is anything between us. In any case, I'm not the kind of person who loves writing letters."

"I knew I could rely on you."

As she stood up, she stared at me with a revealing look, as though making certain I would do what she had asked. She shook hands with me to say goodbye, and then walked away.

I watched her go, confidently standing tall and erect as she walked between the tables. Then I paid the bill and left.

I found Wadia busy preparing a tray of potatoes in the oven, so I got down to work on the revised copy of the voiceover until I was done with it. Then I called Antoinette and offered to bring it to her after lunch.

"I have two spare tickets to an Arab concert," she said. "How would you and Wadia like to come? You could bring the voiceover and I would bring the check for your payment."

I called out to Wadia and told him what Antoinette had suggested. He agreed to go.

"We'll do it," I told her. "Only, would it be possible to be paid in cash, rather than by check? I won't have time to cash it tomorrow."

"I'll try," she replied.

The concert began at seven. That gave me enough time to eat and review the voiceover one last time. At six forty-five, Wadia and I took a taxi to the American University in Beirut.

There was a large crowd in front of the concert hall and Antoinette was hard to find. She was wearing a light fake-fur coat over the usual pair of jeans and slender high-heel shoes.

She squeezed my hand warmly, and I kissed her on the cheek. We went up to the entrance, but a policeman came over to us and pointed to her purse. She opened it and pulled out a gun that she offered to him. The policeman put it in a side storage area, after giving her a receipt. A young man next to me pulled out his gun, getting ready to hand it over. Wadia and I walked through after declaring we had no weapons.

We had a hard time finding a place to sit. I noticed the tense atmosphere that dominated the hall, as well as the excitement of the audience.

"It's the first time that people are out at night in Beirut since the killing of Bashir Ubayd," Wadia observed.

I handed the voiceover to Antoinette. She gave it a quick glance and put it in her bag. She handed me an envelope that contained my fee.

"If you want to make any adjustment in the text," I said, "or if there turns out to be any problem with it, write to me."

She nodded in agreement. I turned my attention to the printed program that Wadia handed me. The concert was made up of songs by *Sayed Darwish*, and some of Leila Mourad's songs composed by Daoud Hosni, as well as some Umm Kulthoum numbers composed by Zakariyya Ahmad, in addition to the poem "They taught him how to be hard", by Abd al-Wahhab.

I leaned over Antoinette and whispered to Wadia, "Did you notice that the selections in the program are all Egyptian?"

Finally, the curtain raised on a Lebanese ensemble, with the musicians sitting in a row in the front, and the male and female choristers behind them. The concert began with a well-known song by Sayed Darwish made famous by Fairuz, "Visit Me Once Each Year", followed by two of his songs about various professions – "The Cart Drivers" and "The Pickpockets".

It was an excellent performance and the applause was thunderous. I was swept away by a feeling of elation. When the ensemble sang "That's What Happened", the pent-up dam burst.

Written more than sixty years ago, the song, with lyrics by Badia Khairi, went:

> *What happened, happened, so don't blame me:*
> *You don't have the right, for we are not free.*
> *How can you say I'm to blame, my brother,*
> *When the wealth of our land belongs to another?*
> *Talk to me first about the things we need,*
> *Then you can blame me for my misdeeds.*
> *Instead of them gloating over our plight,*
> *With your hand in mine, we'll stand and fight.*
> *We are one people,*
> *Our hands are strong.*

Tears flowed from my eyes like a flood. I couldn't stop them. I sobbed without restraint. I sensed that Wadia and Antoinette were exchanging glances.

"What's the matter?" Antoinette whispered in my ear.

I didn't answer her, but abandoned myself to weeping.

A little later, it was intermission, and I dried my tears. We went out to the garden of the American University to smoke. Wadia reminded me of our student days, and the tears started up again, pouring from my eyes in spite of myself.

He put his arm around me, and began patting my shoulder. Soon a sense of calm came over me, and I dried my tears. I was able to keep control of myself for the rest of the concert.

The audience clapped for a long time when the program ended. The ensemble played an encore of some of its songs, and then we finally left our seats and moved slowly to the door. Everyone was dragging their feet, as though they hated to go back to their homes.

Antoinette reclaimed her gun and we left the concert hall. We had barely stepped out onto the street when we heard the sound of gunfire nearby.

Shouts went up from different places; some people ran, while others brandished their guns.

"Run," shouted Wadia.

Antoinette took off her shoes and clutched them in her hand along with her purse. She carried the gun in her other hand. We set off running, while she led us through streets that took us away from the neighborhood.

We heard no more gunshots, so we slowed down, and finally stopped, out of breath. We heard the sound of a speeding car coming up behind us, so we pinned ourselves against the wall for protection. A military jeep, enclosed on all sides, sped past us. We followed its blinding headlights as they danced on the walls of buildings and fell on an old poster that had the famous photo of Gamal Abdel Nasser where he seems to be sad and dejected, immediately following the 1967 defeat.

Wadia offered to let Antoinette stay the night with us, but she refused and insisted on going back to her house in East Beirut. So we put her in a taxi and we took another to the apartment.

# 26

My last day in Beirut began with overcast, cloudy weather. Wadia was still sleeping, so I had my breakfast while reading the papers, which carried news of a new Israeli attack on South Lebanon. There were several photos of houses destroyed as a result of this attack, and of the victims lying in hospital beds.

I got my suitcase ready, cleaned the room and made the bed. I did the same thing in the kitchen and living room. Finally, I took a bath and put on my clothes. In the meantime, Wadia woke up and had his breakfast. When I went back to the living room, I found him getting ready to go out.

"I'll be back before tonight to go with you to the airport," he said.

"You don't have to do that," I responded. "I can order a taxi."

"I'll order it for you. Is six o'clock all right?"

"That's fine."

He headed to the door, but I stopped him, saying, "If you're coming back early, call me first. I might have a female visitor."

He promised he would, and left the house.

There was a bottle of whiskey on the desk, so I poured a

glass and sat down to drink it. A little before noon, the phone rang.

Picking up the receiver, I said "hello" in a flat, mechanical tone.

Lamia's scolding voice reached me: "You're in a bad mood."

"Hi," I said, using the same tone.

"Why didn't you call me?" she asked.

"Didn't you tell me not to? And you promised to call *me*."

"I couldn't."

"Did you get the contract and the advance?"

She didn't answer my question, but asked me in turn: "What time are you heading to the airport?"

"I'm leaving here at six."

"Is Wadia there with you?"

"No."

"When is he coming back?"

"Tonight. Why?"

"I'll come over in an hour."

"Will you have the contract with you?" I asked.

"We'll talk about that when I get there."

I drained my glass and poured another one. By the time she came, I had had three more glasses.

She took off her coat, under which she had on a crimson skirt and an olive-green sweater with a low neck that revealed a blouse of the same color. She tossed her purse and the yellow envelope that contained my manuscript on the chair. She threw herself onto the couch.

Her hair was pulled back into a ponytail.

"Coffee?" I asked, still standing.

"I don't want any," she replied.

I sat down in front of her and lit a cigarette.

"Do you know what we realized about the gunman who attacked Abu Khalil? There was no trace of him. No one else saw him. It's obvious he made up the whole story."

"Why?"

"To convince us that we needed him, after he got the sense that I would be getting rid of him. You know, I'm afraid of him sometimes? I suspect he was a sniper during the early part of the war."

"What was his original job before the war?"

"I think he worked in sales, or was a building security guard."

"Was he the one that planned the explosion?"

"No. That's another story. We know who did that, and we've come to an agreement with them."

"Who?"

"I can't tell you.

"Adnan talked to me yesterday," she said after a moment. "I read him several paragraphs from your manuscript. The paragraphs that can cause problems and prevent it from being distributed in Arab countries. He told me he can't assume the responsibility for publishing it in the current circumstances."

I lit another cigarette.

"You could have told me that on the phone," I pointed out.

"You're in a bad mood," she said.

"Your friend came to see me yesterday."

"Jamila? How?"

"She called me and asked to meet me."

"What did she want?" she asked, perplexed.

"She asked me to break off my relationship with you."

She became angry.

"Sticking her nose in! I've had it with her. She's always that way with my friends."

"Why?"

She stared at me with her eyes wide and innocent-looking: "I don't know."

"She told me everything. I mean about the relationship between the two of you."

Her face went pale. "I don't understand," she said.

"You don't have to play dumb. I'm not asking you to explain yourself."

"Why should I have to explain myself?" she shouted furiously at me. "I can do what I like."

"Exactly."

"Is it my fault I can't stand you men and your boorishness, your egos and your lies?" she went on in the same agitated state. "You don't know what Lebanese men are like. Their whole lives revolve around paying in installments, joining the rat race, and producing a son to carry on the family name."

"They do that on account of you women."

"I know. That's why I always go back to him. Generally I prefer men."

I laughed and her anger dissipated. She smiled.

"You're a free woman," I said. "As long as you're happy."

"I only knew happiness when my mother was by my side. She was strong. I wanted to be like her, so I took part in demonstrations."

"When you were in college?"

She nodded. "Can you believe I used to shout out slogans for Palestine and Gamal Abdel Nasser, and against imperialism? Sometimes I shouted slogans for Mao Zedong."

"And then what happened?"

"My mother died. Then I got married. I couldn't find the cause that would sweep me off my feet."

"Because you only love yourself."

"How did you know?" she said, mockingly. "Actually, I love my body."

"I'm being serious. You only take. I challenge you to recall one time that you gave."

She smiled and gestured with her chin at the couch, saying, "Lots of times. With you, for example."

"With me you took without giving," I said.

She stood up and walked over to me, then sat on my lap.

"Don't you want to give me something before you travel?"

She looked appealing, her face flushed with emotion. I put my arm around her waist and she leaned against my chest.

"I didn't finish telling you what Adnan told me," she said. "He is prepared to take a risk on your behalf. Because of the promise he gave you. But in this situation, you will have to relinquish all your rights."

"Is that all?"

"No. There's another idea. There is a Swiss company that is interested in publishing the book."

"In Arabic?"

"Of course."

"I didn't know the Swiss read Arabic."

"We will distribute it to Arab readers."

"In Switzerland?"

"No, dummy. Use your brain. The book didn't leave a single Arab regime unscathed. And then there's the sex in it.

What is the only place where it can be distributed without restrictions?"

"Lebanon," I volunteered.

"Lebanon isn't a distribution center. It's only a production center. There isn't a publisher in his right mind who would think of relying on Lebanese readers alone. Only one place can easily print and distribute the book."

"Where?" I asked, puzzled.

"I didn't think you were this stupid. Israel, of course. There are more than one and a quarter million Palestinians thirsting to read something in Arabic."

I lit a new cigarette and noticed my hand was steady.

"Write us a letter authorizing us to act on your behalf," she went on. "We'll take care of the whole thing. It will be a lucrative deal, and you'll be able to get some of the advance before you leave."

I raised an eyebrow.

"Are you paying in cash or in kind?" I asked.

She slapped my chest playfully. "You're terrible!" she said. "You don't deserve to be treated nicely."

She leaned over me and put her cheek up against mine.

"*You know, you haven't slept with me yet,*" she whispered in English.

I placed my palm on the triangular opening of her sweater, and ran my hand up her neck, up to her clavicle. My fingers probed the base of her neck, and I felt her skin.

"Do you like my neck?" she whispered.

She pushed her head back to give me an opportunity to admire her neck, and I put my fingers around it.

She closed her eyes and a purple tinge appeared on the skin of her neck, spreading to her chin and cheeks. The place where I touched her neck was soft and tender, and I gently pressed on it.

"Hey," she said in a faint voice. "You're hurting me."

I suddenly sensed that I was fully erect. Without letting go of her neck, I undid my pants with one hand, and pushed her clothes to the side. Then I leaned on top of her and raised my right hand to her neck. I clutched it between my fingers while thrusting into her body.

A mysterious glow burned in the space of the room, coursing through my body and my entire being. My fingers continued to press on her neck muscles and their bulging veins, while my body moved on top of her.

Her face began to contort with pain. Her lips slackened into a moan, and her neck and face turned red. But I paid no mind. The fire was lit before me. My semen was welling up inside me and was on the point of bursting out and gushing forth. Every squeeze of my fingers on her neck became a step toward the edge of the pitch-black abyss, where the exploding volcano was, and absolute ecstasy.

# 27

I didn't choke her, and I didn't have my orgasm. She gathered her strength and roughly pushed me off her. She was able to free her neck from my fingers. She jumped up and stared at me in alarm, while I collapsed into my chair, breathing heavily, my limbs quivering.

She raised her hands to her neck and moved her lips, but her voice was stuck in her throat. Without caring about her appearance, she grabbed her coat and bag, and hurried to the apartment door. She opened it and rushed outside.

I listened to her footsteps on the stairs. Then I slowly got up, adjusted my clothes, walked to the door and closed it.

The sun had set, and it had grown dark more quickly than usual. I turned the light on in the living room. I walked to the library and picked up a bottle of whiskey. I wrenched off the cap and took a swig directly from the bottle.

I looked for the pack of cigarettes, and found it on the floor beside the chair. I lit a cigarette with trembling fingers and sat back down.

I smoked the cigarette down to the end and stubbed it out in the ashtray. Then I walked to my room and brought my carry-on and suitcase out to the living room. I picked up the envelope that held my manuscript and put it back in the secret compartment in my suitcase.

I felt surprisingly cold and put on my jacket. I took a mouthful from the whiskey bottle. I looked at my watch, then lit a cigarette and went back to my seat.

After a while I heard a car horn, and I walked over to the balcony. I found a taxi in front of the building. I closed the balcony door, and checked to make sure I had my passport and plane ticket in my pocket. Then I slung the carry-on over my shoulder and picked up my suitcase. I cast a final glance around the apartment, then turned out the light and left.

# Glossary

*al-Amal*:  Newspaper belonging to the Phalangist Party.

**al-As'ad, Kamil (1932–2010):**  Shiite Lebanese politician from a powerful family in Lebanon's south. He served as speaker of the Lebanese parliament several times, including from 1970 to 1984.

**al-Atrash, Sultan Pasha (1891–1982):**  Spiritual and political leader of the Druze tribes of Jebel Druze in southern Syria. Leader of a Druze revolt against the French in 1925.

**Ali Pasha, Muhammad (r.1805–48):**  An Albanian soldier who came to power in Egypt in the wake of Napoleon's invasion and expulsion. Although nominally a viceroy of the Ottoman sultan, he became powerful enough to invade the Middle East, occupying Lebanon and parts of Syria. He is known as a reforming ruler who set Egypt on an early path to modernity.

**al-Manfaluti, Mustafa Lutfi (1876–1924):**  Egyptian author of essays and sentimental short stories.

**Amal militia:**  Armed Shia faction in the Lebanese Civil War, which grew out of the earlier Movement of the Dispossessed founded by the Shii Imam al-Sadr.

**Arab Deterrent Forces:**  Peacekeeping forces sponsored by Arab League countries that were deployed across Lebanon starting in November, 1976. Their purpose was to take over peacekeeping duties from the Syrian Army, although Syria continued to provide the majority of ADF troops in Lebanon.

**Bamahaneh:** The official, semi-independent magazine of the Israeli Defense Forces.

*bey*: A term of respect, originally Turkish, roughly equivalent to "lord". Frequently used to refer to dignitaries and men of high position in the Ottoman Empire, but now mostly obsolete and old-fashioned-sounding in the Arab world. "*Ya bey*" is used when addressing someone directly as a *bey*.

**blue bone:** Slang derogatory term for a Christian.

Capucci, Hilarion (1922–) Greek Catholic bishop born in Aleppo. An outspoken supporter of Palestinian rights and an opponent of Israel.

**Chamoun, Camille (1900–87):** President of Lebanon from 1952 to 1958, when his illegal attempt to secure himself another presidential term led to a brief civil war, a deployment of American Marines, and his eventual removal from office. In 1975, the grant of exclusive fishing rights off Sidon made to a private company he headed, a move that was strongly protested by local (mostly Muslim) fishermen, was one of the catalysts for the outbreak of the civil war a few months later. He was a founder of the National Liberal Party, which was part of the rightist, Christian-dominated Lebanese Front.

**Darwish, Sayed (1892–1923):** Egyptian composer widely considered the father of popular music in the Arab world.

**Deir Yassin:** Name of a Palestinian village near Jerusalem where 107 Palestinian Arab inhabitants were massacred by the radical Israeli paramilitary group Irgun in 1948.

**Deuxième Bureau:** The Lebanese government's bureau of military intelligence.

**Druze:**  A secretive Muslim sect which traditionally has been considered heretical by other Muslim groups. The Druze, under the leadership of Kamal Jumblatt, generally allied with the leftist Lebanese National Forces (LNF) during the civil war.

**Eddé: Raymond (1913–2000):**  Moderate Maronite leader.

**Fairuz (1935–):**  Professional name of a Lebanese singer beloved across the Arab world.

**Fatah:**  A Palestinian nationalist group founded by Yasser Arafat in 1959, which soon joined the PLO, and eventually came to dominate it.

*fedayeen*:  Literally, "those who sacrifice" or "those who redeem". A term that came to mean Palestinian militants and unofficial fighters.

**Feisal (Emir Feisal bin Hussein bin Ali bin al-Hashimi) (1883–1933):**  Oldest son of the sharif of Mecca and a leader of the Arab Revolt against Ottoman rule during World War One. After the war, the Emir Feisal was the king of the short-lived Arab Kingdom of Syria, before becoming the first king of the newly established monarchy of Iraq from 1921 until his death twelve years later.

*fellah(a)*:  Egyptian term for the traditional peasant class in rural Egypt along the Nile.

**Frangieh, Suleiman (1910–92):**  Maronite politician and head of a powerful clan from Zgharta near Tripoli. President of Lebanon 1970–76.

**Gemayel, Bashir (1947–82):**  Youngest son of Maronite leader Pierre Gemayel, and militia commander of the rightist, Christian Lebanese National Forces during the civil war.

**Gemayel, Pierre (1902–84):**  Founder of the Phalangist Party and patriarch of the Gemayel clan, one of the strongest Maronite clans during the civil war.

***ghutra***:   A white cotton headdress generally worn by men from the Gulf countries. Can be worn with or without the black cord known as the *'iqal.*

**Green Line:**   The dividing line (drawn as a green line on maps) separating West and East Beirut, strongholds of the Muslim and Christian sides in the civil war.

**Guardians of the Cedars:**   Strongly anti-Palestinian, Lebanese ultra-nationalist militia.

**Gur, Mordechai (1930–1995):**   Israeli general and politician who served as chief of staff of the Israeli Defense Forces from 1974 to 1978.

**Habash, George (1926–2008):**   A Palestinian militant and leader of the Popular Front for the Liberation of Palestine, a Marxist organization that rivaled the PLO and was more closely allied with the Soviet Union.

**Haddad, Saad (1936–84):**   Defecting Lebanese military officer who formed the South Lebanon Army to defend Christian enclaves in southern Lebanon and collaborated closely with Israel.

**Hamra Street:**   Name of a popular commercial street in West Beirut, known for its restaurants and cafés. Also refers to the surrounding neighborhood.

***hatta***:   A checkered Palestinian scarf (usually red or black against a white background). Can be worn on the head or around the neck. Partly because Yasser Arafat was rarely seen without it, it became associated with the Palestinian resistance movement.

**Imam Musa al-Sadr (1928–78):**   Born in Qom, Iran. Radical religious leader of Lebanon's downtrodden Shii community. In 1973, he founded the Movement of the Dispossessed, which claimed to represent all the underprivileged of Lebanon, not just Shiis.

**Iyad, Abu:** The name most commonly used by Salah Khalaf (1936–91), Fatah's second-in-command and head of its intelligence wing.

**Jumblatt, Kamal (1917–77):** Radical Druze leader who founded the leftist Progressive Socialist Party. A fervent Arab nationalist, he was a vocal leader of the Muslim/leftist front during the civil war.

**Karami, Rashid (1921–87):** Sunni Lebanese political leader from Tripoli who served as prime minister several times from the 1950s until his assassination in 1987.

*lebneh*: A tangy yogurt cheese eaten as an appetizer or spread.

**Maronites:** A Lebanese Christian sect in communion with the Roman Catholic Church. The "informal agreement" that has organized Lebanese politics since the country's independence guarantees that the president of Lebanon is always a Maronite.

**Martyrs' Square:** A well-known square in central Beirut, Sahat al-Shohada, named for sixteen Arab nationalists hanged there by Ottoman authorities during World War One.

**Maslakh-Karantina (the "Slaughterhouse-Quarantine" district):** Adjoining urban neighborhoods in East Beirut near the port that by the 1970s had become overcrowded slums. Populated mainly by poor Shiis, Kurds, Armenians and Palestinians, it was controlled by the PLO. Most notorious as the site of a massacre of its inhabitants committed on January 18, 1976 by Christian militias as part of their drive to consolidate control over East Beirut.

**Mourabitoun ("the Sentinels"):** A Nasserist organization founded in the 1950s, which was revived during the lead-up

337

to the civil war and which allied with other leftist militias in West Beirut.

**Movement of the Dispossessed:**   *See* Amal militia.

**Nasser, Gamal Abdel (1918–70):**   Fiery, charismatic president of the Republic of Egypt from 1954 until his death in 1970. As the foremost champion of Arab nationalism and a vocal proponent of Arab unity, Nasser was an inspiring political leader for a generation of Arabs in newly independent nations of the Arab world in the 1950s and 1960s. He enacted sweeping nationalization programs and ran a repressive regime domestically.

**Phalangist Party:**   A right-wing Christian party (and militia) founded in 1937 by Pierre Gemayel. Dominated by the Gemayel clan, the Phalangists became a major force on the Christian side during the civil war, and strenuously opposed the Palestinian presence in Lebanon.

**Popular Front for the Liberation of Palestine (PFLP):**   Soviet-backed Marxist–Leninist Palestinian resistance group founded and led by George Habash. At the time, the second largest organization in the PLO after Fatah.

**Ravagers**: An Israeli term for Palestinian militants.

**Saad, Maaruf (1910–1975):**   A popular Sunni politician from Sidon who was allied with the Lebanese left and with Nasserism. He championed local opposition to the monopolistic privileges granted to Camille Chamoun's Protein Company. In late February 1975, he was shot – possibly by a Lebanese Army sniper – during a protest and died a few weeks later. His death became a rallying cry for the Lebanese left and Palestinians opposed to the Lebanese government, and was one of the triggers for the outbreak of civil war that spring.

**Sahat al-Burj Square:**   Sahat al-Burj, meaning "Tower Square", was a central square named for its clock-tower. It was later renamed Martyrs' Square, but the neighborhood around it was notorious for brothels.

**Sa'iqa:** A Palestinian militia led by Zuhayr Muhsin formed and controlled by Syria's Baathist regime.

**Salam, Sa'ib (1905–2000):** Sunni Lebanese political leader who served as prime minister several times from the 1950s to 1972. During the civil war, he was a major ally of the Saudis in Lebanon.

**Sentinels:** *See* Mourabitoun.

**Syrian Social Nationalist Party (SSNP):** A proto-fascist political party founded in 1932 explicitly modeled on European fascist groups, and promoting a national identity encompassing much of the territory historically known as Syria.

**tarbush:** The fez. Round red cap with a flat top commonly worn by men in the Middle East in the nineteenth and early twentieth centuries.

**Tigers:** Short for "Tigers of the Liberals" (*Numur al-Ahrar*), they were a militia linked to the National Liberal Party, part of the rightist, Christian Lebanese National Forces coalition during the civil war.

**zaatar:** Arabic for "oregano". Also the name given to a spice mix used to flavor bread or olive oil.

# Acknowledgments

Behind every book there are always other books, and people other than the author.

Whether through practical assistance or moral support, this book owes its existence to my wife, as well as Ra'uf Mas'ad, Mohi al-Labad and Muhammad Berrada.

As for the books, they are: *Lebanon's War*, edited by Galal Mahmud and photographed by Abd al-Razzaq al-Said, who lost his life while doing his job following the Israeli destruction of West Beirut in 1982 (Dar al-Masarra, 1977); *Diaries of the Lebanese War* (Center for Planning Affiliated with the Palestinian Liberation Organization, 1977); *The Lebanese Crisis*, by a group of scholars (The Arab League Educational, Scientific and Cultural Organization, 1978); *The Great Bloodletting of Lebanon*, by Sami Mansur (Cairo Arab Center, 1981); *Tell Zaatar* (Palestinian Women's Union, 1977); *The Litani Operation*, by Ashraf Elias Shufani (*Occupied Palestine* magazine, 1978); *The Tragedy of Lebanon*, by Jonathan Randal (Hogarth Press, 1983); *Autumn of Fury*, by Muhammad Hasanayn Haykal (Beirut, 1983); *The War and the Experience of the Lebanese National Movement*, by Muhsin Ibrahim (Beirut al-Masaa, 1983); articles by Bakr al-Sharqawi in the magazine *Ruz al-Yusuf*, 1976, and articles by 'Isam Sharih in the magazine *al-Duha*, 1982; *Capucci*, by Haydar Haydar

341

(Ibn Rushd, 1978); *Good Morning, Nation!* by Ra'uf Mas'ad (Matbu'at al-Qahira, 1983); *People Under Siege*, by Mahjub Umar (Dar al-Arabi, 1983); *Pages from the Boy's Workbook*, by Hani Fahas (Dar al-Kalima, 1979); *Beirut's Nightmares*, by Ghada Samman; *Zahra's Story*, by Hanan al-Shaykh; *Little Mountain*, by Elias Khoury; and "Beirut – Up From the Rubble," by William S. Ellis with photographs by Steve McCurry, *National Geographic*, February, 1983.

And thanks to my friends who were kind enough to read the manuscript and offer their opinions on it: Saad al-Din Hasan, Ghanim Bibi, Nadia Muhammad Yusuf, Yusra Nasrallah, as well as others whom circumstances do not allow me to name.

*Sonallah Ibrahim, December 1983*

# Translator's Afterword

It has been a privilege to translate Sonallah Ibrahim's *Beirut, Beirut*, not only because it is a powerful work by a major author, but because it successfully blurs the genres of journalism and fiction, blending the rigor of the former with the narrative demands of the latter. Is this a work of fiction with a heavy dose of names and facts? Or is it a history lesson (like Antoinette's film) in the guise of a novel? Either way we view *Beirut, Beirut*, it is obvious that Ibrahim's own journalism background informs his approach to fiction, as it does in his other novels. As Robyn Creswell has pointed out in a 2013 profile of Sonallah Ibrahim in the *New Yorker*, "Ibrahim's fictions are full of real or invented documents. They stick out of the surrounding text like exposed structural beams, as if he were purposefully drawing our attention to the archival labor involved in writing."

The "archival labor" that Ibrahim put into *Beirut, Beirut* – with its tallies of civilian deaths, its enumeration of war crimes, and its revealing cinematic anecdotes – is amply demonstrated by his frequent quotations from headlines and the list of sources he includes at the end of the book. The republication of this novel in 2014 offers us an outsider's contemporary view of the destructiveness and brutality that overtook Lebanon during a decade-and-a-half of civil war.

What struck me most as I translated it is how it offers a window into a historical event that is at once very familiar and increasingly distant. On the one hand, the web of political relationships that launched and prolonged the Lebanese Civil War – a pattern of internal sectarian divisions manipulated by regional and international powers for their own ends – is a familiar one in our time. At the same time, the geopolitical alignments of late 1980 (the period when the novel is set) seem quite remote: the left/right affiliations of the various factions, for example, reflected an overarching Cold War reality that no longer sets an agenda for global politics. At the same time, Islamist political groups are notably absent among the factions the narrator describes and encounters.

Because so much of the book involves real events and public figures, the translation has involved a good deal of research on my part. I have made use of the author's list of sources in order to locate and use the original wording of excerpts taken from those sources originally published in English.

The French colonial presence in Lebanon complicates the spelling of names in translation, since a translator is often faced with the dilemma of choosing between 1) a standard transliteration of an Arabic place name; 2) a commonly used French spelling; and 3) a less common English spelling. In some cases, where a Lebanese public figure had a well-established presence on English-language news databases such as Reuters or the *New York Times*, I used the most commonly-used spelling there.

I have generally not translated the names of city squares and other place names in Beirut, with the exception of the

Sahat al-Shohada, which is familiar to visitors under its translated name, "Martyrs' Square."

Throughout the text, Ibrahim refers to Lebanon's state intelligence bureau by its official Arabic name, "al-Maktab al-Thani", which is itself a translation of the French term "Deuxième Bureau". To better reflect the French influence on the institutions of the Lebanese state, I have chosen to refer to Lebanon's espionage office by the French term, "Deuxième Bureau", rather than the more prosaic "Intelligence Bureau", or, even worse, "Second Office", a literal translation that would simply puzzle Anglophone readers.

Occasionally, the Arabic text refers to Yasir Arafat by his informal name of "Abu 'Ammar". I have chosen to refer to Arafat by his actual name in my translation. Although "Abu 'Ammar" will be familiar to Arabic readers, I didn't want to risk confusing the English-language reader with an unfamiliar name.

Finally, given the specific historic and cultural details in a novel such as this, it was inevitable that I would need to rely on friends and colleagues to help me with particularly difficult references. I would like to thank Salah Chebaro, Ari Hagler, Zaki Haidar, Michel Moushabeck, Nadia Naqib and Alon Tam for their assistance in untangling some knotty words and unusual expressions in the text. As always, I take responsibility for any errors within.

Chip Rossetti